BEYOND
THE RIDGE

Visit us at www.boldstrokesbooks.com

By the Author

Three Days

One Touch

Secrets and Shadows

Second to None

Beyond the Ridge

BEYOND THE RIDGE

by

L.T. Marie

2015

BEYOND THE RIDGE

ISBN 13: 978-1-62639-232-8

This Trade Paperback Original Is Published By
Bold Strokes Books, Inc.
P.O. Box 249
Valley Falls, NY 12185

First Edition: January 2015

CREDITS
EDITOR: CINDY CRESAP
PRODUCTION DESIGN: SUSAN RAMUNDO
COVER DESIGN BY SHERI (GRAPHICARTIST2020@HOTMAIL.COM)

Acknowledgments

This story has had quite a history. It's been a ten-year process so I thought it would be fun to share the journey with you, the readers.

When it comes to romance, I would have to guess that most stories start with at least one if not both leading characters. This has been true for all my stories, with the exception of this one. *Beyond the Ridge* actually started with Dax, a purebred stallion who belongs to the character, Coal Davis. I've always had a love for animals, and writing a story where an animal has a strong connection with one of my characters was a joy.

I completed my first draft of *Beyond the Ridge* in 2004. Since then, there have been dozens of drafts (and I do mean dozens) and too many changes to count. In 2008, I adjusted the storyline to coincide with the gay marriage ruling in California. Like many others, I was excited during this time and even more excited that I had a story that could go along with its outcome. So you can imagine my disappointment when the ruling was overturned a few years later.

In late 2009, I submitted *Beyond the Ridge* to BSB. They took it into consideration but decided that they would rather initially publish another story I had submitted. So I shelved *Beyond the Ridge* and worked on what became my first BSB release in 2011, *Three Days*.

I've released four books since then, and have learned so much from many of the key players at BSB. After that first release, I've tried to apply many of the lessons taught to me by Rad, Vic, and now Cindy to Jay and Coal's story because I never gave up on the dream of publishing this book. As I'm writing these acknowledgments, it's hard to believe that after all this time, it will actually be put in print. I'm excited that their story will finally be told, but like all stories, it would have never been possible without the help of some key individuals.

First off, I'd like to thank Rad for giving me the chance to tell this story. I enjoy being a part of BSB, and I hope this story makes you proud.

To Vic for guiding me early on with a round of edits that really helped pull the story together.

To Cindy for helping me fine-tune my craft. I know there will be many more adjustments in the future, but I'm looking forward to the process with you.

To my wife for encouraging me to write this story all those years ago. All I can say is, I did it!

And finally to my readers for continuing to read my stories, listen to my audiobooks, and reach out to me with all your good thoughts. All I can say is You Rock!

Dedication

To Tina

My constant companion, my lover, and my best friend.
I'm looking forward to a lifetime of laughs with you.

Ti Amo

CHAPTER ONE

C oal Davis extended her hand to Julio, the person who had been responsible for taking care of her horses in her absence. She looked forward to resuming their care even though that meant returning to the life she'd tried so desperately to escape.

"Good-bye, Julio. Thanks for everything."

"You no need to thank me, Ms. Davis," Julio said, his thick accent making his you sound like ju. "You say good-bye to your momma for me."

"I sure will. Here's the money she promised plus a little something extra from me."

"You no have to do that." His eyes glinted when she handed him a few folded up hundred-dollar bills. He quickly pocketed the money and folded his hands around her hand, shaking it vigorously. "I love taking care of your horses. But thank you. Gracias, Ms. Davis."

"You're welcome."

She climbed to the top of the fence and hooked the toe end of her boots through the wooden slats waiting while his truck exited the property. Once she could no longer hear the sputtering of his tailpipe, she closed her eyes and relished in the sound of silence. Nature's music had always been a soothing balm to her soul and a strong reminder of all that she had missed in the past few years while finishing up her MBA in the bustling city of New York. Country-style living fueled her blood. It made her appreciate the simpler things in life, especially since her life tended to be riddled with complications. As she inhaled the pungent scent of manure warming in the afternoon sun and gazed out over the familiar landscape of lush green pastures and wide-open spaces, she had to admit she missed the picturesque setting. But as she stared up the dirt path that led to her parents' home, what she didn't miss was being under her family's constant scrutiny.

The reason she'd chosen to finish school in New York City was that it gave her a form of escape. The three-thousand-mile separation had been equivalent to standing on the viewing side of a one-way mirror with the bonus of her family, her father mainly, not being able to stare back. For once in her twenty-seven years, she didn't have to worry about the Davis name and all that applied to it. The possibilities for a new life were as open to her as flowers welcoming spring. She'd been given the chance at freedom, acceptance, maybe even love, although with her disastrous relationship track record she'd be cautious of that journey in the future. But as she sat there wondering how it all changed so quickly, the only thing she felt was trapped.

A distinctive whining alerted her that her large purebred stallion, Dax, was close by. He'd always been the one constant in her life that made growing up a Davis bearable. When she was sad, lonely, or craved escape, she'd saddle up her horse and ride into the hills for hours. As she grew older, those rides turned into all-day adventures, usually resulting in a secluded picnic and a nap below a willow tree. There'd been countless times on those rides when she thought of never returning to the life she'd been born into. But unlike her dreams of leaving everything behind, reality was not that simple.

Her whistle caught Dax's attention as he quietly grazed on the long blades of grass a few yards away. The well-known signal triggered him into action, and she admired the raw power he projected as he picked up speed and glided effortlessly over the earth to greet her. She dug into her pocket and pulled out one of his favorite treats as he stopped in front of her and prodded her with his head.

"That's all you're getting for now," she said, scratching behind his twitching ears. "Go play with Oak and Willow."

Dax nudged her again to no avail and snorted, making her laugh at his persistence. His wide-set eyes were dark, almost mysterious as they locked on Coal's. She could almost see his eyes crackle with intelligence, and when it became apparent she would win the test of wills, he turned away from her and raced to join the other horses. It had torn at her heart having someone else take care of him while she was away, and she was thankful that she could once again spend time with her stallion. His companionship was essential now more than ever, especially since she had few people in her life she could talk to about her family without fear of it somehow getting back to them.

After giving her black Stetson a pat to secure a few of the loose strands that had strayed into her eyes, she tilted her chin toward the afternoon sun, enjoying the radiating warmth. She could have stayed perched in that position for hours, but a vibration against her leg notified her of an incoming call. She pulled her smartphone out of her pocket and checked the caller ID.

"Hey, Mom."

"Hello, dear," Jane Davis said. "Are you home?"

"Actually, I'm hanging out by the barn."

"Good. I was starting to think you were avoiding me."

Not you. Just Dad. "Sorry. I've been busy since I got back. You know, with the house and all."

"That's exactly what I want to talk with you about. I'll take the golf cart and meet you in five minutes." Her mom hung up without waiting for a response leaving Coal to wonder what could be so important that her mother needed to come down to the barn to talk instead of having her travel up to the house. Her best guess was probably because her dad was home, and privacy in Thomas Davis's house wasn't high on his priority list, unless it pertained to him.

Being born a Davis had always been more of a blessing than a curse. Rules needed to be followed, and traditions were expected to be upheld. Being the only heir to the Davis name came with a lot of responsibility she didn't ask for or want. She never complained about growing up wealthy, especially since past experience had taught her that she had access to many of the luxuries a lot of children could only dream of having, including health. Being wealthy, though, came with a price sometimes, be it friendships or sexual relationships. Sadly, she'd learned long ago that her last name represented a dollar sign to most people, and she'd learned to resent it. But what she hated most was that her family responsibilities were always placed above her happiness and were constantly being thrown in her face.

Her entire life was about obligation—obligation to school, family, and now to the one thing that threatened to alter her existence.

She was sick of all the accountability, and learned firsthand that money could buy anything or destroy it. While growing up, she'd thought she'd learned many lessons about the almighty dollar, but until a few days ago, she didn't understand the full scope of the ugliness that money and power brought with them.

Why her, she thought as she gripped the fence harder and felt pieces of wood splinter underneath her fingers. Why did her grandparents tether her to her father? It would have been so much easier if they'd just left him everything. Maybe then this guilt over making a decision she so didn't want to make wouldn't be keeping her up at night. But after the shock of the news wore off, she'd realized that had been their plan all along. One thing the Davis family knew how to do was pack on the guilt.

Fuck 'em, she thought. She had other things to dwell on such as the remodeling of the generations-old family home, the only gift from her grandparents that wasn't tied to her father in any way or riddled with stipulations. Mental plans began to form as she decided what to do with the two-thousand-square-foot home that was badly in need of repair. In addition to rebuilding the front porch and adding a back deck off the master bedroom, the interior floors needed refinishing and the old single-pane windows needed to be replaced with something more energy efficient. She didn't mind a little hard work and looked forward to a little hammering and some demolition to take her mind off her family problems. Eventually, she'd have to hire someone to do the things she couldn't, but she'd cross that bridge when she came to it.

Her house was situated a few miles down the road to the right of the forked path adjacent to the pasture. Her parents' house followed the left fork, their path lined by hundred-year-old willow trees. The only reason she'd accepted the house was to repair it and sell it in the near future after the other financial matters were settled. No way could she fathom living this close to her father any longer than she had to. Just the thought caused her anxiety to flare to unhealthy levels. A few months tops and then she'd need to make some very tough decisions.

Many of the finer touches she planned for her home would make it warm and inviting, unlike the large Colonial-style home that she referred to as a prison while growing up. True, her mother had an eye for textures and patterns and kept the home stylishly updated, but it wasn't the decorations or furniture that made her avoid the house like the plague.

She gazed at what she could make of the far left bedroom window of her parents' home. She'd plotted many escapes from that spot and recalled dreaming of Prince Charming riding in on his horse and carrying her away to a faraway place and a different life. That fairy tale seemed amusing to her after all these years especially since Prince Charming's face had changed quite considerably since the last time she thought about that particular fantasy. Now she imagined dark hair, smoldering eyes, and of course, *he* would be a *she*.

Ha! What would Daddy think of that happy ending?

She was about to hop off the fence when a sleek Jaguar approached from the front gate. As the sporty silver rocket shot past her, it kicked up dust and spooked the horses.

"I hope he chips his paint," she said. Dax appeared by her side and she grabbed his reins to steady him. "Did you see that car, boy? Obviously one of Daddy's friends."

Thomas Davis had many friends, most of them living within the city limits of Woodside. He was born and raised in the area and had always loved the opulent community. Woodside was known for housing some of Hollywood's biggest stars and some of the richest people in California. With its large plots of open land, Woodside also offered many of these people the privacy they required. There tended to be some older money as well, families who had lived in the community since the days of farms and cattle ranches. These were the people like her grandfather, who had made their fortunes early on. Due to the staggering home prices within the small community, outsiders were only seen when they were employed for jobs as gardeners or hired help. She'd learned long ago that mixing in with people below her social class was frowned upon by her family. She'd lost many friendships throughout the years because of this fact, most people staying clear of her once they met her father.

No one could quite measure up in his eyes, whether it was due to their personalities or their family's social status. She could recall a dozen lectures from him about the values of society and how her role would be important to carry on the family name. Of course she didn't agree with most of his ideals, which tended to be an ever-present source of contention between them.

The few people that had passed his litmus test always had an agenda attached to their friendship. All, that is, except for her best friend, Angel, who happened to be the daughter of her father's best friend. Finding out that people wanted to be friends with her because of her social status or the political power that her father brought to the table made her wary of other people's motives and led to a number of trust issues that she didn't know if she could ever overcome.

"Hi, sweetie!" Jane Davis brought the golf cart to a stop next to the fence as Coal hopped off of it landing within a few feet of her. Her mom hadn't changed much over the last year, and she still marveled at her mother's youthful good looks, finding it hard to believe she would be turning sixty next month. Hopefully, those genes carried over to her. God knows she didn't get her height. "Why didn't you come up for lunch?"

"Not hungry." Coal tilted her head as her mother leaned forward to kiss her cheek.

"You're never hungry." Her mom reached up to pet Dax just above the nose when he whined from the other side of the enclosure. "I think he's trying to get your attention. He missed you when you were gone."

"He doesn't want my attention. Do you, boy?" Coal laughed as Dax probed her mother's jacket pocket. "He wants more carrots."

"He is persistent."

"Yes, he is." *Pretty much like all the males in this family.* "So what was so important that it couldn't wait until later?"

"Isn't that obvious, Coal? Really. I talked to you about all this on the phone last week."

She fought to recall the conversation, but how could her mom expect her to remember anything especially after her father dropped the bombshell of her grandparents' will on her? After that mind-numbing experience, she was lucky she remembered her own name.

"I came to find you because I need to know when you plan to start the renovations," her mom said. "I have a few good contractors in mind, and all of them said they could start immediately."

And allow Daddy to have some say in the remodel? No fucking way! Her dad was always trying to find some way to intrude on her life, and she swore that when she returned, things would be different this time around. "Mom, I told you. I'm planning on doing a lot of the work myself. Besides, I don't want Daddy involved. We're still not on speaking terms, and I can only imagine what he thinks about me moving back to the area."

"Well, for one, you're his daughter, Coal and he loves you. What makes you think he doesn't want you here?"

"Uh, maybe because he still looks at me like I'm an ugly green monster with three heads. And I won't change who I am." *No matter how much it threatens his political ambitions.*

"Honey, that's not true. Just give him some time. He'll come around."

"Time, Mom? He's had three years! This family's had three years. How much time does everyone need? I am who I am, and this family needs to get over it!"

"Honey, calm down." She stopped Coal's pacing with an arm wrapped around her shoulders. "You know how he is. He's old-fashioned and stuck in his ways. You have to remember you've been put in charge of something very important. Something that means a lot to many people who aren't as fortunate as us. Let's take it a day at a time and wait and see what happens. All right?"

Coal nodded and gathered the strength she was used to summoning when it came to dealing with her family. She took a deep breath and steadied herself. "Yeah, okay."

"So, about the contractors, dear, when do you want them to start?"

"Mom—"

"Just listen." Coal's stubbornness was a trait she had inherited from her father, but her mother always possessed the ability to get her to listen to reason. That and her mother was the master when it came to use of the guilt card. "I know you want to do a lot of the work yourself, but with everything else going on right now, you can't do it all. I promise, your dad will have nothing to do with it, but that doesn't mean I don't want you to try and get along with each other. Besides, I'm your mother and want to help with this. You know how much I like remodeling projects. Don't take that opportunity away from me."

"Really, Mom?" Coal groaned. "The guilt card right from the gate?"

"Is it working?"

"You know it's not that I don't appreciate your help. But I really wanted to do this on my own."

"I know, Miss Self-Sufficient, but I would feel so much better if you had a small crew to lift the heavy things. Please."

"First guilt now begging? You're killing me here."

"Yeah, but that smile means it's working." She placed her palm on Coal's cheek. "You remind me so much of your father when those dimples appear."

She closed her eyes, trying to draw from her mother's strength. Her mom seemed to be the only one in her family who ever truly accepted her. Probably because she wasn't born a Davis, just married one. "Fine…whatever. But Daddy stays out of it or no deal."

"Thank you," her mother said in obvious relief. "With that settled, I have errands to run and calls to make. See you later, sweetie."

As her mother drove away, Dax leaned his head over the top of the fence and rested it on her shoulder. She buried her face into his thick neck and inhaled the familiar scent of dust and sweat tinged with honey, the contact as comforting as a safety blanket. Just when she started to breathe easier again, the nerve-irritating screech of tires on dry pavement sent a chilling reminder of the reason she'd returned home.

Images of twisted metal and two body bags lying in the street finally caused the tears to fall unchecked. Her grandparents' death had been all over the news, their horrific car crash sparking a chain of events that would forever alter her life. Their death added one more shackle to her already constrained existence, making her wish that being a Davis wasn't a life sentence.

She allowed the tears to fall, including the ones she'd held back during the reading of the will. They'd left her a house, and an inheritance, which tied her to the one thing in her childhood that had meant the world to her. Regrettably, they'd also tied her to her father in the worst way. Even in death, her family members had found a way to manipulate her.

Getting angry and focusing on the positives was the only way she could keep a clear head in this fucked up situation. Maybe with her temporary job and a new project to fill her time, she could forget about her family troubles and look forward to the challenge and the physical work ahead. Without a purpose to occupy her mind, she was likely to lose what was left of her sanity.

The sun was beginning to set over the western ridge, so she whistled for Dax and the other two mares to join her inside the barn. Once they were settled and secure, she walked down the narrow dirt path that led to her newly acquired home and pulled off her boots upon entering the unlit house. The electrician was due to arrive Monday, so until then, she'd have to use a flashlight to help navigate her way through the house and up the winding staircase. Just like the rest of the house, the master bathroom was in need of a major overhaul, and as the old shower faucet creaked in protest, she lit a few candles that were resting on the pedestal sink and prayed for five minutes of hot water to soothe her aching muscles. Of course, she could have stayed with her parents during the remodel process, but she'd rather reek of manure for a year than take the chance of running into her father.

She plopped down onto the Aerobed not caring that it was partially deflated. Without electricity, there was no way to re-inflate it unless she wanted to take a trip back to the barn, and she was far too tired for that. As she crawled beneath the covers, she hoped to fall asleep immediately. But the instant she closed her eyes, thoughts of the will and her father's new role in her life caused her to bolt upright and gasp for air as she felt the familiar fist of anxiety wrap its powerful grasp around her throat. This sudden surge of panic had happened every night since the reading of the will, and she could blame it on loneliness, but she knew she'd only be fooling herself. What couldn't assuage the pain of her new reality was that her destiny had once again been chosen by her family, instead of her family giving her the option to choose whatever path in life suited her journey.

CHAPTER TWO

Jay absently hammered in a few more framing nails, securing the last window that would complete her projects for the day. Her mind had been wandering from the job most of the afternoon, still consumed by her all-night sexcapades that left her exhausted and pleasantly sore. Showing up late that morning had put her an hour behind schedule so as four o'clock approached, she knew she'd better hurry before her ball buster of a boss caught her daydreaming again.

"Fuck!" Jay allowed the heavy Craftsman hammer to fall to the ground and cradled her hand close to her chest. Her thumb began to throb as the blood rushed to the injured area. She shoved the digit into her mouth as if that would stop the pain.

"I told you, you needed to pay more attention," her boss, Dino, said. He shook his head in obvious disbelief. "That's the second time this week."

"Bite me, Dino."

Dino DiAngelo was not only her employer but also her first cousin. They had been short-handed ever since their other cousin, Vinny, broke his leg when he fell off a fifteen-foot ladder. Dino couldn't afford to have another employee out on disability, but she knew his irritation stemmed more from his concern for her safety. "Let me see your thumb."

Jay refused with a shake of her head.

"Damn it, Cuz. Let me see!"

"No." She picked up her empty soda cup and stuck her thumb inside using what remained of the ice to keep the swelling down.

"Fine, be a stubborn ass!"

"Takes one to know one." Dino had looked after her ever since she was old enough to remember. Since their fathers were brothers and her home situation had always been less than ideal, she spent a lot of time at Dino's house getting dirty and creating things from scratch, like the tree house she and her other cousin, Dakota, used to sleep in when they were kids. He was older than Jay by four years, but they were so much more than cousins by blood. In her heart, he was her brother. Her best friend. "See," she said. She held out her thumb for him to inspect. "All better."

The tension lines eased from around his eyes that were one shade darker than her own. "Damn it, Jay. You need to be careful. Uncle Tony would have my nuts if you got hurt."

Jay hated it when he brought up her father's name in any context. After all their years growing up together, he should know better than anyone that her dad could give a shit about anything that happened to her. "Cuz, I don't know if you noticed, but I'm almost thirty years old and can take care of myself."

"How the hell does twenty-seven equate to almost thirty? I'm thirty-one for Christ's sake. What does that make me, almost forty?"

"You said it." Jay bumped his shoulder playfully.

"You think this is funny, don't you?"

"Hell, yeah. How many people get to taunt their boss and still get paid? Now, help me frame the rest of this in so we can go the hell home."

"Sure, but you're going to have to keep your legs crossed a little longer than you have planned. We need to make a stop before I drop you off at the shop. I have another job to bid on, and if I get it, I think it will carry us through the summer."

"Yeah? That would be sweet. I was planning a road trip to Seattle to do a few small jobs for Dakota because she wants to give the restaurant a facelift, but if you got the work, I got the time."

A new job was just the news she needed to hear. Lately, things had been even tighter than usual financially, and she'd been stressing over how she was going to get through the summer if Dino didn't find them some work.

"Damn. I'd hate to take work from your cousin. She going to be okay with that?"

"She'll survive. She said the offer was open-ended so I can take care of it during the holidays when our business here slows down. By then, Vinny should be healed and can cover for me for a few weeks. Honestly, I'd rather stay here for work if it's an option."

What she'd never tell him is that she could barely afford gas let alone a trip to Seattle. Every time a bill arrived in the mail, she couldn't sleep for days wondering if she'd be able to pay it on time. She'd never been late with a payment yet, but if work became scarce, which happened often in the contracting business, she might have to think about a change in occupations. She'd even go back to washing dishes if that meant keeping her pride intact.

"Good, because I'm going to need your help. If we get this gig, it's only going to be you and me. The lady of the house's daughter wants to do some of the work herself, but I was told it needs a full overhaul and she needs help with acquiring the permits."

"Sounds easy enough. Where's the house?"

"Woodside."

As Dino loaded a few more tools into his truck, she caught him peering at her with one of those sideways curious looks. *Woodside. Was he nuts? After everything that had happened?* The prime location meant the job would undoubtedly turn over a nice profit, but that didn't stop her from worrying that someone would recognize their last name, which would surely cost them both the job. "This explains why you've had that shit-eating grin on your face all day. How much is this gig?"

"Don't know. I have to see the extent of the work. The woman on the phone said complete remodel so you know what that means. Full remodel plus Woodside equals bank."

Jay wanted to share his enthusiasm but couldn't cut past the fog of worry to crack a smile. She wouldn't voice her concern because she needed the job. Without it, she'd be broke in no time, and there was no way she'd ask her cousin or anyone for a handout, even if she was living on the streets. Hopefully, whoever planned on hiring them had never heard of the DiAngelo name.

After securing the window, she packed her tools away and joined Dino in his truck. "So, you really think this will keep us busy for the summer?"

"And then some. Relax, will you? Let's go check it out. I'll have a better idea of the numbers after we give it a go see."

They traveled the winding two-lane road through the hills of Woodside until they came upon the driveway that led to the Davis home. Dino turned left at the main gate, following the directions to take another left at the fork in the road. Once they cleared a patch of trees, they parked in the circular driveway in between a metallic silver BMW and a black Porsche Carrera 4S. They were met by a striking older woman wearing a green silk shirt and expensively tailored black slacks.

"Hello, I'm Jane Davis." She extended her hand to Dino. "Welcome."

Dino removed his hat before taking her hand. "Hi, I'm Dino and this is my cousin, Jay."

"Nice to meet you, ma'am." Jay scanned the plush surroundings, trying her best not to appear uncomfortable. She gave the elegant blonde with the welcoming blue eyes one of her best smiles, and when the woman returned it with one of her own, the tension dissipated from her shoulders.

"Pleased to meet you both. Let me take you to the house."

They followed the golf cart down a narrow dusty road coming across a home nestled among a patch of oak trees that Jay remarked would have to be scaled back if the Davises decided on doing any necessary roof repairs. Dino removed a notebook from his front pocket as he exited the truck and jotted down a list of supplies and tools required for the job while Jay opted for a complete tour of the house. She examined every room for signs of potential problems, from structural abnormalities to possible termite damage considering the age and deterioration of many of the wood surfaces. There would be no way to tell the extent of the electrical problems or water damage, evident in the yellow discoloration of many of the walls, until she removed most of the sheetrock for further evaluation. Regardless, the master bedroom deck was unsafe and needed to be completely rebuilt, along with the roof that would need to be replaced with something newer and more durable. After probing the house inside and out, Jane handed them a list of specifics for the interior of the home. Jay was so focused on the list in her hand that she didn't see the person headed through the front door as she was headed out.

"Whoops! Sorry," she said to the woman she'd just knocked to the ground. She could swear she saw lightning flash in the blonde's eyes and would have thought them hypnotic if they didn't appear as cold and remote as an Alaskan glacier.

"No problem." The woman ignored Jay's outstretched hand and stood, brushing off her butt with her Stetson.

"I'm really sorry. Are you sure you're okay?" The more she studied the cowgirl with the intense gaze, the more she could see the similarities between the younger woman and the elegant Jane Davis. Suddenly, it dawned on her. This was Jane's daughter. *Fucking perfect! What a great first impression.*

"I'll live," the woman said and motioned to Jane with her finger. "Mom, can I see you in the kitchen?"

"Of course, dear. Could you two please excuse us for a moment?"

As soon as mother and daughter were out of earshot, Dino motioned with his head for her to follow him outside. "Way to go, Cuz. You just knocked the big boss lady on her ass."

Like she needed a detailed account of her fuckup. She kicked at the wooden porch with her work boot, her eyes remaining glued to the kitchen door. The familiar weight of failure hung heavily in the pit of her stomach, and she wondered how long it would take either of them to return to tell them both thanks but no thanks.

❖

"Mom, who are those two?" *But more importantly, who is she?*

"It's just the contractors, dear—Jay and Dino DiAngelo. They were inspecting the house. I would have asked you to join us but didn't know you'd be back from your ride so soon."

Coal had taken Dax up the eastern ridge for an afternoon ride when she spotted the white work truck entering through the front gate. As she rode briskly back down the hill to check on the new visitors, she spotted Jay climbing out of the truck. She also noticed the shorter, stockier man with her, but had to be honest, he wasn't the one who had caught her attention.

"Mom, I thought we were going to discuss this."

"We discussed it yesterday and you agreed to help. Nothing fancy. Besides, it's only the two of them. They'll do whatever you need."

Oh, she needed something all right, and it was more contact with the hard body that had slammed into her. Jay DiAngelo was one tall drink of cold water on a hot day. The naturally tanned skin, her long, lean form, and those honey eyes would have left her mesmerized in any other situation. Being cool around her mother had been difficult, especially when Jay flashed her that cocky "I know I can affect you" grin. The hand that Jay had extended to her was obviously used for hard work. Contractor's hands—callused and strong. Her temper had got the best of her when she ended up on the floor, but her anger didn't stem from the fact that she would have a nice bruise later. This Jay DiAngelo was the hottest woman she'd ever seen, and her mother wanted to hire her to work around her house all summer. *This couldn't be happening.*

"Does it have to be those two?" Coal pointed through the kitchen window at Jay and Dino involved in what appeared to be a very animated conversation. Both contractors looked as though they were swatting at flies with their hands, the well-known Italian trait not surprising considering their last names. "I mean *look* at them, Mom."

"Look at what? You know I find Italians adorable, and besides, they came highly recommended by the Stephens. I've seen their work. They're reasonable and quite good."

Oh, she was sure Jay DiAngelo was good at a lot of things, being a contractor not top of her list.

"Honey, what is it?"

Coal tried to focus on what her mother was saying, but as Jay leaned forward to pick something up off the living room floor, she couldn't help but stare at the way her ass filled out a pair of black Levi's. "Whatever! You want to hire them, fine. All I ask is that you let me know their schedule so that I can make myself scarce."

"Why do you need to leave while they're here? They shouldn't be too much of a distraction."

Interesting choice of words. "Just get me the schedule."

Jay stepped aside, giving Jane's daughter plenty of room to pass. When she turned the corner and disappeared, Jay was left without a doubt that she'd lost her summer income. *Damn, Seattle, here I come.*

"So, can you both start Monday?" Jane asked.

"Wouldn't you like a bid first?" Dino shook her hand in excitement.

Jay wanted to punch him for asking the question. As far as she was concerned, they were being given a second shot. What was that old saying about not looking a gift horse in the mouth?

"That's not necessary. You two come highly recommended, and I'm sure the bid will be fair. If you need anything for the job, please come see me because Coal does not wish to be bothered."

Coal. Hmm...different. I like it.

"Yes, ma'am, and thank you." Dino ushered Jay out the door before Jane had the chance to reconsider. Once they both climbed into the truck and closed the doors, Dino let out a sigh of relief. "Wow, Cuz, we dodged a bullet there. Time to celebrate."

Jay threw him a sideways, uninterested look. "I don't feel like drinking tonight. I'm tired and need to catch up on some sleep."

"Oh, come on. One beer. That's all. This is a big deal."

He was right. It was a huge deal, but she still couldn't shake that nagging feeling in the pit of her stomach. "One. No more. Then I need to get some shut-eye."

"What the fuck's wrong with you?" he asked as he started the truck. "I thought you'd be excited. This is a shitload of money, Jay."

"Sorry." She thought about telling him she still didn't feel comfortable working in this particular area, but she thought better of it. "Guess last night got the better of me."

"I knew it was something. And how was Felicity?"

"Felicia."

"Whatever," he laughed. He never could keep up with her frequent conquests. "So, how was she?"

"A memory. Now let's go get that beer."

Coal straddled the top of the corral fence, watching the DiAngelos' work truck make a right onto the main highway and disappear around the first bend. Absently stroking Dax's head as it rested on her thigh, she pictured the woman who had not only knocked her down but had unknowingly piqued her curiosity. Jay DiAngelo was as mysterious as she was handsome. Animal-like in the way she moved and studied things in detail, including Coal when Jay didn't think she noticed. She'd avoided those smoldering eyes as she walked past her but could still feel the heat from them on her skin and was surprised she hadn't gone up in flames. She'd only known one other woman who had also captured her attention instantly. She shook her head as if to erase the ancient history. No sense digging up things that needed to stay buried.

"Coal?"

Coal glanced over her shoulder to find her mother standing a few feet away. "Did we forget something?"

"No, but I can tell you have something on your mind. Are you nervous about the remodel?"

Coal tilted her head back to study the blue sky that was now marred with imposing white clouds. "No, just tired," she said and let out a sigh. "I haven't been getting much sleep since the will reading, and it's catching up to me."

"I noticed. I just didn't know if you wanted me to notice."

"Everything will be okay. I promise. I think things will be better once we start the work on the house."

"Okay, as long as you're sure." Her mom patted Coal's knee. "Would you like to go out for dinner tonight? Your dad's working late so it would be you and me."

"Sorry, I can't. Angel's back from Italy, and we're meeting up in about an hour."

She'd been relieved when Angel called her earlier that day to say she was back in town after spending three months in Rome. She had to dump her family troubles on someone, and Angel was always the perfect solution. Angel's father was Judge Justin Parker, who also served on the California Supreme Court with Coal's father. Judge Parker was the only liberal judge out of the seven, and thankfully, Angel was as open-minded as her dad.

"I'm glad Angel's back safe. Tell her I said hello."

"I will. Thanks, Mom."

Her mom climbed into the golf cart and drove away as Coal returned her thoughts to the sexy contractor she'd just met. She hoped after she and Angel talked about the mess her life was in, Angel could help her get her priorities straight. If not, it was going to be a very long summer.

Chapter Three

Coal entered Woodside's local eatery to find Angel sitting at the bar nursing a beer. The cozy, informal restaurant held many childhood memories, and with its barn-like atmosphere and checkered tablecloths, it was as down-home as the town of Woodside was ever going to get.

"Hey, I missed you." Coal threw her arm around Angel's shoulder before giving her a kiss on the cheek. She climbed onto the adjoining barstool and flagged down a waitress for a beer.

"Hey, babe. Been forever. How's things with the fam and dear old dad?"

Not only was Angel's family as liberal as Coal's was conservative; Angel was as outspoken and flamboyant as Coal was reserved and cautious. The True Religion jeans molded to Angel's long legs, and the crimson boots matched the color of her stylishly cut hair. Her white spaghetti-strap tank displayed lean arms tinged with a hint of color, and her green eyes sparkled like polished emeralds. Angel's cavalier attitude made her Coal's opposite in every way, and Coal admired her for it.

"Eh, the usual."

Angel tilted her glass, stopping it halfway to her mouth. "Seriously, that's what I get after not seeing you for six months? A shrug and an incoherent sound? I see circles under your eyes, which means you're not sleeping, and honestly, you look like you got run over by all your horses."

One thing Coal could always count on was Angel's brutally honest opinions. No matter what the circumstance, Angel's no-nonsense attitude was refreshing, especially since life's experience taught her that what one said to one's face was sometimes different from what they actually believed. "Why are we friends?"

"Because you need someone to tell you the truth instead of blow smoke up your ass. Oh, and my quick wit. Let's not forget that."

"Remember when I said I missed you?"

"Yeah."

"I take it back."

Angel laughed. "Sweetie, you'd be lost without me. But seriously, you look exhausted. Have the nightmares returned?"

Thankfully, the waitress had picked that exact time to place a beer in front of Coal. She took a healthy sip, but the cool gold liquid did nothing to quench her thirst. After her earlier encounter with Jay DiAngelo though, she wondered if any liquid could. "Yeah, but they're not as bad as a year ago."

The nightmares had finally subsided as Coal worked her way back into a routine while living in New York. But once she returned home, suffered through the will reading, and tried unsuccessfully to make peace with her father, they returned—more powerful and more intense than ever.

"Maybe moving home wasn't a good idea. You know you can always stay with me."

"Thanks for the offer, but I didn't move home. I moved *near* home. Besides, I have to do this. My father and I have a lot of crap to work out, and it's the kind of stuff that can't be wrapped up with a phone call."

"Your father…Jesus, your family has always been too hard on you, *except* for your mother. I mean who cares about what happened? You're an adult and can sleep with whoever you damn well please. If he wasn't such a conservative bastard who's looking to make a political statement, maybe—"

Coal silenced Angel by placing a hand over her mouth and nervously scanned the small room. She couldn't have this conversation in a restaurant, especially one two miles from her home.

"Sorry," Coal said and removed her hand.

"No. I'm sorry. It's hard to keep my opinions to myself because I was there. I saw what all that did to you. But let's not rehash the past today. I'm here about the infamous will reading. Let's have it."

"You might want to get another one of those." She pointed to Angel's beer. "And a shot. After I tell you this story, you're going to need it and maybe a few more."

Angel motioned for two more beers as Coal leaned toward her and rested her folded arms on the bar.

"When I got the call that my grandparents died, I was devastated. A few days later, I arrived home, but I was still in shock. That night, we visited the family attorney and he tells me my grandfather has left me in charge of their ranch in Half Moon Bay. I also inherited the old family home down the road from here and some money."

"Wow, that's awesome. So what's the problem?"

"Just wait. It gets worse."

"Hold on a sec. You just told me they left you cash and a house. Not to mention you're being left in charge of the ranch where you've spent a large part of your life. Financial stability, a good job and a reason to get some distance between you and your parents. I'm clearly not understanding the *worse* in this situation."

"Well, if you'd stop interrupting." Angel was never one for long, drawn out stories. She motioned for Coal to continue. "Did I ever talk to you about my grandfather?"

"I know a little. But it's been a long time."

"He was someone I really looked up to," Coal said as she recalled a time when life was so much simpler. "If you remember, I worked at the ranch a lot of weekends during the school year and used to stay with him for a month every summer."

"What I remember is you being obsessed with the ranch to the point you even wanted to give up going to prom so that you could work there."

"Not true. I didn't want to go to prom because Dad fixed me up with Tommy Windell when I didn't choose a proper date." Coal used her fingers to emphasize the word proper.

"Eww. He had the worst teeth—"

"Angel, focus."

"Sorry. Continue."

"Granddad loved one thing and that was horses. Probably where I got it from. Anyway, when his brother Walter died at fourteen from cancer, Granddad wanted to do something in his honor. A few years after Walter's death, he started Horses for a Cure. He bought the large ranch out in Half Moon Bay and completely remodeled it so that children with special needs and crippling diseases could ride horses to aid in their rehabilitation. When I went off to school, I got my MBA hoping to use my education to do something similar. I guess since I used to help him with those kids and am familiar with the workings of the ranch, he's put me in charge of the entire operation."

"That's great! So still, I'm waiting for the part where I want to drink myself into a coma."

"That's because I'm not done. You see, my grandfather also taught me the values and responsibilities of wealth, along with his philosophy of helping others. Unfortunately, my father still doesn't share those values, and doesn't believe in, as he puts it, 'wasting his time on the unfortunate.' Granddad knew all too well what my father valued, and knew that if he left him in charge, he'd dismantle the program and find other uses for the land that were more suitable to him."

"No way. He would do that?"

"In a heartbeat. That ranch sits on twenty acres of beachfront property. It would be worth millions to some developer. So because of that issue, Granddad left me with fifty percent. But guess who owns the other fifty?"

"No fucking way!"

"So way."

"But, sweetie, why would your grandfather do that? You just told me that he was worried that your dad would destroy the program. Partners with your father doesn't make any sense."

A mixture of anger and pain swelled within Coal, causing the beer sitting in the pit of her stomach to burn its way back up her throat. "According to my dad, it's because of my lifestyle."

"What!"

"Shh. You're going to draw attention to us."

"So what? Jesus, Coal. This is such bullshit!"

"Angel, please keep your voice down." She glanced nervously around the room. "I know it is. But I guess Granddad didn't like the idea of me being a lesbian either. So three years ago, he changed his will. He must have thought my father could talk some sense into me. It's written that every year, the money in the trust will be released to the program in specified increments. But to release the money, it will require both our signatures. I'm listed as the operating manager of the ranch, but my dad has more of the financial say. If at any time the program comes into question for any reason, it's up to him to decide what to do with the rest of the trust. That means he can also sell the ranch without my authorization. He told me after the will reading that if I continue with my 'conduct unbecoming of a Davis,' he will find better uses for the money. That means the program and the ranch will be put out of business and the jobs of all those who are employed and all those kids who depend on that ranch will be the losers. I have sixty days to decide if I want to take on the responsibility. If I decline, my dad is left fully in charge and that ranch will be as good as gone."

"This may sound harsh, but I say fuck 'em. Sign everything over to him now and let those people's lives weigh on his conscience. Case closed."

"If it were only that simple," Coal said in exasperation. "And you know I can't do that. He may not have a conscience, but I do."

"You said your grandparents left you some money. Can you use that?"

"That ranch takes more than I'll ever have. It has fifty horses and two-dozen ranch hands. They do receive outside donations from a number of sources, but nothing that could come close to covering all the expenses. Granddad had been so independently wealthy that he could have financed it himself if he'd needed to. Besides, it's one or the other. I either do this thing with my dad or I'm out."

"But maybe you could get some big name donors. People give millions to charity all the time. Look at Jerry Lewis."

"Jerry Lewis," Coal laughed. "Be serious. And could you see me doing a telethon? Not to mention, do you really think people are going to give money to a program where my dad is causing resistance on the other end? You forget, he's thinking about running for political office. He's got too much clout."

"I see your point." Angel appeared as frustrated as Coal felt. "So what does this mean for you?"

"It means that the ranch remains untouched until I make a decision."

"So you do plan on going along with this idiocy?"

"As of this moment, I don't have a choice."

"Sure you do. We all have choices. I feel sorry for those kids, but this is such crap! And does your mother know all this?"

"No," Coal said. "She knows about the will reading but not about what my dad said to me afterward."

"Why not? She's the only level-headed one in your family. Talk to her. She'll know a way out of this."

"No," Coal said again, this time with more conviction. "My mom thinks my dad walks on water. Besides, what if I do tell her and she confronts him? I've long ago given up on repairing my relationship with him, but I wouldn't be able to live with myself if I did anything that could possibly mess up theirs."

"Don't you think that's being a little melodramatic? Your mother is not going to hold you responsible for what happens in their marriage. But whatever. It's your fam and your call. Do you have any type of plan at all?"

"Tonight"—she held up her beer in toast—"my plan is to get drunk. After that, I'll have to play it day by day until I figure this all out. If I say screw it, like you suggested, to those kids, it would be the equivalent of unplugging a patient who needed a ventilator to survive."

"I get all that, but Christ, Coal! You're not a martyr. You are who you are, honey. Your family has been handling you your whole life. It's time to take the reins and live."

Coal leaned into her and hugged her. Angel's "I don't give a shit" attitude was one of the reasons she loved her so much. "I know that, but I can't allow my father to destroy the only hope these kids have in their desperate hours. I'll figure out something, but it's going to take time."

"That's the spirit." Angel moved to her feet and stretched. "When I get back from the restroom we're going to put our heads together and figure something out."

Coal wanted to share Angel's enthusiasm, but the day and the conversation had worn on her. Nothing could change the fact that her dad would be looking over her shoulder every chance he got. All these damn stipulations to make sure he could keep her in check. To make sure she lived by the family's rules—as unconventional and archaic as they were.

After ordering two hamburgers and a side of sweet potato fries, Coal rested her arm on the bar and laid her chin in her hand. She was so deep in thought trying to figure out a way to get out of her current predicament that she didn't register the person reaching in front of her to grab a menu until that person was practically leaning on top of her.

"Excuse me. Sorry. Didn't mean to bump into you."

"No problem," Coal said and spun in the stool to find Jay DiAngelo standing before her looking all dusty and dirty and downright appetizing. Jay's hair was disheveled and damp, evidence of wearing some kind of hat. Her black racerback T-shirt clung to her torso like a second skin showing off small, firm breasts and defined deltoids, no doubt from hours of working with heavy tools. Her powerful thighs were clearly outlined underneath a pair of snug jeans that hung over a pair of black work boots. But what paralyzed her from speaking was the color of Jay's eyes. Even in the dim lighting they flashed a brilliant amber and the more Coal sat there dumbstruck, the darker and more dangerous those eyes became.

"Hi." Jay extended her hand in the awkward silence. "I'm sorry we got off on the wrong foot earlier. I'm Jay DiAngelo."

Coal stared at Jay's hand like it was a hot burner, scalding her if touched. She remembered the feel of that hard body from earlier and couldn't risk not reacting if she touched her again.

"Look." Jay slowly pulled her hand away and tucked it into the pocket of her jeans when Coal didn't extend the courtesy. "I hope I didn't hurt you earlier?"

"I've been thrown harder from my horse. Let's forget it, okay?" Coal knew she was being short, but the woman did strange things to her, and she couldn't risk staring into that warm gaze much longer without melting into a huge puddle. She turned back around to focus on her beer instead.

"As long as you're sure." Jay placed her menu back into one of the holders. "I'm glad you're all right. Have a nice weekend."

"Wait!" Coal spun back around causing more than just Jay's head to turn in her direction. "I thought you were going to order something?"

"I was, but I don't think I'm hungry anymore."

"You don't think? You mean you're not sure?"

"Actually," Jay's charming grin returned and she took the menu away from Coal, slowly slipping it out from between her fingers. "I'm starved."

Oh, God. She's flirting with me! In that instant, Jay reminded Coal of a person from her past. The cocky grin. The flash of interest in her eyes that ignited the irises. Oh yeah. She knew that look, but this time, she refused to allow it to affect her. "Try the hamburger. It's the best thing on the menu."

"Thanks for the tip." Jay's grin faltered, and she didn't appear quite as confident. "Oh, and thanks again for giving us the job. The list your mom gave us is impressive."

"It is a lot," Coal said, glad to have moved onto a safer topic. "It started out a lot smaller, but you know how it is."

"Sure do. So, are you really okay? I know I keep asking, but you did hit the ground pretty hard."

"Please, don't worry about it. I fell on my ass, which meant I was cushioned well."

"I doubt that," Jay said.

"You can't help yourself, can you?"

"Is that a trick question?" Jay's grin made them both laugh. "And actually, I'm only trying to make polite conversation. I didn't mean to make you uncomfortable."

"You didn't," she lied.

"Good, because I'm harmless. I'm glad I ran into you because I was meaning to ask where you'd like us to start first?"

"Good question. Does it really matter?"

"To some it does. A complete remodel is a huge stress so if there's a space you'd like us to work on first to help take away some of that stress, it will help keep you happy, which will make our job easier."

"I never thought of that. Let's say, I'll have you start in the bedroom first."

"What a great idea."

When Jay's eyes flashed again, Coal was thankful that the waitress picked that moment to return with her meal. Jay DiAngelo wasn't just a handsome contractor. She was charmingly dangerous, and Coal was in for a long few months. "Good, then everything's covered."

"Sure," Jay said but with a little less confidence. "Enjoy your meal and I'll see you on Monday."

Jay moved to the opposite end of the bar just as Coal picked up the beer list and pretended to be engrossed in the choices. *Did I really just say the bedroom is where I want you to start*? She tried not to appear too obvious as she looked out of the corner of her eye at Jay leaning quietly against the wall closest to the front door. She'd never met anyone who had this type of effect on her. Jay was a walking orgasm, and damn, she knew she hadn't been laid in a while, but these reactions to a woman she had just met were bordering on ridiculous. She was twenty-seven, not seventeen!

"What did I miss?" Angel asked. She looked over Coal's shoulder and smiled as she returned to her seat.

"Jesus!" Coal jumped as if shocked. "You almost gave me a heart attack."

"Don't think I could claim responsibility for that. Do you know her?"

"*Who* are you talking about?"

"Oh please." Angel rolled her eyes. "You think I didn't notice tall, dark, and absolutely butch standing over there by the window? I saw you two talking. Well, flirting was more like it."

"We were not flirting," Coal said under her breath, hoping Jay couldn't hear them.

"Tell it to someone who will believe you. I also noticed you can't keep your eyes off her. So what gives? And put your eyeballs back into your head before I have to pick them up off the floor."

She didn't want to get into a long discussion over a woman she secretly wished was a choice on the dessert menu, so she only told her what was relevant. "My mom hired her to help with the renovations on the house. She starts Monday."

"Really." Angel's voice dropped in pitch. Apparently, she liked what she saw too. "So how's her...uh...work ethic?"

"Stop that. And I know nothing about her."

"Semantics. You're going to get to know her. Tell me you're not interested?"

"Fine. I'm not interested."

"Would you be mad at me if I was?"

"Suit yourself," Coal said, keeping her eyes pinned to her beer.

Why should it matter if Angel was interested in Jay? After all, Jay DiAngelo was nothing more than a distraction. And with the current mess she was in, she couldn't afford to have any other curve balls throw her off her game. At least, that's what the practical side of her brain was telling her. The other side, the primal side that wanted to eat Jay alive until not even her bones remained, was shouting at Angel to keep her damn hands off!

"You're lying," Angel nudged Coal with her shoulder. "And I was kidding. You don't have to be on guard with me, sweetie. I'm not your family. I love you, no matter what."

"I know," Coal said. She wrapped one of her arms around Angel's shoulder and tugged her close. "But you're wrong about one thing. You're more my family than my own family."

The sound of the door chiming forced her to turn around to find Jay was gone. Probably best that she no longer had the distraction. And maybe if she sat there long enough, she'd begin to believe it.

CHAPTER FOUR

Coal sat stiffly in front of her father's antique mahogany desk, but as far as she was concerned, it might as well have been a firing squad. The stench of stale cigar smoke permeated the air, and as the red leather chair engulfed her, memories from her childhood came roaring back of all the times he'd lectured her in that very spot.

She had been in the middle of giving Dax a bath when he'd had his office assistant summon her to his home office. She hated being called to the office because she could never remember a time where being in that room meant that anything positive would happen. From the anal look on her father's face, she doubted today would be any different.

"Hey, Dad. Beverly said you wanted to speak to me?"

"Coal, sit down," her father said without visually acknowledging her.

"I am sitting down." Even after all this time, he still couldn't look at her. He sat rigidly in his executive leather chair, representing everything she'd come to resent. And if it weren't for their subtle similarities, the high eyebrows and straight nose, the kind that parents passed on to their children, she'd have her doubts that this man was actually her father.

Her father was just as he appeared to be, a conservative, uptight human being with distaste for anyone who didn't see eye to eye with him on what he considered issues of moral importance. He'd spent many years serving on the California Supreme Court as one of their most respected judges. People admired his decisions even though her gut told her some decisions weren't always based on the law. With talk about his possible run for governor next year, all eyes were on every case he presided over.

She impatiently waited while he finished signing a few more of the legal documents that currently held his attention. A particular document caught her interest, something to do with gay marriage, but he quickly closed the folder before she had a chance to finish reading the heading. Without so much as offering her a passing glance, he swiveled toward the large bay window and looked out over the garden. Except for the slight graying at his temples and a few more worry lines around his eyes, there were no other outward signs that he had recently turned sixty-three.

When he finally turned in his chair, he narrowed his steely gray eyes in obvious disapproval. "Coal, you really should eat more. How are you ever going to meet a man who finds you attractive if you remain so thin?"

Fucking unbelievable! Trying to keep the venom out of her voice, she did her best to match his neutral tone. "I'll take that under advisement, Dad. But as you know, that will never be an issue for me. I doubt you called me up here to discuss my eating habits and my weight, so what gives?"

"Watch your tone, Coal," he warned her. "I called you in here because we haven't talked since the will reading. I wanted you to know that I stand by your grandparents' decision. It is not my intention to take control of the ranch, but I will if you see fit to carry on in an un-Davis manner."

Yeah, I kinda got that. "That's great, but we already had this conversation. Anything else, because I got a lot to do before work tomorrow?" Coal wanted to scream. She wanted to throw something. But visions of choking him until the smug look slipped from his face were consuming most of her thoughts.

"Let me make it clear. This family is going to come under a lot of scrutiny in the next few months because of my possible run for the governorship. So you need to consider your actions very carefully from now on. I'll be watching you closely, so I don't expect any more of this nonsense from you. You have a responsibility to this family, first and foremost, and I expect you to meet that responsibility head on. You are a Davis, and I will expect you to act as such."

Coal pushed out of her chair and stormed to the other side of the room. "I have always taken my responsibilities seriously, *especially* when they have concerned this family." *If I didn't, I wouldn't be standing here taking this shit from you.*

"If that's true, then as a member of this family, I will expect certain things from you."

"What *things*?"

"For instance, I will eventually expect you to get married and have a family."

"You're joking, right?" How dare he ask that or anything more from her? Like they hadn't already taken enough.

Her father looked at her over his reading glasses, clearly not understanding her sarcasm. "If you're asking me if I'm serious, then the answer would be, yes, I am."

Feeling the words as though he had slapped her in the face, she gritted her teeth in an attempt to rein in her temper. In fact, a slap would have been preferred over what he was suggesting. "I have a newsflash. Unless gay marriage becomes legal in the State of California, which I don't see happening anytime soon, I can't see marriage as a possibility for me. Unless you know something I don't?"

Her dad narrowed his eyes. "How dare you!"

"How dare me? I'm only considering these ridiculous terms because I believe that Grandpa's work was important, unlike you who has no moral conscious and would have no problem destroying other people's lives because I don't fit the family mold. But I will not allow you any more control of my life. If the fact that I'm a lesbian ruins your political plans then that's your problem. But I will not"—Coal leaned toward him and slammed her palm onto his desk—"subject myself to any more lectures from you on this topic. Case. Closed."

"You will not speak to me in that tone." He rose to stand toe-to-toe with her. "And you will *never* use that word in my presence again. The only term that applies to you in this house is 'daughter,' and even that is a cause of shame for me now. You will honor this family or that ranch is history. That I promise you."

Coal refused to release his unwavering gaze, and her jaw ached from grinding her teeth. "Anything else?"

"No. Just as long as we understand each other."

"Actually, I will never understand you. Ever!"

She raced down to Dax's stall, slamming the door so hard it threatened to rip from its hinges. Wood chips flew in all directions, spooking Dax into the far corner. Pacing wildly, she looked for something to throw. When she heard footsteps on the stone path, she turned to find her mom in the doorway.

"What's wrong?" her mother asked.

"Did you know, Mom?"

"I have no idea what you're talking about. All I know is that I saw you nearly destroy the barn door so I came to see what's going on."

"Did you know why Dad called me to his office today?"

"Put the pitchfork down and stop acting crazy before you give Dax a coronary," her mother said. When Coal complied, she took another step closer. "I knew he wanted to talk to you. Tell me what he said."

"Screw said. How about told? He expects me to get married. Have kids. With a man! I just don't fucking get it. Why can't he love me for who I am?"

"Are you sure you didn't misunderstand his intentions?"

"No, Mother. I know damn well what his *intentions* are."

"Honey, he's been under a lot of stress since his parents died. And now with the added political pressure, I'm sure he didn't mean any of it."

"Jesus, Mom!" Coal combed her hands through her hair, grabbing two fistfuls in aggravation. "You're always covering for him. He meant it…every word. I don't know if I can do this. I want to carry on Grandpa's work. I really do. I just don't think I'm strong enough to share the responsibilities with Dad."

Her mother pulled Coal into the comfort of her arms and kissed her on the temple. "You're the strongest person I know, honey. If anyone can do it, you can. But right now, it sounds like you need a break." Her mom made two clicking sounds with her tongue, and Dax responded by making his way cautiously toward them. "Take Dax for a ride."

"I'm not in the mood."

"It wasn't a request. You both need to calm down after your tirade, and you know it will make you feel better. Besides, it will give me a chance to talk with your father."

"Do you really think you're going to change his mind?" Coal said. She kept her voice low, careful not to spook Dax again. He lowered his head so that she could put her arm around him, and as she began to stroke his nose, she could feel his calming effect already on her. "Be realistic. He hates me."

"Don't confuse stubborn pride for hate. You two are more alike than you think, which is the reason you're always butting heads. Now go. Let me worry about him."

"Come on, Dax."

The farther they raced through the open pastures and the more distance she put between herself and home, the more the tension eased from her body. Her mother had been right. Riding always gave her time to think. But tonight she'd need more than her steadfast stallion to take her mind off her troubles. What she needed was a friend and a few strong drinks. And she knew just the person to call.

"He said what?" Angel yelled so loudly into the phone that it ratcheted Coal's headache up to migraine status. "You've got to be fucking kidding!"

"I wish I was." She rested her head in her hands and closed her eyes, the stress of the day finally zapping what remained of her energy.

"What an asshole. I mean, I know he's your father, but *damn*."

"You're not offending me. He is that and much more, but that's not why I called. I need a drink."

"We both do," Angel said in a much happier tone. "Spice it is."

"Angel, we can't. If someone recognizes me, the ranch will be sold to the highest bidder."

Spice had been the go-to place ever since they had been old enough to drink. It had been a small, family-owned restaurant before it was converted into the only lesbian bar in the entire South Bay. Women of all types frequented the bar, looking for a good time in more ways than one.

"Stop worrying. It's so far out of this snobby town that no one will recognize you. Besides, you've seen the kind of people that frequent that club. They're lucky they can afford a beer let alone a mansion. Come on," Angel urged playfully. "I'm not talking about someone to share a U-Haul and a turkey baster with. And don't you dare tell me you're going nun status."

Coal laughed. A career her dad might actually be proud of. "Of course not. But until—"

"Damn it, Coal! You're not talking me out of this. We need a couple of good women tonight to take our minds off of *your* problems. I'm not talking about forever. I'm just talking about a hot body and maybe even some mindless sex. If you find someone that interests you, you can even bring them back to my place. What do you say?"

Coal groaned. God, a tall, warm body did sound appealing.

"I'll take that as a yes. I'll be there in thirty."

Coal wanted to argue, but when Angel set her mind to something there was no changing it. She hung up the phone and ditched her robe for her favorite pair of white Wrangler's and a pastel yellow tank that showed off ample cleavage. Maybe a few beers and a hot butch could help her forget everything for a few hours. After the day's events, it sure couldn't hurt.

CHAPTER FIVE

Jay absently peeled off the label on her longneck bottle watching as a scattered few danced to the loud techno beat. Smoke shrouded the dimly lit room like thick tule fog, and for whatever reason, she began to second-guess her decision for her evening entertainment.

As she leaned against a barstool to observe a number of single women surrounding the dance floor, she realized for the first time in a long time that she wasn't looking for a hookup. Her odd mood left her feeling disconcerted. When did sex with any woman who was willing not seem appealing? Two nights ago, she'd been okay with it. Hell, she'd orgasmed so many times with Felicia's mouth around her clit she was surprised she could walk yesterday. She wondered what had caused the drastic change in her mood since then. The only difference in her life was her new job and her new employer, but that couldn't be the reason. Could it?

What was it about Coal Davis that made her feel like she was falling without a net to catch her? Talk about being off-balance. She hadn't been able to get her bearings since their first run-in yesterday afternoon. She'd never met anyone like her. One minute, that appraising gaze raked over her, warming her skin to the point where she thought she would go up in flames. The next, Coal refused to look at her. And why couldn't she find the restraint to not flirt with Coal? Truth was, she couldn't help herself. Thankfully, the redhead appeared before she skirted any other boundaries and risked her employment. By the way they'd hugged one another, the two women were apparently close but she didn't want to waste any more time thinking about why that bothered her so much.

Enough with trying to figure out her new employer. Starting Monday, she'd keep her head low and do the job she'd been employed to do. The rest of her weird feelings she could compartmentalize as a normal reaction to a beautiful woman. But for now, what she knew for sure was there was nothing like sex to get her back into the game.

As she moved to the edge of the dance floor, her libido sparked to life with a combination of the throb of the heavy bass echoing through the wooden floors and the hot, sweaty bodies that bumped against her. She closed her eyes and soaked in every sensation, allowing her body to absorb the electrically charged energy around her. Her arms began to tingle as the current raged below her skin, flowing through it as easily as the blood coursing within her veins. When she opened her eyes, her heart continued to skip wildly but it had nothing to do with the reverberating beat.

She thought she imagined Coal sitting alone at a table in the back of the bar. She moved into a dark corner, content to watch her for a few minutes. Suddenly the music stopped. And when the fog cleared and the lights dimmed, the bar transformed from pulsing and crazy to hypnotic and sensual.

"This set is for all you lovers out there."

A familiar eighties love song caused dozens of women to pack the twelve-by-twelve dance floor. From her angle of the room, she continued to observe Coal who had no idea she was being watched. As scores of people became wrapped in each other's arms, Jay fought with the idea of going to her. Coal looked sad, but more than that, she looked weary. She should keep her distance. Coal was a client and not just any client. She lived in Woodside. A town where she promised she'd keep a low profile. But her feet ached from not moving. Her palms began to sweat. And when her body demanded she moved, she finally gave in to temptation even though the consequences could be catastrophic.

"What the hell," she murmured. She downed the last sip of beer and placed the bottle onto a nearby table. Her motives were nothing more than a dance. And honestly, what would one dance hurt? She weaved between chairs, careful not to bump into those locked in intimate embraces. As she approached Coal from behind, she placed her hand on her shoulder. "Excuse me. Would you like to dance?"

"No, thank you..."

Jay smiled as the words died on Coal's lips. She ran her hand down Coal's arm, not stopping until warm fingers wrapped around her own. She tugged, and Coal followed wordlessly out onto the dance floor. She liked how Coal's fingers naturally intertwined with her own, and as they reached the outer edge of the wooden surface, she turned and pulled Coal into her arms.

She rested her chin on top of Coal's head still not believing she found the guts to ask her new employer to dance. Coal had looked so vulnerable, so undeniably defeated as she had sat at the table all alone staring aimlessly into space as if she were plotting an escape. She'd seen those types of looks on the faces of others before. It spoke of a need to replace something missing in their life. She'd gotten a small glimpse of the life Coal Davis led and found it hard to believe she could need anything. But whatever essential part of Coal was missing, it had put that longing expression on her face. Even though she couldn't place it, that something had compelled her to act.

Normally when she found a woman attractive, her motives were clear. Sex was not only the top priority, it was the only priority. She'd never needed anything beyond sex. Which made this situation even more confusing. Whatever this was between them felt different. Not that she couldn't picture their bodies wrapped in a naked embrace. That image became more vivid as she inhaled Coal's scent, an intoxicating mixture of tropical flowers and coconut. If Coal were any other woman, Jay would have already lowered her head to her neck and tasted her skin until she'd had her fill. She would have run her tongue along the ridges of her ear until Coal was a puddle in her arms. But Coal wasn't just any other woman. Coal had been cordial but undeniably distant since the day they'd met.

Maybe Jay should have heeded the signs and kept her distance. She'd known Coal Davis for what, two days? And yet, instead of respecting the walls that Coal kept erecting between them, she kept trying to tear them down.

When did she start pursuing women who didn't give into the chase? If a woman wasn't interested in her, then there were a lot of fish in the sea. Where she trolled, she'd always found women who not only took the bait but devoured it and often begged for more. But not only did Coal refuse to bite, she was good at altogether ignoring her. That alone should have been warning enough. But pushing for conversation in the restaurant and asking Coal to dance proved this situation was like no other that she'd ever encountered. The question was, what made this woman different?

As she moved them around the dance floor, she made sure to keep Coal safe by being a buffer against the swarms of people who kept bumping into them. As Coal ran her fingertips up and down her neck, Jay tried not to respond to the feel of cool skin against her hot flesh. When she cradled Coal's head against her chest, she could never remember fitting so well with another. Couldn't remember the last time she wished the music would never end. But like all good things, they did end, and as people began to clear the dance floor, Jay released Coal and buried her hands into the back pockets of her jeans when she couldn't find another use for them.

"I enjoyed the dance," Jay said. "Can I interest you in a beer?"

"Thanks, but I need to go." Coal motioned for the door as she slowly backed away.

"Sure. I understand." Although she didn't understand Coal's reaction or her odd feelings when it pertained to her. "Good night."

Jay waited until Coal pushed through the door before she removed her hands from her pockets. Funny, they were shaking, but she chalked it up to nervous energy and still feeling exhausted after a long, hard week. Regardless, the night had lost its appeal. Maybe after another drink, she'd call it a night too and get some much-needed rest.

Coal couldn't catch her breath and the balmy night air wasn't helping matters. She had to get away from the bar and as far away from Jay as possible. She didn't know much about her, but what she did know was scaring the crap out of her. Jay reminded her too much of the one person who swore she loved her above anything else. Jay and her ex, Taylor, didn't look anything alike, but the familiar spark of attraction was unmistakable, and she'd be damned if she allowed anyone to get that close to her again, especially when there was so much more than just her sanity to lose this time around.

She should have trusted her instincts and avoided going to the bar. It wasn't that she was against non-committal sex. In reality, she preferred it ever since her last disastrous relationship. It helped keep her private life as hush-hush as possible, and a little release now and then helped keep the burning desire of having a lifelong relationship at bay at least until the next time she thought about it. It's not like she had to worry about that anyway. There'd only been one person who had ever made her want more. Now there was a memory that didn't warrant the use of brainpower. One minute, she was in love. The next, her entire world had been turned upside down.

After spending the first half hour watching Angel grind her hips between the legs of a good-looking brunette, she'd been ready to go home. She didn't think she could feel any worse until the music turned slow, erotic. As Angel moved into her partner's arms, she tried to remember the last time she'd been held by another. Tried to remember what it had felt like to surrender under someone's touch. She'd wanted to flee, and then Jay appeared. All it took was one look from her, and she was lost.

In the comfort of Jay's embrace, she allowed their dance to carry her away from all the stress in her life. They hadn't spoken. They didn't have to. Locked flawlessly like matching pieces in a puzzle, she'd felt so complete. So alive. When she'd caught the faint aroma of sweat mixed with cedar, she had wondered what it would have been like to place her lips on Jay's throat and taste the heady scent. In those strong arms, she'd forgotten about all her family troubles. About all her responsibilities and the expectations placed on her by others. For once in what felt like forever, she'd become completely lost in someone else, and it felt good. Really good. She tried to commit every sensation to memory, from the feeling of Jay's hands as they rested along her lower back, to every muscle that coiled tightly around her. When Jay had moved sensuously against her, she recalled Angel's earlier comment about mindless sex. Just the image of a naked Jay hovering above her with a sheen of sweat glistening off her body made her realize that sex between them would be anything but mindless. That's when she realized she had to make an excuse about leaving or else make a huge mistake.

"Where are you going?" Angel asked from behind. "And what's with the race to the finish? Do you know how hard it was for me to chase after you in these three-inch ankle breakers?"

"I'm going home. It's late and I'm exhausted."

"Home? But I just saw you dancing with that gorgeous butch—"

"You just don't get it, do you?" She took a steadying breath as a week's worth of frustrations finally got the best of her. She was also still painfully aroused from her dance with Jay and ran a trembling hand through her hair hoping it didn't show. "I'm not supposed to be dancing with gorgeous butch women. If you forgot, I'm supposed to be laying low until I can figure out what to do about all this shit I'm knee-deep in. I told you earlier I was worried that I'd run into someone I knew. Now what am I going to do if she says something to my parents?"

"Oh, please. What's she going to do, take out an ad? Look, I don't know what you're supposed to do, but we were supposed to be having fun tonight, remember? It was just a dance."

Tell that to the intense throbbing between my thighs. "You're right. I guess I'm more tired than I thought."

Angel cupped Coal's face with both hands. "You don't have to apologize to me. If sleep is what you need, we'll go. I'm sorry I'm pushing you. You know it's because I only want you to be happy."

Coal closed her eyes, feeling the weight of Angel's words sink in. "Yeah. Me too."

CHAPTER SIX

Jay stretched out on the newly constructed porch railing with a soda in hand and peered out into the pasture for any sign of Coal and her horse. Every afternoon around the same time, she managed to catch sight of her riding one of the horses over the first ridge before disappearing into the hills behind a patch of oak trees. She spent all her breaks in that very spot and loved watching Coal do what she was obviously born to do.

Jay had never seen anyone exude such confidence when she rode. Coal was beautiful around her horses and commanding without hesitation. Since their dance, Jay had thought of little else, but what still kept her off balance was Coal's constant Jekyll and Hyde routine. When she'd first approached her, Coal appeared about as wary as an untamed horse. But then their hands touched and she had guided Coal out onto the dance floor and into her arms. She recalled how Coal's head had rested in the crook of her shoulder. Could still feel Coal's breath on her neck. Still smell the sunny freshness of Coal's unique scent. But then the dance ended, and as if a veil had been dropped, that once inviting gaze turned to one of disinterest and as black as a stallion's coat.

Asking Coal to dance? Talk about having guts of steel she didn't know she possessed. It wasn't that she was a stranger to being the aggressor or turning on the charm. Being the one in control had always been okay with her, and most of the women she went home with expected it. But with Coal, she never felt like she was in control. And when Coal had wrapped her arms around her shoulders, not only did she feel powerless, she felt as though she were falling—gripping at the air frantically as if in a free fall without a parachute. These weird feelings had left her uneasy ever since.

When she couldn't sleep at night, she remembered Coal's cool fingertips gliding along her heated skin. Remembered how right it felt to have Coal wrapped in her arms. Coal was solid from all her years of riding, but soft in all the right places. She was beautiful and sexy, and the thought of Coal anywhere near made Jay's pulse race and her sex throb uncontrollably. Those memories had not only been the cause of many sleepless nights but a countless number of orgasms. But even though these images stirred her blood, she had to keep in mind that Coal Davis was not an option on her menu.

Besides the fact that their social classes were very different, Dino would kill her if she slept with a client. Not that any of it would matter anyway. It wasn't like she had chances to be tempted since Coal left most days before she arrived. Except for occasionally spotting her on horseback, she wondered where Coal spent most of her mornings. She had no idea why Coal had taken a passive interest in the remodel of her own home, but her mother did make it clear from the start that Coal didn't want anything to do with the daily details of the process. Something told her that she had become part of the reason for Coal's lack of involvement. Could that be her ego talking? Probably. She wasn't used to women being resistant to her charms, but it appeared she'd finally met the one woman who could. The problem was it mattered too much that Coal could resist, and until she figured out why, she imagined a lot more restless nights ahead.

Disappointed that she wasn't going to get the opportunity to see her, she pulled the project list from her pocket and studied the handwriting that could only belong to Coal. The writing was smooth, the letters bold—a clear reflection of Coal's ever-changing moods. She caressed each letter with her fingertip, touching each one as if she were touching Coal's skin. Now there was an experience she would never forget, especially since she doubted it would ever be repeated.

"Hey, Cuz," Dino shouted from below. "Jane Davis called and said she had a few additions to that list in your hand. She left a message saying if she wasn't at the house, she'd be down by the stables. Can you go see what she needs while I finish up that baseboard in the living room?"

"Got it."

She placed the list into her pocket and removed her tool belt from around her waist. Digging out a sandwich from her lunch bag, she decided that the short walk would do her some good, and maybe if she was lucky, help her push all thoughts of what would never be aside.

Coal had spent the first part of her morning straddling the window frame inside Dax's stall. With her left leg dangling outside the sill and her right resting on a hay bale inside with her chin cradled in her hand, she sat mesmerized, observing Jay working diligently in the eighty-degree heat. Even at a distance, Jay's sleek, powerful form was awe-inspiring. It had been a week since they'd shared a dance, and still she couldn't forget how it had felt to be held in Jay's arms. Today those arms were sleeveless, and Jay's button-fly jeans weren't leaving much to the imagination. The sweat that had accumulated on her skin made those clothes stick in all the right places, and what she wouldn't pay to trade places with that shirt.

She'd spent the earlier part of the morning in Half Moon Bay sorting through all the financial paperwork regarding the acquisition of the ranch. She'd met with a few of the ranch hands, helped take care of a couple of horses, but what had made her morning was listening to a little boy's laughter while he rode around in circles on one of the horses.

Dominic Trujillo had just turned five and had recently gone through his second round of chemo. He had been diagnosed with acute lymphocytic leukemia, or ALL, at the age of three and according to his parents, his condition wasn't improving. All Dominic ever talked about, while lying in his hospital bed, was riding horses. So when Dominic was strong enough to travel, they made the drive from Oregon to spend a few days at the ranch. The Dominics of the world were the reason she couldn't allow her grandfather's dream to fail. These kids were innocent victims of life, and she'd be damned if she would allow her father to take one more thing away from them.

She'd made the short drive back over the hill around an hour ago and had planned on cleaning out Dax's stall. That is until she spotted

Jay and forgot about her priorities. So instead she'd spent the last twenty minutes watching closely while Jay installed two of the porch supports. With every swing of her hammer, Coal couldn't concentrate on anything but the rippling of her muscles. As she'd continued to sit there ogling, she wondered if Jay had thought at all about that dance. That one dance had ignited a fire within her that refused to burn out. She'd been smoldering ever since. The memories still burning like embers never completely dying.

The days since had been spent avoiding Jay at all costs. She couldn't risk running into her because she couldn't control her body around her. Just seeing Jay made her wet. So instead, she spent time at the HMB ranch, tended to the horses and concentrated on the remodel.

She straightened when Jay climbed onto the roof and shielded her eyes from the bright morning rays. For whatever reason, Jay appeared to be scanning the stables and the pastures beyond. The question was why?

Coal turned her attention to the three horses grazing within the gate's boundaries and didn't notice anything out of the ordinary. Turning her attention back to Jay, her body became momentarily paralyzed when Jay tilted her chin toward the sky and reached into her tool belt for a bottle of water to douse her head. The combination of Jay's body silhouetted by the sun and the water cascading down her chest and neck shifted Coal's body into overdrive. She tried swallowing around her sand dry throat and ran her tongue along her bottom lip, pretending to experience the taste of a few of those clear, sweet droplets. As the water dipped down the center of Jay's chest, she adjusted her sitting position when her jeans became a tad bit tight from her near orgasmic fantasy. With her mind elsewhere, she wasn't paying any attention to her footing. And when the heel of her boot caught on a loose board inside the stall, she went tumbling out the window, thankfully landing onto a few hay bales below. Dax placed his head through the window opening and snorted as he shook his head at her.

"What? Never seen a girl make a fool out of herself before?" she asked. Dax bobbed his head and stomped his foot. "Whatever, Mr. Perfect. Go away. I'm busy gawking at the help and you're blocking my view."

She pushed his head out of the way to find that Jay was no longer anywhere in sight. Knowing it was probably for the best since she hadn't gotten any of her chores completed, she spent the next half hour hosing out Dax's stall. She tried everything she could think of to take her mind off of Jay, including humming some of her favorite tunes, but nothing could erase the images of those biceps flexing when she'd hoisted a couple of two-by-fours onto her shoulders or how her quads flexed beneath her jeans as she squatted to fix a few planks on the new bedroom deck. She wondered what it would feel like to have those muscles quiver under her fingertips. Would they become rock hard or would she possess the power to turn them to butter as she used her tongue to outline every firm curve?

These thoughts were exactly why she had left the day-to-day remodel dealings to her mother. She had no chance of running into Jay that way. No chance of them making small talk and getting to know one another on any level. For the last week, that plan had worked perfectly. But with every day that passed, she was starting to regret not taking a more active role. After all, it was her house. Besides, she wanted to see how the installation of the crown molding and gas fireplace in the bedroom was coming along. She planned on making her home as green as possible, and swapping out the log-burning fireplace had been a good start. But it wasn't thinking about the warmth of a fire on a cold night or the soaring temperatures that made her skin slick and blood boil. It was thoughts of Jay lying down in front of that fireplace with the flames dancing across her bronzed skin that brought a healthy glow to her cheeks and a rush of moisture between her legs. She became so lost in the images of licking a naked Jay that she accidentally sprayed Dax with the hose, receiving a nasty snort from her stallion.

"Whoops! Sorry, boy." She turned the nozzle to the off position as Dax let out a high-pitched whine and stomped his foot. "All right. I said I was sorry. But give me a break. I was just getting to the good parts."

Dax snorted again and bumped her with his nose, making her laugh as she wiped a shaky hand across her forehead. It had to be lack of sleep that was clouding her judgment. She didn't have time for these kinds of thoughts, especially with everything going on in her life. Maybe a good night's sleep would help clear her head, help put life into perspective.

It could also be lack of sex that kept her from thinking about much else. Jay was smoking hot, of that there was no doubt. She'd spent many nights fantasizing about Jay but the orgasms that followed were hollow and she felt lonely afterward. The last time she'd actually shared a bed with someone was while she'd been living in New York. But like the countless times before, she'd left before the other woman awoke. She still hadn't got past the ache of old hurts and wondered if she'd ever be strong enough to put it all on the line again. Although that thought scared the crap out of her.

Too tired to think about much else, she contemplated stretching out on a hay bale to catch a few z's. All the nights of very little sleep since the will reading were catching up to her. Since the argument with her father, most of her early mornings at the ranch were spent trying to sort through most of the finances. The Half Moon Bay operation was a lot larger than she'd anticipated which made not being able to work out some sort of compromise with her father a non-option. Besides the children who needed the ranch for their rehabilitation, some of the employees had been there for decades. Could they find other jobs if the ranch was no longer operational? She guessed, probably not. Then there was the notion of figuring out what to do with the rest of her life. She eventually wanted a relationship and possibly a family. Kids weren't a priority now but with the right woman, she could see living a fulfilling life.

Irritated that all those plans would have to be put on hold until the rest of her life fell into place, she decided to stick to her current daily plan until she could figure out a better one. The plan had worked so far because she never stopped until her hands were blistered and she could barely keep her eyes open. Last night, she'd been so focused on installing the shelves in her walk-in closet that by the time she'd finished, she'd run out of energy to put her bed frame together. Working until she was too exhausted to think helped her feel as though she were gaining some control over her life. She believed the more she organized the smaller things, the more the chaos that swirled around her would eventually spin itself out.

Putting aside all thoughts of Jay and everything she needed to do, she took out Dax's brush and gently massaged his face. He laid his head against her body, welcoming the attention as she hooked her hand through his bridle, holding him steadily in place. As she caressed between his nose and eyes, he stood unflinching, evidence that her attentions were having a calming effect on him. She started to fall victim to the steady cadence of his breathing, and soon she closed her eyes and thought of nothing at all.

❖

"Hey," Jay said. "Come on. Open your eyes for me."

Jay had walked into the barn a few seconds earlier, watching in horror as Coal fell to the floor. She'd been admiring Coal's gentle approach around the large animal, fascinated by the sight of Dax's demeanor around Coal. Seeing the two together had almost been hypnotic. The bond between the two was as strong as any trusting relationship she had ever witnessed. She hadn't been able to move. Hell, she didn't want to move, until she saw Coal collapse, and then without hesitation she knelt next to Coal and pulled her into her arms.

"Huh?" Coal's glazed expression was evidence of her confusion. She placed her hand on Jay's jaw. "Jay, what's going on?"

Thank God, you're alert. "You fainted. Try not to move."

She was still troubled by Coal's ashen appearance and didn't want her to risk hurting herself further. Coal had hit her head when she fell and would most likely have a nice bump later. Except for their brief conversation at the restaurant, this was the first time she'd actually been close enough to Coal in the light of day to study her striking features. Coal's eyes were definitely her most expressive characteristic and were now clouded with pain and something else she couldn't place.

"I'm fine," Coal said. "Help me up."

"Are you sure?" Jay didn't want to let Coal out of her arms. Coal was still shaking and very pale. "Maybe I should get your mom."

"No! Please," Coal said, more alert. "Just help me to my feet."

Jay lifted Coal with ease but refused to remove her arm from around Coal's waist. "Is there something I can get you? Water? Anything?"

"Really, I'm fine. I don't know what happened. I didn't eat much earlier so that's probably it."

"I have a candy bar in my pocket. Would you like it? Maybe it'll help."

"That's sweet of you, but no thanks." Coal moved away to lean against a pile of hay bales and Jay felt the loss instantly. "I'm actually feeling much better."

"Are you sure?"

"Yes," Coal said and smiled weakly at her. "Did you need something?"

"Your mother left a message saying she had some additions to your list and that she'd be down here by the barn. I haven't been able to locate her, and we've come across a few problems that need to be addressed," she said more calmly than she felt. Every instinct screamed at her to take Coal back into her arms, but she had to respect the distance Coal had put between them. "Do you know when she'll be back?"

"I didn't even know she was gone," Coal said and ran a tremulous hand through her hair, a sure sign she was still not a hundred percent. "What are your questions?"

"If you're up to it, it'll be easier if I showed you. Then you can decide what you want us to do about them."

"Sure. Let me take care of Dax and I'll be right with you."

Jay waited outside while Coal secured her horse and locked the gate behind them. As Coal's strength returned, Jay began to breathe a little easier. "He's a very beautiful animal. Is he yours?"

"Yes. He was a present from my father for my fifteenth birthday. He really is beautiful, isn't he." It wasn't a question.

"Yes, he is." *But not as beautiful as his owner.*

"So these issues. What are they?"

"Dry rot for one," Jay said not being able to keep the disappointment out of her voice. She hated to relay the bad news but dry rot always meant termites, which usually resulted in thousands of extra dollars' worth of repairs. "It looks like we're going to have to also replace the supports for the deck, not just the planks like we'd first planned."

"If it has to be done. Did you find dry rot anywhere else?"

"No. But we should also replace the beams attached to the house since it appears they've never been treated."

Coal nodded as if she agreed with everything Jay was saying. "What else?"

"Thankfully, that's it for now."

"And this couldn't wait until the end of the day?" There was no anger in Coal's question, only curiosity.

"It could have, but if we can get the order in before five, the lumber company we use said we can have those beams by the end of the week. It will help speed up the process and save money and time in the long run."

"That was thoughtful of you."

"Yeah, that's me. Thoughtful," Jay said dryly, hoping the humor would take the sting out of the bad news. When Coal smiled back, Jay was happy to see pale pink returning to her once ashen cheeks.

"Speaking of delays, why didn't you drive out to the stables? It would have been faster."

"Technically, it's still my lunch break and I needed some exercise."

"Exercise? You've got to be kidding. You've been running around all day lifting things and jumping off of roofs. How much exercise does one person need?"

"I didn't realize you've been watching me so closely, Ms. Davis." The knowledge that Coal had spent time observing her sent a jolt of excitement coursing through her.

"Who said I was watching?"

"You did. But it's cool. And you have my permission to watch anytime."

"Permission?" Coal laughed as they climbed the porch steps. "You know, if that head of yours gets any bigger, it's likely to explode."

"Funny thing, my cousin says that to me all the time." Jay followed Coal inside, and after taking a quick tour of the house and getting all her questions answered, she heard Dino yelling to her from the truck. "Guess that's my cue. Thank you for answering my questions."

"Jay, wait!"

"Forget something?" Jay paused halfway down the front steps and turned to look at Coal over her shoulder.

Coal approached and placed a hand on her forearm. "I wanted to thank you. You know, for earlier."

"Not necessary." Jay registered the softness of Coal's skin along her arm as something passed between them, something she had no words to describe. The answering flash in Coal's eyes told her she felt it too. "But I'm glad you're all right."

"I'm fine, really, but could you not say anything to my mother? I would appreciate it."

"About what?" Jay said with a wink before sprinting off to meet her cousin, for the first time not caring the least bit that she could be flirting with disaster.

CHAPTER SEVEN

Coal couldn't relax as thoughts of Jay coursed through her mind like a raging river after a storm. The fading orange skyline meant it would be dark soon, but it was still too early to sleep, not that she'd be able to anyway. Ever since coming to in Jay's arms earlier that day, her body had been overcome with crackling nervous energy, the kind that made her nerves tingle as though a thousand bugs were crawling all over her skin. Since she couldn't relax and cooking wasn't an option considering her kitchen had been completely gutted yesterday, she grabbed her keys and went in search of dinner.

Twenty minutes later, she climbed onto a barstool and ordered a tall Guinness and a cheeseburger to go, recalling the last time she'd visited the once old horse barn that had been converted into a restaurant when she'd been about five years old. Angel had bought her a chocolate sundae to help cheer her up after Taylor had walked out on her without another word.

The restaurant hadn't changed much in the past three years. Dozens of tables were scattered throughout the thirty-by-thirty space, each adorned with red checked tablecloths that matched the waitresses' shirts. Old coach lanterns hung from the wooden walls, and pictures from the local fairs and community events lined every available inch of wall space. There had been a time when many happy family memories had been shared within these walls. Sharing a milkshake with her parents on a Saturday afternoon had been the closest thing to tradition that she could remember. Today she was here to drink alcohol, to drown those memories until she forgot them and the pain.

As she watched the many couples enjoying their evening out, she was reminded that she'd once had a dream to share her life with someone. What a fool she had been to believe she had finally found the one person she could give her heart to. Who would desire her above everything else, including what they stood to inherit. Instead, she'd learned another valuable lesson on the things money and power could destroy. The more she sat there and saw that sense of belonging etched into their faces, the more she couldn't stop the envy from coursing like poison through her veins.

As she sipped her beer, she decided that from this day forward, the self-pity had to stop. Lots of people had lives that were a lot tougher than hers, the kids that relied on the ranch for one. Those children didn't have years to live. Some of them had cancer, brain tumors that left them with nothing more than mere days left to fill with happy memories. She had never seen one of those kids complain about the hand they were dealt. That reason alone was one of many that made her want to fight harder to keep her grandfather's legacy alive.

She swiveled around on her barstool intent on taking a quick trip to the restroom when she stood and accidentally bumped into someone coming back from the way she was headed. Even if her eyes weren't open and she wasn't familiar with the solid body now plastered to hers, the heady scent of fresh cut wood was unmistakable.

"Well, it seems we keep running into each other," Jay said.

"Seems that way," Coal said, her voice an octave lower than usual. When Jay's cocky grin surfaced, Coal felt her knees grow weak and she placed one hand on the nearest stool to steady herself. Just another reminder of how dangerous being around Jay DiAngelo could be.

"So, hey!" Jay stepped back, the grin fading. "Are you here for dinner or a quick drink?"

Coal moved carefully around Jay, trying her best not to touch her again. "I needed something to eat so I came for one of their hamburgers. They're the best in town, if you haven't tried one. How about you?"

"I'm here with my cousin. After we left your place, we went to finish up another small job and got hungry. Would you like to join us? We have extra room at the table."

"Thanks for the offer, but my order's to go." The offer was tempting, but she didn't need any more temptation where Jay was concerned.

Jay shoved her hands into the pockets of her jeans and began to rock back and forth on her heels. Coal didn't know if Jay was aware of the nervous habit, but she liked the idea that she wasn't the only one who felt a bit off balance when they were around each other. "Well, if you'd like to join us while you wait, Dino and I are sitting right over there."

"Thanks," she said and glanced over Jay's shoulder to find Dino waving to the both of them from a table in the corner of the room.

"It's good seeing you."

"You too."

Once she locked the bathroom door behind her, Coal was able to take her first full breath. Why did Jay have to be so fucking sexy? Jay always reminded her of a young horse, skittish and a little wild. Maybe it was because at times Jay seemed guarded around her, which she found intriguing for someone who most of the time exuded a cocky self-assuredness that she couldn't decide if it made her want to hit her or kiss her. Regardless, during those temporary bouts of shyness, Jay's body language screamed she needed to be cautious. If that were true, then why didn't Jay trust her and why did Coal feel the desire to earn her trust?

The more she paced in the tight space the more she realized she was the one being cautious, actually ridiculous. Jay had merely asked her if she would like to join them while she waited for her food, not ask her out on a date. She was her contractor, after all, and there was nothing wrong with being social until her food arrived.

She glanced at her reflection in the bathroom mirror, quickly straightening her clothes and finger combing her hair. Once she entered the dining area, she picked up her beer and moved to join Jay and Dino at their table before she had the chance to change her mind.

Jay looked as edible as ever stretched out in her chair, her long legs crossed at the ankles with her hands folded behind her head. One corner of her mouth lifted into a half smile when Coal stopped and pointed to the chair next to Dino.

"Does the invitation still stand?"

"Of course," Jay said.

"Thanks. The waitress said it would be at least ten more minutes."

"What's the rush? We can buy you a drink if you'd like…ow!" Jay grimaced and leaned forward to rub her leg.

"What happened?" Coal lifted the tablecloth and noticed Jay rubbing her shin but was more interested in the questioning look Dino was throwing in Jay's direction.

"I hit my leg on the table. Happens a lot since they're long." Jay glared at her cousin.

"My cousin's a klutz, Ms. Davis," Dino said. "But we would love to get you that drink."

"No, thank you, Dino. And please call me Coal. Like I said, I can only visit for a few minutes. I really do have to get back."

"What's the hurry?" Jay asked. "You just got here."

"Tomorrow's the Fourth," Coal said not able to keep the bitterness out of her voice. Just the idea of having to spend hours socializing with her father's colleagues and friends made her rather face a stampede of wild Mustangs.

"You don't have to explain anything to us," Dino said. "My cousin can be *nosy* sometimes."

"I'm not that nosy," Jay said. "Just trying to make conversation."

"It's okay. My parents throw a huge barbecue every year for the Fourth. It started out small twenty years ago, but now it's become this major event. We usually host around two hundred people."

"Sounds like fun. We're Italian so we understand large gatherings." Jay looked up as Dino stood and stretched. "Where are you going?"

"I forgot my wallet inside the truck. Excuse me, ladies. I'll be right back."

Dino disappeared through the swinging doors leaving Jay and Coal alone at the table. Coal's demeanor changed and Jay studied her as she nervously kept scanning the restaurant. The last time she'd seen anyone that uptight her father had been sitting in a courtroom during his trial receiving his sentence from the judge. She placed her hand on Coal's arm, making her jump. "I'm sorry, but you look a little tense. Everything okay?"

"I'm fine. Guess the day has taken a lot out of me."

"Are you still feeling dizzy?"

"No," Coal said more quietly. "Just tired. But thanks again for earlier. I'm glad it was you who found me."

"Glad I could help." Jay cursed inwardly at the waitress's rotten timing. She placed Coal's food bag in front of her and mumbled a thank you when Coal handed her a tip. "Are you sure there's nothing I can do?"

"Maybe there is one thing." Jay arched an eyebrow. "Would you come to the barbecue tomorrow? Look at it as my way of saying thank you."

Jay remained quiet for a moment. She could think of nothing but wanting to get to know Coal on a more personal level, but a family barbecue... "Wow...that's uh...nice of you. I need to check my schedule—"

"Hey, if you're busy, I understand."

"I'd love to," Jay said quickly before she found a way to back out. *What the hell am I doing?*

"Perfect," Coal said and grabbed her dinner. "How does seven sound?"

"Sounds like a plan. I'll see you tomorrow then."

Jay waited until Coal's car was no longer in sight before placing her head into her hands. What had possessed her to agree to attend a party thrown by the Davises tomorrow? Talk about putting her foot in her mouth. She had to find some excuse because there was no way she could hang out with the likes of the Davises. They were way out of her league.

While Jay was plotting her out for tomorrow's festivities, Dino took that moment to drop into the seat next to her. "Cuz, what are you doing?"

"What are you talking about?"

"You know damn well what I'm talking about. She's our client, and you don't mess with the clients. I need this job, Jay, and so do you. Besides, that dame's got money. What the hell would she want with your poor ass?"

Leave it up to Dino to spell out all her troubles for her. She didn't ask or want his input, but that didn't mean he wasn't right, which angered her even more than the fact that what she did on her off time was none of his fucking business. "I'm not *doing* anything with her. I asked her to sit with us to be polite. That's not going to affect our job."

"Bullshit! I've seen that look in your eyes before. I can tell you're interested in her, and by the way she looks at you, the interest is mutual. Nothing better happen between the two of you. Because if it does, I'm going to pull your ass off this job. Capisce?"

The only time Dino ever spoke Italian was when he was pissed or trying to make his point clear. She understood all right. And she didn't like what he was implying one bit. "Perfectly," she snapped. She pushed away from the table. Suddenly, she'd lost her appetite.

❖

"Jay, is that you, darlin'?" Shiloh yelled from the bedroom, her heavy Texas accent as syrupy as the day Jay had first met her.

"Yeah, it's me," Jay said and deposited her keys onto the coffee table. She walked into the kitchen to retrieve a beer. "When did you get back?"

"A few hours ago. We had to stop over in Paris due to mechanical problems. Sorry I didn't call, but my cell doesn't work out of the country."

"No problem. I wasn't staying around tonight anyway."

"Ooh, why?" Shiloh emerged from her room wearing a pair of skimpy white shorts and a colorful floral blouson top. Her blond hair was wet, a sure sign that she'd just stepped from the shower. "Got a hot date?"

"Nope." Jay plopped down onto the worn leather sofa, throwing her feet up onto the coffee table that was littered with a week's worth of newspapers.

"I see you gave the maid the week off while I was gone."

"Yeah, well, I've been busy."

"Oh my." Shiloh plopped down next to Jay and placed one hand on Jay's thigh. "Who put the spur up your butt today?"

Jay threw her a sideways glance. "Where the hell do you come up with those expressions?"

"Honey, I'm from Texas. Nobody speaks English there. All we have are expressions. So come on, tell me what's bothering you."

"It's nothing, Shi. I'm a little on edge is all."

"On edge? Sweetie, you're so sexually frustrated right now you look like a firecracker ready to pop." Shiloh swiped Jay's beer out of her hand and downed the remaining contents.

"Have some," Jay said sarcastically before snatching the can back from her overbearing roommate.

"Don't mind if I do. So, what's got your tail in a spin, darlin'?"

Jay didn't want to have this discussion with her. She'd already caught enough shit from Dino about what she should and shouldn't be doing. She didn't want to discuss the barbecue tomorrow or her jumbled feelings when she was around Coal.

"Well?"

"It's nothing, Shi. You know me. I haven't been laid in a few days and I'm getting the itch is all."

"Got someone particular in mind to scratch it?"

Jay shrugged. "Maybe, but I don't think I'm on her radar."

Shiloh let out a hearty laugh. "Darlin', you're on *everyone's* radar." Shiloh moved to stand behind Jay and rested her hands on her shoulders, kneading the tight muscles. Jay's body relaxed as she let out a satisfying groan.

"No, I don't think so." *In fact, if I am on this one's radar, I better duck, because I get the feeling that Coal Davis knows how to shoot.*

"Believe me." Shiloh leaned forward, her lips inches from Jay's ear. "I don't know who this woman is, but no matter what you think, when you walk into a room, everyone notices."

Jay tilted her chin back, staring into her eyes. "Even you?"

They had never been anything more than roommates, but Jay couldn't deny the hint of sexual tension that had always hung between them. She never acted on it because she knew from experience how fast sex could end a good friendship.

"Yes, sweetie." She kissed Jay affectionately on the cheek. "Even me."

"Why?"

"Because you're one sexy woman. Now, enough with all this blabbering. Go take a shower since you smell like sweat and sawdust. Then we'll get out of here. I need me a good woman tonight too, and I know the perfect place."

"Oh, yeah." Jay turned to face her just as Shiloh disappeared behind her bedroom door. "And just where might that be?"

Shiloh peered around the partially open door. "Like you don't already know the answer."

CHAPTER EIGHT

Coal nodded pleasantly as if she were listening to the man who had been talking incessantly since her father had introduced them. Chinese water torture would have been preferred to the constant ramblings of Jefferson Tyler Sutter, who, as he explained, was a Harvard Law graduate. She didn't care that he had recently taken on a position at one of the largest law firms in Silicon Valley, nor did she care for his pompous attitude. As he explained about her father's suggestion that she take a day to show him around the area since he had just moved to California, thoughts of dumping her glass of Pinot over his head came to mind. Mercifully, her mother motioned to her from the opposite side of the yard, which meant she was saved from an embarrassing scene and Jefferson's starched white polo would remain stain free. "If you would excuse me. My mother needs my help. Nice talking with you."

"Let me know if you'd be interested in giving me that tour of San Francisco," Jefferson said, but Coal was already pushing her way through the crowd.

She stopped to greet a few of her mom's friends before sneaking away to wait out front for Jay. Although she couldn't wait to see her, she knew inviting her to the party had been a bad idea. She'd do her best to keep Jay away from her father. It would be hard but not necessarily impossible since he very rarely left his built-in barbecue when he entertained. She could only imagine his perception of Jay, especially since Jay didn't go out of the way to hide the fact that she was a lesbian, and it had very little to do with her looks. Sure, she was more handsome than beautiful, but it really came down to the way Jay regarded her. Coal had experienced that appreciative gaze the first day they'd met. Jay hadn't ogled her like some men had done in the past, nor was the look disrespectful in any way. Since their first run-in, she tried to ignore the nervous ripples in her belly every time Jay threw one of those heated looks in her direction. She'd witnessed admiration, curiosity, and even something a little dangerous. From anyone else, she would have felt uncomfortable. But with Jay, she craved that flicker of what only could be desire, even if Jay wasn't aware of it.

She also was intrigued that Jay didn't appear put-off by her family's wealth or their position in society. Jay's relaxed, easygoing nature was a comfort and was drastically different from the power-hungry uptight people her father kept in his close circle. Many of those people filled her parents' home tonight. They were the phony types, the ones who could throw out a compliment and still wear an insincere smile. Wealth and influence ruled their existence, and Jefferson was part of that world. She wasn't stupid. She knew he wouldn't have looked twice at her if she wasn't Judge Thomas Davis's daughter. She sighed in disgust. Being a pawn in her father's chess games was really getting old.

The rustling of bushes behind her made her jump. When she looked down, she let out a nervous laugh when one of the neighborhood cats appeared and crouched in an apparent effort to check out the festivities. It didn't matter who or what it was as long as it wasn't her father trying to introduce her to another single man. His behavior had been bordering on distasteful all evening, and if it continued, his wrath be damned, she would find a way to disappear for the rest of the night.

Why couldn't he accept that her life was hers to lead? She'd made many mistakes in the past, but mistakes were to be learned from. Maybe if he hadn't found out about her being a lesbian the way he had, he could have been more tolerant. Maybe he could have even embraced the idea. But as she thought about his actions all evening, she shook her head in disgust realizing she was only fooling herself. The Davis family reputation would always be more important to him than her happiness. That unfortunate reality she'd known her whole life. She only wished it wouldn't hurt so damn much to accept it.

❖

Jay parked her truck in between a red Ferrari and a brand new Aston Martin, seriously regretting accepting Coal's invitation to this party. Everywhere she looked there were cars that cost more than she made in years. Anxiety twisted in her chest, and her hand clenched where it rested on the shifter. *You can do it. Put the truck in reverse and go before anyone sees you.*

"Something wrong?"

Startled, Jay peered through the open driver's window and noticed Coal staring at her curiously with one hand resting on the door. She cut the engine. So much for her escape plan. "No. Thought I forgot my jacket at home, but I found it shoved underneath my tool belt." She grabbed the black windbreaker and stepped from the truck.

"Jacket? It's eighty degrees out here. What's really going on?"

"Nothing."

Coal reached for her hand and slid her fingers through Jay's. "It's something. You were going to leave. Why? And I want the truth. No bullshit."

Jay fought for an answer but was too focused on the way Coal's thumb was rubbing over her knuckle to think about the question. Funny how such an innocent act could cause a tidal wave of blood to seep south. She swallowed hard knowing she shouldn't allow Coal to touch her because what she really wanted far surpassed a single touch. But as she stood there studying her surroundings, Dino's words sank in. She couldn't hang out with these people, and it was foolish to believe otherwise.

"The truth? I feel out of place here. I'm a contractor who drives a beat-up pickup and works for my cousin. Look at your parents' house… these cars in the driveway. I can't relate to this, Coal. I'm sorry."

"Jay," Coal whispered and squeezed her fingers. "If it makes you feel any better, I feel the same way. I'm here because my family expects it of me. Honestly, I'd rather be anywhere else." *Preferably somewhere with you.* "So, please, will you stay?"

"Okay," Jay said reluctantly. The near pleading note in Coal's voice was too much. "I've never been to your parents' house, so how about a tour?"

When Coal agreed, she followed her down a paved stone path that weaved through a small garden. As they entered the house through a patio door off the kitchen, Jay listened with genuine interest as Coal answered her questions regarding the architecture and interior design.

"Your mother decorated the entire house without help?"

"She sure did," Coal said. "Decorating for her is like doing a jigsaw puzzle. She has an incredible eye when it comes to pulling patterns and textures together."

"You can say that again. These rooms are like works of art." Jay took in the solid oak floors and matching beams. "Does she have her own decorating business?"

"She would love you if she heard you ask that. But no. She thought about it a few years back, but her other interests keep her really busy."

"Is she helping with the decorating of your house too?"

"She wanted to, but I want to complete that project myself. Make it my own, you know?"

Jay understood completely. Her dream had always been to be able to build a home from scratch. Put her personal signature on every touch. Another dream that would have to wait. "Well, from what I've seen of your color and wood choices, you have an amazing eye too."

A tinge of pink raced its way up Coal's neck and across her cheeks. Jay had the urge to chase the color with her tongue and turned to study a painting on the far wall hoping she hadn't been too obvious.

"Thank you."

They moved into the great room where a large stone fireplace consumed half of the far wall. Coal explained how her father refused to use anything but local stones for its creation, but Jay was only partly listening as her mind began to wander with inappropriate thoughts. She pictured Coal stretched out on a bearskin rug in front of that fireplace. Imagined chasing the shadows from the flames with her fingertips. Coal would be beneath her. She'd tease each nipple with her tongue before she continued her descent—

"Jay?"

"Hmm?"

"Did you hear anything I just said?"

"Sure," she lied. "The fireplace is unique."

"Fireplace?" Coal gave her an odd look. "I was telling you a story about the fabric for the couches that my mother had to special order from France."

"Oh right. Sorry. Guess I have a lot on my mind."

"Penny?"

"Huh?"

"You know...for your thoughts."

Not for a million dollars. Although reliving that fantasy would definitely be in her future, probably as soon as she got home and crawled in bed. "I'm thinking you promised me a meal."

"Come on then." Coal motioned outside with her chin. "Let's go say hi to my mom and then I'll do my best to put some meat on those bones."

They briefly stopped to talk with Jane before they joined the crowd gathered around three large buffet tables covered with epicurean delights that could satisfy even the fussiest eater's appetite. The spread reminded her of those pictures she'd seen of cruise ship meals with the first table filled with trays of barbecue chicken, steak, and tiger prawns that were the size of her fist. She placed a steak and two prawns on her plate before heading over to the salad table, which was full of varieties that ranged from mixed fruit to Caesar. By the time they arrived at the dessert table, neither one of them had room on their plates.

"Man, you guys take this fattening up thing seriously. I've never seen so much food in my life."

Coal laughed. "I doubt that. I've been to a few Italian feasts and remember having to be rolled to my car more than once."

"True statement. When my aunt Rosa cooks for the family, I have leftovers for a week!"

They picked a table near the edge of the yard that had a great view of the entire house and beyond. As Jay scoped out the dozens of nearby tables, her anxiety returned as she tried to ignore the many probing gazes preying upon her.

"Hey," Coal said and placed her hand on Jay's arm. "You're shaking."

She tried to break a roll apart, but her hands were trembling so badly that she ended up dropping it into her plate instead. "I know, sorry. Guess I'm not used to large crowds."

"Why did you come then?"

She looked up from her plate and could only come up with one answer. "Because you asked me to."

"Oh, Jay," Coal said and rose with plate in hand. "Grab your plate. Let's get out of here."

"Are you sure? I don't want to take you away from your friends."

"They're not my friends," Coal said with a trace of bitterness. "Come on. I know the perfect spot."

Coal led Jay around to the front of the house where they sat on the stone steps to enjoy what was left of their meals. They'd spent the last half hour talking about some of the world's rare forms of wood and the differences in modern architecture when they heard footsteps approaching. Jay saw Coal tense before she turned to find two men standing directly behind them. One of them she didn't know, but the other was unmistakable. As she stood to face them, her worst nightmare had become a reality.

"Coal," the slightly shorter man said in a deep baritone. "Who's your friend?"

"Dad," Coal said, her stiff body matching the hard set of her jaw. "This is Jay. Jay, this is my father, Thomas Davis."

"Jay," he repeated, nodding toward his extended hand as if suggesting shaking it wasn't optional.

"Nice to meet you, sir."

"And this is my dad's best friend, Judge Justin Parker."

"Justin's fine." He took Jay's hand and shook it firmly. "Have we met? You look very familiar."

"I don't think so, sir." She tried to keep her voice steady even though she couldn't imagine a worse scenario. The one family she'd tried so hard to avoid was friends with Coal's family. *Fucking unbelievable!*

"Jay, if I may ask, how do you know my daughter?"

"Dad," Coal said quickly. "Jay works for the company Mom hired to remodel my house."

"So you're the one my wife has been raving about for the last few weeks. She says you do great work."

"Thank you, but it's my cousin who should get all the credit. I'm sorry to do this, but it's getting late and I should go. It was nice to meet you both, sir." She turned to Coal. "Ms. Davis, thanks for the great meal. I'll see you Monday."

Coal forced a smile as Jay bounded down the stairs and disappeared into the night. She wanted to go after her, but with her father standing there with a cigar between his lips and a dissecting expression, she knew it wasn't an option.

"Coal, Angel wanted me to tell you she was sorry she couldn't make it tonight," Judge Parker said.

"It's okay. I'll call her tomorrow so we can catch up," Coal said absently, not being able to think of anything except Jay and how she'd looked like she'd wanted to crawl out of her skin a minute ago.

"I think it's time you rejoin the party," her father said. "There are a few other people I would like you to meet before the night's up."

"Tom," Judge Parker said. "I hate to butt in, but I can hear your wife calling you. We all should get back, but before we do, you walked away during our argument. You know this gay marriage issue isn't going to go away. There's going to be a vote and we should talk—"

"Justin!" her father's eyes flashed with warning. "This is not the time or place for that discussion."

So that's what those documents were the day she was summoned to his office. They were the arguments for and against legalizing gay marriage in California. She remembered an article on the Internet mentioning how the court was supposed to vote on the issue soon, and her father would be one of the deciding votes.

Judge Justin Parker had been a friend of her father's for over thirty years. They attended Yale together and had managed to keep their friendship alive throughout the years even though their views of the law were polar opposite. Where her father was conservative, Justin Parker's liberal views made for a good balanced argument between them. Besides the fact that he was Angel's father, Coal had always liked and respected Judge Parker, and was happy that he also served on the California State Supreme Court. Unfortunately, he was the only liberal judge out of the panel of seven, which meant many decisions didn't tip in his favor.

Great! Well, we all know how you're going to vote, Dad.

"I apologize and you're right. It can wait until Monday. Now, come on." He threw an arm around her father's shoulders and led him back toward the backyard, leaving Coal to stare after them. "My wife has been bugging me to ask you about your famous barbecue sauce. I told her I would get the recipe out of you one way or another."

Coal stood motionless still reeling from the last few minutes. The gay marriage argument of all things, and her father would be one of the people who would decide the fate of thousands of couples? She didn't know how to process this new information, but the familiar roar of a large engine brought her out of a daze and forced her into action. She raced down the steps in time to see Jay's retreating taillights. Jay must have seen Coal waving at her because the truck stopped and Jay stepped from the still idling vehicle.

"Forget something?" Jay asked.

"Actually, yes." She stepped closer to Jay. "I forgot to tell you I really enjoyed our time together tonight."

"Me too. Cold?"

Coal looked down to find that she was unconsciously rubbing her forearms, but it had nothing to do with the temperature. She was anxious because she didn't want Jay to leave and she needed to find an excuse for their evening not to end. When Jay reached behind her seat and pulled out the windbreaker from earlier, Coal played along as Jay placed it around her shoulders. She caught the familiar scent of smoked cedar tinged with a hint of orange, and her stomach did a pleasant flip.

"Thanks." Coal's heart pounded in her throat, but it wasn't from her recent marathon sprint. She couldn't ask Jay to stay, especially after meeting her father. Which left her with another idea. "Look, I know you said you had to go, but there's going to be an awesome fireworks display in about a half hour not too far from here. I was wondering if maybe you would like to go watch it with me?"

Jay's lips parted in surprise. "What a great idea."

❖

Jay made a left onto a dirt turnout, following Coal's instructions to pull over next to a railing with a posted sign warning of a sheer drop. From their vantage point, they could see out over the entire South Bay and as far north as San Francisco.

"You're right. The view from here is awesome." Jay pulled a blanket out of the back of her cab and laid it over the hood of her truck.

"Would I lie to you?"

Coal climbed up next to Jay just in time to catch the first explosions of color raining down over the valley below. Loud booms and cracks echoed in the night sky mixed with the occasional whistle from a bottle rocket. The metallic smell of gunpowder tickled her nose as the temperature slowly rose all around them. But the heat that caressed her body wasn't from the fireworks or the humid July night. All her energy was focused on the position of Coal's thigh where it rested along hers and how she fought with the urge to touch her.

"I'm sorry about earlier," Coal said just as Jay looked up to witness a happy face appear in blue overhead then evaporated as if its presence had never existed.

"For what?"

"For my father. He can be a little…intense sometimes."

"I noticed. Has he always been like that?"

"Sometimes he's worse. That was his low-key persona, probably because Judge Parker was there and my dad isn't big into scenes. He wants everyone to think he's in control all the time."

At the mention of Judge Parker's name, Jay tensed. She couldn't wait to get out of there the moment she recognized him. She had to get off this subject. Find a way to keep the conversation moving along and away from a topic she did not want to discuss, especially with Coal. The problem was she was having a hard time focusing on the scene all around her instead of the one playing out next to her. "Parents like control. They can't help themselves. I think it's in the parental manual." *Trust me, I know from experience.*

"Yeah, well, I think my dad takes that manual a little too seriously," Coal said her voice tinged with sadness. "I think it's weird Judge Parker thought he knew you. Are you sure you've never met him?"

"Not personally." Jay gritted her teeth. She didn't want to lie to Coal, but this wasn't a conversation she could have with her. Her job, her income, and her reputation would suffer if she came clean about the reason she tried so hard to avoid the Parkers. She answered the best she could without giving much away. "But I do know who he is."

Coal placed a hand on Jay's thigh. "Hey, relax. It's just us now."

"I'll try, Ms. Davis."

This time, the flash that erupted in Coal's eyes had nothing to do with the explosion of colors that rained down upon them. "If you call me Ms. Davis one more time, I'm going to smack you."

"Violence? That's not very becoming of a lady, *ma'am*."

"Cut it out!" Coal slapped Jay playfully on the arm.

"Okay, okay." Jay laughed. "Coal it is."

"Better. Now that that's settled, how about telling me something interesting about the mysterious, Jay DiAngelo."

"Mysterious? Me? I think you're giving me way too much credit."

"Why don't I be the judge of that?"

"Not much to tell," Jay said. "I go to work everyday, bring home a steady paycheck, and on the weekends, I like to let loose with a few beers and hang out with friends. So if you need a word to describe me, how about we go with boring."

"You're so not boring. Boring is prep school and parties where people sit around and talk about their mutual funds. I'm falling asleep just thinking about it."

"Do they really do that?"

"And more, but I want you to stay awake for the fireworks. How about telling me where you grew up?"

"North Beach. Lived there most of my life until I moved to Redwood City a couple of years ago after Dino hired me."

North Beach, better known as Little Italy, was located in the city of San Francisco and bordered popular tourist areas such as Chinatown and Fisherman's Wharf. Over the years, the once predominately Italian neighborhood had transformed into an eclectic mix of ethnic groups, although one could still find a large number of Italian restaurants throughout.

"Cool! Do you know I've never been there and I've lived in this area all my life?"

"How is that possible?"

Coal shrugged. "What can I say? I'm a country girl at heart. I've visited the big stuff in the city. You know, Alcatraz and Coit Tower. I even saw that windy road once."

"You mean Lombard Street?"

"Yeah, that's the one. I don't know why I can't remember that name. But back to North Beach. Do you miss it?"

"Kind of. I have a lot of great memories, but it's a lot different there now than when I grew up. I used to walk around the neighborhood, and let me tell you, I knew everyone. I'd bring some of the older people their groceries, and I delivered newspapers until they started hiring people who had to have their own cars. And the Italian delis," Jay said and rubbed her belly. "You could find one on every corner. I spent most days working off all the free meals people gave me by walking the hills back and forth to school. Now it's a big tourist area and is too commercialized for me."

"Sounds a lot like Woodside, except for the Italian delis of course. Everyone knows everyone in this small town, and walking is a way of life around here because of all the land, unless you own your own horse or drive a Mercedes!" They both laughed.

Jay enjoyed Coal's laugh. It was deep, hearty, the kind of laugh that made others smile no matter the occasion. As another firework exploded sending a multitude of colors streaking through the sky and the smoke faded, she turned to find Coal smiling so brightly that the backdrop of moonlight failed in comparison. "Did you go to college around here too?"

"For a short while," Coal said quietly. Her shoulders slumped forward and her hands gripped the blanket below. Whatever memory Coal had of that time was obviously too painful to voice so Jay reverted back to a safer topic.

"You never told me what your dad does for a living. He seems like a pretty important man."

"I thought you knew," Coal said. "He's a State Supreme Court justice. Just like Judge Parker."

"He's a judge?" Jay repeated absently, not even realizing she'd spoken out loud. So much for thinking there couldn't be a worse scenario than when first finding out the Parkers and the Davises were friends.

"For over twenty years."

A loud explosion overhead caused them to focus on the dozens of colors as they rained down in the clear night's sky. The finale was so deafening it had given Jay time to compose her thoughts. The evening was turning out to be overwhelming. Running into the family that could make her life hell if they wanted to, finding out about Coal's father's occupation and his friendship with the Parkers, and having these raging feelings for a woman she needed to stay away from was too damn much. As the color display came to a close, it gave her the perfect excuse to end the night before things got too far out of hand.

"That was an awesome show." Jay jumped off the hood of the truck and began to quickly gather their things. "We should probably head back. I'm sure you're being missed by your family, and I have to get home."

Coal leapt off the truck, landing within inches of Jay. She reached for her hand and squeezed. "Everything okay?"

"Of course. It's just getting late and I have an early start tomorrow."

The excuse worked as they climbed into the truck, remaining mostly silent for the short trip back. Coal mumbled a good-bye to Jay when she dropped her off at the main gate, but Jay could sense the cold that had settled between them like a sheet of impenetrable ice. She waited until Coal disappeared beyond a row of cars before making her way down the hill and back to the reality of her life. After the night's events, she needed a hard dose of reality before she made a mistake that could cost her much more than she'd ever imagined before.

CHAPTER NINE

Jay walked arm in arm with Shiloh down the busy street crowded with locals and tourists excited about the yearly Half Moon Bay street fair. The small seaside town hosted the local art and wine festival every year and was known for attracting people from many different communities throughout the Bay Area and beyond. Main Street was popular for its numerous restaurants, live entertainment, and small, family-owned stores. After grabbing a sandwich and something to drink, Jay spotted them a table underneath a tree to enjoy their lunch in the shade.

"You've been looking a little green around the edges all morning, darlin'," Shiloh said. "You feeling okay?"

Jay took another bite of her turkey sandwich hoping it would somehow fill the empty void in the pit of her stomach, but knowing that no food could. She hadn't felt right since dropping Coal off last night. Not being one to talk about her feelings, even with someone she considered a close friend like Shiloh, she kept the information to herself.

She'd met Shiloh at a party over a year ago, and they'd clicked right away. At the time, Jay had recently moved into her apartment and was looking for someone to share expenses. Coincidentally, Shiloh had just moved to the area and found herself in the same situation. Since Shiloh was a stewardess and always on the go, she was the perfect choice since Jay liked her privacy, especially when it came to entertaining her numerous hookups. They spent a lot of time hanging out together when Shiloh was in town, and at first glance, probably, it appeared to most people like they were an item. "I'm fine. Didn't sleep much last night, is all."

"You don't have to tell me that. I heard you walking the floors all night. Like my granddaddy used to say, if you got a bull stepping on your chest, best have a friend get him off before he crushes you."

Jay laughed. She loved Shiloh's use of idioms even though half the time she didn't understand what the hell she was trying to tell her. "You're granddad sounds about as crazy as you."

"You're damn tootin'." Shiloh winked at Jay. "Oh look! It's Jeannine."

Shiloh waved frantically at a stunning six-foot brunette as Jay took another sip of her beer. "Have I met her?"

"Don't think so. I work with her at the airline. Don't hightail it until I get back, you hear? I'll never find you in this crowd."

Shiloh disappeared in the direction of the handmade jewelry stand positioned directly in front of the town's oldest grocery store. With Shiloh gone, she was at a loss of what to do. Deciding another beer was the best solution, she stood to go stand in the obscenely long line when she spotted Coal already in line, her arms filled with packages.

"Hey, what are you doing here?" Coal asked in surprise.

Jay could barely keep her eyes off of Coal who looked edible in a pair of denim shorts, a snug pink tank top that highlighted two perky breasts, and a pair of white sneakers. She looked younger than Jay remembered and didn't seem pissed, only welcoming, which, after last night, she took as a good sign. "I was going to ask you the same thing."

"I always come to the annual street fair. It's the perfect time to buy supplies for my horses. I get them there." Coal pointed to the local feed and fuel store, which was one of the only stores that supplied food and accessories for horses in the area. "Besides, the food is great and the beer is even better. I was about to get a beer and a hotdog. Would you like to join me?"

"I would. But you see, I came with a friend and seemed to have lost her." She glanced around for Shiloh, but didn't see her anywhere among the throes of people pushing their way down the blocked off two-way street.

"It's no problem if you need to go."

"No, I'm cool. And let me get that." She pulled the last twenty from her wallet to pay the vendor for two hotdogs and beers. The vendor gave her three dollars change, and she shoved the money back into her wallet refusing to think about how she'd be able to afford lunch for the next few days. She was now officially broke until payday, but having the chance to hang out with Coal was worth a few missed meals. As she stared at Coal dressed in designer clothes, her hands filled with bags from the trendy shops that lined Main Street, it was a harsh reminder that they lived in two very different worlds. Until recently, she'd never questioned her modest upbringing. Maybe because she'd come from a family where pride stemmed from a hard day's work. Building and creating new from old gave her a purpose. She'd always been proud of who she was. But the more she hung around Coal and saw how the other half lived, the more she realized that pride alone would never be enough to measure up in Coal's world.

"That's sweet of you. Thanks."

"You're welcome. How about we eat and walk? There's some great shops just down the street."

"Perfect plan."

She wasn't going to question why all appeared to be forgiven after the way she'd acted last night. Once she'd dropped Coal off at her home, she'd spent the rest of her night thinking about her own rash behavior. She'd freaked when she ran into Judge Parker. Then, to make things worse, she found out Coal's father was also a judge. But not just any judge. One of the most powerful judges in all of California. When she'd arrived home, she thought about calling Coal. Telling her that she was sorry for the way she'd acted. But what was she going to say? She couldn't tell Coal about what her own dad's actions had almost cost her. It was bad enough she was still paying off the attorneys and the second mortgage on her aunt's home. That was something she'd never told anyone, even Dino. No, she couldn't risk it or her job, not that she didn't think Coal wouldn't fire her anyway come Monday morning for nothing more than being a jerk. So instead, she'd paced all night long, hoping that Coal could forgive and forget. From Coal's reaction to her today, maybe that was exactly what happened. Or so she hoped. "So, what did you get for your horses?"

"A new saddle. This one actually." Coal pointed to the window of the local feed store. "I liked the chestnut color compared to the medium brown. What do you think?"

"I think it's beautiful. Love the rose detail along the edges. What else did you get?"

"I only came for the saddle but then slipped into shopping mode and bought a new harness, a lead, and a bunch of other stuff. You know how it is."

"Sure." *Not really, but I can play along.* "Where is it all?"

"I couldn't carry all that stuff, silly. It's being shipped to my house."

"Oh, right."

She'd always felt a little foolish talking about subjects she couldn't relate to, and she knew zero about horses. Appearing uneducated in any way bothered her, especially since all she had to show for her twenty-seven years was a high school diploma. She remembered her dad calling her an idiot when she blew her only chance at a college education, an education she'd sacrificed to save his ass. Even though she didn't have a choice at the time and knew in her gut that she'd made the right decision, his words had cut deep. As the unwanted memories crept back in, she didn't realize Coal was trying to get her attention until she felt Coal link her fingers through hers.

"Hey, you look lost in thought. Want to talk about it?"

Jay squeezed back, liking the way Coal's smaller hand felt wrapped up in her own. The touch grounded her, and she felt it everywhere that mattered. "I was thinking I don't know much about horses. Want to share some tips of the trade?"

"Sure, if you're really interested," Coal said warily, as if she knew there was more to Jay's statement than she'd let on. "Horses need shelter for one. The ranch I work at part-time, which is only a few miles from here, has over fifty horses to board then at home we have our own barn so we don't have to pay for housing. Of course there's the upkeep, because between the new horseshoes you need every six weeks and the hay to feed them, it can run around six hundred or more a month per horse. That doesn't include vet bills of course, but that's really inexpensive unless they get sick."

"Do they get sick a lot?"

"Not really. But it does happen."

Jay seemed to consider this. "And you said you work at a ranch a few miles from here?"

"Yeah. Right now it's more of a part-time gig until I get things in order."

"How long have you worked there?"

"Only about a month," Coal said sadly. "When my grandfather died, he left it to me."

"Hey." Jay squeezed her hand. "I'm sorry if I brought up bad memories."

"You didn't," Coal said, her voice rough with a mixture of pain and what sounded a lot like regret. "I guess I'm still not used to the idea of him being gone."

"I understand," Jay said. When her mom had walked out on the both of them when she was young, it had taken her years to get over the pain of that loss. Coal's situation was a bit different though. When someone died, there was never that lingering hope that they'd return. Some holes just couldn't be filled. "Question. Where do you find the time to run a ranch? Even part-time."

"What do you mean?"

"Well, most days I see you working with the horses at home, and I can tell when I come to work the next day that you've done small projects on your home after we've left for the day. When do you have time to run a ranch that has fifty horses?"

This time when Coal smiled, the light that emanated from her seemed to come from her soul. "Amazing with your busy schedule you can keep such close tabs on me."

"Well...I..." She laughed. "Okay, you got me. But I can tell you love what you do. I've seen you with your horses. I bet training and having them listen to you so well is rewarding."

"Thank you," Coal said and blushed. "But I guess it's no more rewarding than what you do. You get to build things from scratch. Create new things from old. I love your work. It's extraordinary."

How could one compliment from Coal make the weight she had been carrying on her shoulders feel a hundred pounds lighter? "Thanks, but I've seen the work you've done when we're not around. And I've seen you handle Dax. You're pretty great yourself."

"I'm surprised you remembered his name."

"I don't forget the important things," Jay said quietly. She still hadn't let go of Coal's hand, but she was more focused on the pulse point in Coal's neck pounding wildly beneath her skin. She wondered what it would be like to put her mouth there. When she licked her bottom lip, Coal's sapphire eyes darkened.

"And what do you consider important?" Coal asked a little breathlessly.

"Since you asked." Jay stepped closer leaving only an inch separating them. "I find dark eyes amazingly sexy—"

"Jay, there you are," Shiloh said. As if coming out of a trance, Jay turned to find Shiloh staring curiously at the both of them. "Sweetie, I've been looking for you everywhere. I found a painting that would look great in our apartment. Come look at it with me."

"Hey, Shiloh."

Coal quickly let go of her hand and took a step back. Coal's face became unreadable, that once hot gaze now cold and questioning.

"Can you give me a second?" Jay asked.

"Surely." Shiloh threw her arm around Jay's shoulders and smiled at Coal. "Didn't mean to interrupt."

"It's okay. Let me introduce you to Coal Davis. Coal, this is Shiloh. She's my—"

"I should go," Coal said abruptly.

"You sure?" Jay asked. *What's with the sudden change of heart?* "We planned on spending the day here, and it's no problem if you'd like to join us."

"I really have to get home. Thanks for the hotdog and beer. It was nice meeting you, Shiloh."

"Who was *that*?" Shiloh asked once Coal was out of earshot. "She's hotter than a fire cracker on the Fourth of July."

"No one." As Jay watched Coal disappear into the crowd she was left with that all too familiar sinking feeling in the pit of her stomach. "You ready to go?"

"Ooh, that tone says she's definitely someone. And by the way you were staring at her backside, this is newsworthy. Come on, spill. Inquiring minds want to know."

"Leave it alone, Shi," Jay warned her. "Let's get out of here. I think I've had enough fun for one day."

❖

The large grandfather clock chimed four a.m. when Coal threw the paintbrush onto the plastic covered floor and admired her handiwork. She had arrived home late in the afternoon and hadn't stopped working as she tried everything to banish the images of the tall blonde hanging all over Jay.

Words like *sweetie* and *our apartment* had kept her mind occupied and fueled her body into an all-night painting spree. She had to put her anger to good use, so why not use it to her advantage?

After Jay had dropped her off the previous evening, she'd felt empty and out of sorts. Whatever bond they'd tried to form as they watched the fireworks rain down around them had faded along with the colors as soon as they began talking about her family. Then she'd run into Jay at the festival, and things seemed normal between them. She'd thought she'd imagined the barriers that had been thrown up the night before and was excited that Jay had wanted to spend more time with her. One minute, she'd been falling headfirst into Jay's soft gaze, the next a model-like blonde appeared and casually threw her arm around Jay's shoulders as if she'd done it a thousand times. No wonder Jay had been acting as twitchy as a thoroughbred locked in a starting gate when they'd first run into each other yesterday. This most likely explained Jay's abrupt departure the night before and the reason she'd appeared so concerned when she couldn't find her friend that morning. If she thought she had any chance at competing for Jay's affection, it was lost the moment she met the beautiful Shiloh.

Christ, even her name screams sexy.

Originally, she thought Jay's sudden need to return home on the Fourth had to do with finding out her father was a judge. Throughout her life, her dad's occupation had made or broken many friendships. They either wanted to be a part of her world because of her dad's powerful position or they were scared to death of him so they kept their distance. Most of the time, she couldn't care less how people reacted. If they didn't want to be her friend for whatever reason, so be it. But with Jay, it had just hurt.

To think that in a few months her father would be responsible for one of the biggest decisions in California State history that would thrust him into an even more powerful political position. His vote, along with six others, would decide sometime in the spring of 2008 whether gay marriage should be legal in the state of California. It would be a landmark decision, one that could change her life and the lives of thousands of others. That political clout would be needed if he did decide to run for political office. The Conservative Party would give him whatever he required to win at that point, be it endorsements or money. He'd be unstoppable, and she feared even more demanding where she was concerned.

When all the heavy thoughts became too much, she retreated to her room and quickly fell sound asleep. As if in a dream, she heard a soothing voice calling out to her. She struggled to open her eyes as the smoky rich scent of fresh chopped wood guided her gently back from sleep. A feather-light touch softly stroked her face. She groaned as an overwhelming heaviness awakened her body. Unconsciously, she reached out toward the voice and laced her fingers behind a sturdy neck. If this was a dream, she had no plans of opening her eyes anytime soon. She tugged gently but insistently, and yielding lips met her own. She melted into their velvety softness. Heard the answering groan as those lips gave in to her demands. The brush of another's tongue against her own jolted her from sleep. As her vision swam into focus and consciousness returned, she realized the lips she was kissing belonged to none other than Jay.

"Jay?" She was lying in Jay's arms, her head resting in the crook of Jay's arm. This couldn't be real, she thought. She reached out to touch Jay's flushed face, feeling the warmth underneath her fingertips.

"I'm sorry." Jay tried to move away, but Coal refused to release her.

"I think I should be the one to apologize," Coal whispered softly.

"No need. I saw you in here sprawled on the floor and was worried you had passed out again. Are you all right?"

"I am. I guess I was exhausted from working late into the night."

Slowly, Jay pulled away. Coal wanted to protest, pull her back into her arms. But the more awareness returned, the more she remembered why she had worked her body until sleep claimed her.

"I can tell. The painting looks great." Jay moved to her feet. "I should…uh…get back to work."

"Of course," Coal said. She wondered if she'd been able to hide her disappointment as Jay retreated into the adjoining room. She quickly changed her clothes and headed down to the barn to start her morning chores. She needed to do something, anything to forget how it felt to taste Jay's lips. To feel her tongue brushing over hers. She had dreamed of kissing Jay a thousand times since they'd met, but her dreams were nothing compared to the experience. Jay was tender, sweet. God, she was amazing, and if that kiss lasted any longer, she would have forgotten that Jay had someone else in her life. She would have forgotten all her family issues and would have succumbed to those lips and begged Jay to take her. Luckily, Jay had made some excuse about getting back to work, which helped her get her head on straight and allowed the throbbing between her legs to taper to a slow ache. She ignored the constant ringing of the phone in her pocket. She wanted to be left alone, but when her mother appeared in the doorway, she realized she wasn't going to get her wish.

"Why are you ignoring my calls?" her mother asked. "Is everything okay?"

"Everything's *perfect,* Mom." *Yeah, perfect! I finally get to kiss Jay, and she has a girlfriend waiting for her at home.* She picked up a shovel and began cleaning Dax's stall, not getting very far when her mother walked through the barn door and pulled the shovel away from her.

"Honey, you know I hate it when you lie to me. How about you tell me what's got you all wound up today."

"I told you. I'm fine…everything's…*fine.*" *Or it was until I kissed her!*

"Oh well, that's convincing."

"Mom, I can't do this now."

"Is it because of the news this morning, honey?"

"What news?" Since her house had been under construction not to mention she worked sixteen plus hours a day, she didn't have access to television, and she didn't like searching the Net for information on her phone. She had no idea what her mom was talking about, and even if she had, she didn't think anything could distract her from the kiss she and Jay had shared. She figured telling her mother that was definitely out of the question.

"The gay marriage issue. Every news channel is talking about it."

"What about it?"

"The issue is going to the State Supreme Court. If they rule in favor of it, gay people will be able to get married here in California."

Coal felt like a trapped dog being coaxed out of a corner with a bone. Of course her mother was aware that she was a lesbian, that fact was hard to ignore after the way her family had accidentally stumbled upon her secret. But they'd never really had a heart-to-heart about the sensitive topic, and due to her father soon becoming a key player in the state's decision, she'd play the safe card for now until the time came to ante up. "Am I missing something here?"

"No." her mom shrugged. "I just thought you'd be interested is all."

The topic was beginning to agitate Coal, and she needed to do something with her hands. When she couldn't get the shovel back from her mother, she reached for a pitchfork and started shoveling hay. "What makes you think that? I mean seriously, Mom. You already know how Daddy is going to vote. And the court has six *conservative* judges on it. Do you really think the issue has a chance?"

"Actually, I do," her mother said with a sense of confidence that made Coal see her mom for the first time in a very different light. "Think about it. If it didn't, it wouldn't have made it all the way to the Supreme Court."

"Do you really think so?" Coal fervently hoped her mom felt that way, not just for the issue itself, but because it would make her feel a sense of acceptance from one of her family members. "Because it would mean so much to a lot of people."

"Yes, dear, I do. But that's not the reason why I'm here. Jay asked if you have any new instructions for me to give to them before they leave for the day?"

The mention of Jay's name brought Coal's pitchfork to an abrupt halt. "Yeah. Tell her…" *Tell her she's driving me crazy!* "Oh, never mind. I have to go up to the house so I'll tell her myself."

"Are you sure?"

There was a loaded question. She wasn't sure about anything anymore, but she couldn't keep ignoring her responsibilities. They needed to talk and this seemed like the perfect opportunity.

Chapter Ten

For the third time in the past few minutes, Jay measured the opening for the new double mahogany French doors that would open up onto Coal's master bedroom deck. Rechecking her work was essential since making mistakes on special order items could potentially prolong a job and cost her cousin for the error. After the morning she'd had, she'd triple-checked all her work because her focus kept waning since she and Coal had shared that mouth-watering kiss. She wondered what Coal was doing right now—wondered if she was angry at all with her considering she could have stopped the kiss but hadn't wanted to.

She could never recall meeting a woman that made her want so much. Had never met anyone who consumed her thoughts so completely. But she'd learned long ago that want came with a price. That painful lesson was schooled into her the hard way after years of wishing her mother would return, only to be disappointed when birthdays and holidays came and went with no word from her. The more she thought about Coal and her world, the more she realized that Coal Davis was a luxury she couldn't afford. The sooner she got that concept through her thick skull the better off she'd be.

Sweat trickled into her eyes, and she used a bandana to wipe it away. She'd given up on finding her hat hours ago. The temperatures were in the low nineties, and every time she stepped out into the heat, she could feel her skin suffering from the lack of coverage.

"Looking for this?"

Jay glanced over her shoulder to find Coal standing directly behind her, holding her black baseball cap at arm's length. She took the cap and placed it on her head. "All morning. Where did you find it?" She drove another nail into the frame, all the while keeping her eyes glued to Coal.

"Over there by the toolbox. I was trying to figure out why you weren't wearing it since you're starting to resemble a lobster out of water."

"You saying you care about me?"

"I didn't say that," Coal said with a hint of defiance in her voice. "But if you want to risk skin cancer go ahead."

"Well, I think you do." All Jay could do was stare at those incredible kissable lips. Was she playing with fire? Probably. But for Coal, she'd gladly burn.

"Jay, we should talk."

"Uh oh."

She placed her hammer back into her tool belt bracing for a brush-off. The only time she ever heard that tone was when she didn't measure up to someone's expectations or she pissed someone off. The last time was with Dino at the restaurant when he attempted to school her on all the reasons to stay away from Coal. The time before that, it was her father. She pushed that unwanted thought to the back of her mind.

"Jay, relax. I just thought we should talk about this morning."

"What about it?" She knew she sounded defensive, because she was.

"Well, for one, I kissed you and I wanted to apologize."

"No harm no foul. Besides, I'm totally cool with it."

"Really?

Coal crossed her arms over her chest. The defensive posture nearly made Jay laugh. Coal was even sexy when she was mad.

"You might be fine with it, but what is Shiloh going to think?"

"Shiloh?" Jay considered the question. "Why would she care?"

It occurred to Jay that Coal might have the wrong impression of her roommate. She smiled. Was Coal jealous?

"I'm glad you think this is funny."

"Coal," Jay said softly. She stepped closer. "Shiloh is my roommate. Nothing more."

"Roommate?"

"Yeah, as in she rents out one room and I rent the other."

"Oh, well…" Coal began to back up toward the entrance to the master bedroom, blindly searching for the doorframe behind her. "That's uh…great. She's nice. See you later."

Jay couldn't take her eyes off of Coal's retreating form as she pulled out her hammer to continue with her work. The blush that had stole across Coal's face had been adorable and she was so busy looking at the way Coal's hips swayed when she walked out, she missed the next nail she planned to hit altogether and smashed her knuckle instead.

"Ow, shit!" she said with a grimace and dropped the hammer to the floor.

Coal ran through the doorway as Jay cradled her left hand against her chest. Dino was not far behind and stared at Jay in what could only be disbelief. "Seriously, Cuz? I'm going to have to take out hazard pay if you keep this up."

Jay gritted her teeth as if that would stop the throbbing. This strike was much worse than the last two times she'd hit her hand. The previous mishaps had caught her thumb. This time, since her concentration had been elsewhere, she hit the back of her hand and was sure she'd broken it.

"Dino, take a quick drive up to my mom's house and ask her for some ice. I'll wait here with her," Coal said urgently, leaving no room for him to argue.

"I'm on it."

Dino disappeared as Coal gently placed her arm around Jay's waist and guided her onto the floor where she knelt between her outstretched legs.

"Jay, honey, you've got to let me see it," Coal said.

Maybe it was the way Coal called her honey or the way Coal seemed to appraise her with such intensity that made Jay want to give her whatever she wanted. No matter the reason, she unfolded her hand, noting the obvious discoloration and swelling.

She set her teeth against the pain when Coal rotated her hand between both of her own. She couldn't afford for it to be broken and actually let out a sigh of relief when Coal asked her to make a fist and she complied.

"How does it feel?"

Jay heard the question but was too overcome with the gentle way Coal was appraising her to form words. What also wasn't helping were the fantasies she was having of Coal kneeling between her legs. "Like I hit it with a hammer."

"Smartass. Stop dodging the question." Coal placed her palm on Jay's face and moved a sweat-soaked strand of hair away from her eyes.

"I don't think it's broken," Jay said. She could feel Coal's touch all the way to her core. "Probably be fine in a day or two."

"Oh, so you're a doctor now? Because unless you have an x-ray machine outside with the rest of your tools, I don't see how you could possibly know that."

"Coal, I'll be fine. Promise," Jay whispered huskily. As she locked onto Coal's eyes, they became as black as the sea at night. The longer their gazes held, the more the black became hazy, fathomless. She knew that look. This color gave away Coal's wants. Her desires. And it was directed at her. *I know where you got your name.*

"Are you sure? It looks like it hurts." Coal dropped her gaze to Jay's lips. She scooted closer and Jay gripped the floor beneath her fingers. If Coal moved another inch, her knees would press against Jay's center. If that happened, Jay's head and other body parts would surely explode.

"It does, but I've done worse. Look, I want to apologize for not being clear yesterday about Shiloh. I'm sorry if you had the impression—"

Jay looked up when she heard the front door slam and footsteps pounding up the stairs. Coal shot to her feet just as Dino burst through the bedroom door.

"Here's that ice," he said and handed a bag to her wrapped in a towel. "How's the hand?"

"Better, thanks for getting this." She placed the bag over the back of her hand and closed her eyes in an effort to center herself. She had to fight back both the pain in her hand and the swirl of arousal that Coal's presence invoked. "Just give me a few minutes and I should be good to go."

"Good to go?" Coal said incredulously. "You better mean good to go to the hospital because you can't work until you have that checked."

"I can take you now if you want to go, Cuz," Dino said. If he was surprised by Coal's outburst, he didn't show it.

"Hell no! We aren't going to the hospital. Look, it works." She gingerly opened and closed her hand then braced her good hand against the wall and pushed to her feet. She bent forward to pick up the hammer with her uninjured hand and tried to hold a nail in place but swore as it fell from her grip.

"Dino, could you give us a moment please?" The question sounded more like an order.

"I'll be out front if you change your mind, Jay," Dino said and disappeared down the steps. Jay reached into her tool belt for another nail and dropped that one too.

"Damn, I know mules that aren't this stubborn!" Coal swiped the hammer from Jay and held it behind her body. "You're done here today. Now please, go get that hand examined."

"I told you, I'm fine. This kind of stuff happens all the time."

"You're not fine," Coal said softly and placed her hand in the center of Jay's chest. "You're hurt. Please, Jay. For me."

Jay sighed in defeat. She focused on her boots, ashamed for what she was about to confess. Partly because it was true, but partly because she didn't think someone with Coal's upbringing would be able to understand the gravity of her situation. "It's not that easy. What if it's broken? Then what? They put me in a cast and I can't work for what…six weeks? I can't afford not to work. So I'd rather not go."

"Hey." Coal reached out and placed her hand on Jay's jaw. "Look at me."

Jay fell into Coal's steady gaze and forgot about the pain. Forgot about everything. "It's hard to look anywhere else when you're in the room."

"Do other women fall for that line?"

"Sometimes." Jay groaned as Coal ran her thumb across her lower lip. "Look, I'm sorry, for pushing. I didn't realize."

"There's nothing to be sorry about," Jay said. She could feel the soft touch deep in her belly. "How would you know?"

Coal stepped back, dropping her hand to her side. Her gaze became flat, unreadable. "Just promise me, you'll be careful. Okay?"

Feeling the growing distance between them once again, Jay said softly, "You have my word."

❖

How would you know?

The words echoed in Coal's skull as she pushed her way into the barn. She'd heard what Jay had said but knew what she'd meant. *How could someone like you understand?*

She had nearly offered help, even thought about paying for Jay's hospital visit. But after Jay's comment and watching her try to work while injured, she knew Jay would never accept any type of help out of stubborn pride. And Jay was stubborn. And tough. And so downright annoyingly sexy it made her heart hurt knowing that Jay couldn't look to her for comfort.

She'd never taken the time to consider how something as common as an injury could have such an impact on someone's livelihood. Of course, she'd witnessed people's struggles in the past. Had spent a lot of summers watching kids with crippling injuries and life-threatening diseases ride those horses on her grandfather's ranch. In some cases, she even saw the light return to those that knew their world would soon end in darkness. And it stung to know that Jay thought that her social status meant she couldn't sympathize with her in any way.

As the day trudged on, she fought with the deep desire to go check on Jay. She would have done anything to take away her pain. But she also couldn't keep denying she wanted her. And if she had to witness Jay in another unguarded moment, her control would crack. Deciding a ride on Dax would help with her pent-up frustration, she saddled her horse and headed into the hills. The rush of adrenaline and the wind in her face always made her feel as though she had some sort of control over her life. An hour later, they returned, and she pulled out the hose to wash away the large clumps of mud that masked Dax's dark chocolate hair. In the quiet of his stall, she began talking to him like she'd done a thousand times before.

"I just don't get her, boy. She's driving me crazy!"

Dax let out a snort that made her laugh.

"Why can't I stop thinking about her? Oh, and did I tell you I kissed her in my sleep?"

Dax snorted again, pushing his nose into her side. He pulled a gum wrapper from her pocket that she immediately swiped from him. "I don't have any carrots, so stop! Anyway, this is about me, so pay attention. I kissed her, and honestly, I can't think of anything but kissing her again."

Dax stomped his foot and bobbed his head like he agreed.

"Of course it was fantastic, but yesterday I saw her with this knockout blonde and found out that they live together. And then that kiss...." Coal groaned like she was in pain, the good kind of pain that caused a certain body part to swell and throb with the intense need for release. "Jay said they're roommates, but they look like so much more. I'm so fucking confused."

Dax let out a high-pitched whine and knocked Coal's hat off her head.

"Thanks a lot." She picked up her hat and swatted him with it. "Was that your way of agreeing with me?"

Dax bobbed his head again.

"Very funny, smart ass. But the weird thing is, I was a little jealous. How could that be? I barely know her. Ugh...see...crazy!"

Dax made another snorting sound that sounded a lot like a cough.

"*Okay*, you're right. I was a lot jealous. And now I know they're not an item, so what do I do?"

Jay had been eavesdropping outside Dax's stall, her heart soaring with Coal's revelation. She didn't want to let on that she'd been listening so she backed up a few steps and made sure to drag her boots along the dirt path to make her presence known. With a heavy knock, she pushed open the stall door to find Coal and her horse covered in mud from head to toe. The sight was beautiful and strangely erotic.

"Hey." Coal laid the hose by her feet. "Is everything okay?"

"Actually, no. Can I speak with you for a sec?"

"What is it?" Coal moved to her side and picked up Jay's hand, cradling it between her own to inspect it. "Is it your hand?"

"No." She took a deep breath and steadied herself for what she was about to say. She'd been practicing for the past half hour hoping it would be adequate. "I came to apologize for earlier. I didn't mean to snap at you. My problems are not your concern, and I'm sorry if it felt like I took out my frustrations on you."

"Please don't apologize," Coal whispered and moved closer. "I was worried about you. And I was out of line." She rubbed her thumb over the back of Jay's hand. Jay groaned. "Hurt?"

"Christ no. Don't you know by now that when you touch me—" Jay swallowed her next words, afraid that everything she had wanted to say since they met would come pouring out. She wanted to tell Coal that she was all she thought about. That when Coal touched her she forgot about all the reasons why getting close to her on any level was a bad idea.

"When I touch you…what?"

"I feel everything. All at once. Everywhere."

"Well then, how does this feel?" Coal asked before brushing a kiss over Jay's injured hand.

"It's still a bit sore," Jay said thickly.

"It's a good thing then that I have something a lot better than ice."

"You do, huh?"

"Oh, yes."

Forgetting that Coal was a warning sign she should heed at all cost, Jay leaned forward intent on brushing a kiss across Coal's lips when she heard heavy footsteps approach. They both quickly retreated to opposite sides of Dax's stall just as the barn doors swung open admitting Coal's father who was being shadowed by a taller man who looked as though he had recently stepped out of an issue of *GQ*.

"There you are, Coal," Thomas said, although his laser gaze was focused on Jay. "We meet again."

"Nice to see you, sir," she said, although her sights still hadn't left the younger man who was staring at Coal as if he were a cat ready to pounce on his next meal.

"How's the house coming?" Thomas asked.

"We're right on schedule."

"Good to hear. Let me introduce you to Jefferson Sutter. A friend of Coal's."

Jay didn't care for the inflection of the word "friend." Instead, the word preppy came to mind as she studied the tall blond with his perfectly coiffed hair and not a wrinkle in his clothes. His Italian loafers probably cost more than she made in a week, and to make matters worse, he had placed his hand casually on Coal's shoulder as if it was something he'd become accustomed to.

"Dad, what's this about?" Coal sounded about as annoyed as Jay felt, but she made no move to back away from Jefferson.

"Jefferson just relayed to me that during the Fourth of July party, you were gracious enough to offer to take him out on the town. We came to find you since he's free tonight."

"That's interesting. Because I don't remember saying that."

Jay shifted restlessly, not wanting to hear any more about Coal doing anything with Mr. Perfect, or anyone else for that matter.

"It's okay if you forgot," Jefferson said, his tone as arrogant as the smug look on his face. "I was thinking of dinner in the city and a tour of the sights. What do you say?"

"Jefferson, really, I can't—"

"Sure you can. Whatever plans you've made I'm sure can wait," Thomas said, his tone unyielding.

"Dad, I have chores to do. Tonight's not a good night."

"Chores can wait. You have to make time for social outings. You'll learn that after the ranch becomes a full-time undertaking."

"Fine," Coal said. Her tone one of resignation. "Tonight will be great."

"Sir, if you would excuse me," Jay said. She needed to get the hell out of there. "My cousin needs me back at the house. Ms. Davis, if you have anything else to add to the list, I'll be here first thing tomorrow morning."

"Certainly," Coal said. "Thank you, Jay."

Jay sprinted back toward the house, her head spinning from the last few minutes. *If that's how she wants to play it, then fine. I don't want anything to do with women who date men.*

"Quittin' time, Cuz!" Dino shouted from the roof as Jay ignored him and barreled through the front door.

She picked up the first tool she could find and, forgetting about where she was or the consequences of her actions, launched the Philips head screwdriver cleanly into one of the walls. *Too bad that wasn't Jefferson's head.*

"What the hell?" Dino said, more pissed than shocked by her actions.

Jay yanked the screwdriver out from the sheetrock and threw it into her tool chest before slamming the lid shut. "It's nothing. Just a little hole. I'll fix it later."

"No, you won't. You'll fix it right fucking now or you're not leaving."

An hour later, she joined Dino inside the truck, her temper still set to simmer. She wanted away from the job, because she needed to get as far away from Coal Davis as possible.

"You want to tell me what's going on over a beer?" Dino asked.

"No. Just take me back to the shop. I'm not in the mood for company."

"Come on, Cuz. You always talk to me."

Even if she could tell him about Coal without risking getting fired, how could she share her feelings with him when she didn't know how to categorize them? She had never experienced this intense need to want to be with someone so badly before. Not that it mattered anyway. After today, Coal was a closed issue. "I don't want to talk. I need a night out."

"Uh oh." He wiggled his eyebrows playfully. "I know what *that* means. My cousin needs to get laid."

"Exactly."

"Well, I'm glad to see you're still not lusting over our hot client. I thought after the way she had been looking at you today something was going on. Glad I was wrong."

Jay glanced sideways at him, letting out a disdainful snort. "How did she *look* at me?" *Like she cares. She tells her horse all she does is think about me, almost kisses me again, and then in the next breath she agrees to go out on a date. With a man!*

"Like she wanted to eat you for lunch!"

"Fucking right," she said sarcastically. "You obviously can't read women, because I know for a fact that she has other interests."

"And how do you know that?"

Jay stared out the truck window and pointed at the passing silver Jaguar. "Because of him. That would be Jefferson Sutter. Coal's *date* for the evening."

"Cuz," Dino said cautiously. "Do we need to talk about something?"

"Just get me the fuck out of here." She slammed her head against the headrest as he started the truck. She needed a drink and a warm body, hoping that both had the power to banish Coal from her every thought.

Coal stripped off her clothes, angrily throwing them onto the floor in her wake. Once again, she'd allowed her father to tell her what to do, but this time she'd felt as though she didn't have a choice.

If Jay hadn't been there, she wouldn't have agreed to this bullshit night out. She knew this was her dad's fucked up way of getting her out on a date with Jefferson. He'd even brought up the ranch as a warning.

"Night out, my ass." She yanked on the shower faucet and stepped into the hot spray. She poured shampoo into her hands, roughly running them over her scalp as if she could scrub the last few minutes out of her memory.

Before he'd barged in, Jay had nearly kissed her, and unlike that morning, this time wouldn't have been an accident. She'd become so entranced in Jay's hot, demanding gaze that she almost hadn't heard her father and Jefferson approaching. She had watched Jay closely as Jay's eyes followed Jefferson's every move. She hadn't missed the tightness in her jaw when Jefferson had subtly but deliberately touched her. When she'd finally agreed to hanging out with Jefferson, Jay's entire demeanor had changed. Where her body had once vibrated with restrained emotion begging to be released, she had become stiff, detached, her face a mask of indifference.

With towel in hand, she stepped from the shower and stormed into her closet, pulling out a pair of tailored gray slacks and a green silk blouse. She planned to get this night over with quickly, and maybe if she had a little extra time, go for a drink to forget the entire day, everything except for the kiss she and Jay had shared.

With only minutes left before Jefferson was due to arrive, she picked up the phone, needing desperately to talk with Angel. She'd hoped Angel could give her a bit of advice, but after giving Angel the short version of what happened, the advice Angel gave her was not the kind Coal had in mind.

"I can't believe you're going through with this. You do realize this is a date, right?"

"I refuse to think of it that way. Let's just say it's another family obligation and leave it at that."

Angel made a gagging sound. "I hope you're not buying that crap you're dishing out. Because if it was me, I would have told your father to shove it years ago."

"You make it sound so easy. And you know that's not an option right now." This wasn't the conversation that she had planned. She needed a little sympathy, yet this was Angel she was talking to.

"Ah, right. The Davis name. How could I forget? The same name you've been running from for your entire life. Hello! What is with you?"

"You know what. I'm going to go."

"Wait!"

"What?" Coal sighed, putting her hand over her face. As if that would stop the tears.

"Honey, look. I'm sorry. But can't you see it kills me to see you having to put up with all this shit? You know I love you. But I'm also the one person you turn to when no one else will tell you the truth no matter how painful it is to hear. You can't keep choosing to put your life on hold to make other people happy. You need to take the reins and live!"

"You're right."

"Say that again? I want to record it for next time."

"Bite me," Coal said with a small smile. Angel could always find a way to make her feel better no matter how fucked up the situation.

"That's the Coal I know. Tell you what. After you dump Jefferson, why don't you come by Spice? We'll have a drink and you can tell me all about how horrible the night out was."

"Maybe. I'll call you when I get back."

"Awesome. I'm here if you need me. Bye, babe."

Coal hit end on her phone and reached for a Kleenex to wipe her damp face. With ten minutes left to get ready, she ran a brush through her hair and applied a small amount of eyeliner and mascara hoping to cover the dark circles under her eyes. She stared at the woman in the mirror, not happy with the person she saw staring back.

You need to take the reins and live.

Angel's words echoed loudly in the empty house. If she had more guts, she would have spoken up to her father. She would have kissed Jay like she had wanted too. And she wouldn't be showing anyone the town tonight.

Taking one more look in the mirror as the doorbell rang, she took a deep breath and grabbed her purse. This was going to be her last family favor. After tonight, she wouldn't only take those reins; she planned to own them.

CHAPTER ELEVEN

Coal shouldered her way through the packed room trying to make her way to the fifteen-foot section of bar that was adjacent to the postage stamp-sized dance floor. The heavy beat vibrated throughout the crammed room, but even that couldn't compete with the booming voices she had to shout over to order a drink. She had to get away from the crowds. Find a quieter place to sit and gather her thoughts.

She'd called Angel about an hour earlier, telling her about her disastrous evening with Jefferson. Well, at least she thought it ranked high on her shit-o-meter anyway. Since seeing the sights was what she had agreed to, she'd planned to show him around San Francisco's famous Fisherman's Wharf. From there, a short stroll would also give them the opportunity to check out Pier 39, and if the evening had to drag out longer, they could possibly take a short drive to visit the Golden Gate Bridge. But as they entered the city, it became apparent that plans had already been put into motion and that her meddling father had made all the arrangements, right down to dessert.

Jefferson had suggested a trendy French restaurant where, coincidentally, her father visited with many of his high-powered associates on a weekly basis. She sat quietly, listening to him talk about everything ranging from his job to his career plans, politely nodding when she felt it necessary. She barely touched the scallops Provencal he had taken the liberty to order for her, and by the time the crème brulee had arrived, she began complaining of a headache and had asked him to take her home.

Once she'd set foot into her quiet house, loneliness had all but consumed her. When she began to feel claustrophobic, she'd grabbed her keys and hoped Angel hadn't found someone to go home with before she'd reached the bar. With drink in hand, she finally spotted her standing near the entrance to the restrooms talking with one of the butches, who was eyeing Angel as a child would an all-day sucker. Angel was apparently amused by whatever the woman in the motorcycle boots and remarkable arm tattoos had to say because when she tilted her head back and laughed, Coal caught sight of Jay leaning against the back wall engaged in what appeared to be an even more intimate type of conversation.

Maybe it was the second vodka cranberry or the fact that she had been off-kilter all night that made her world seem as though it was spiraling out of control. She wasn't sure. But seeing Jay with Shiloh draped against her made her throat constrict with every breath and the feelings of loneliness to return more powerfully than ever.

Jay's head was resting against the wall, and her eyes were closed while Shiloh whispered something into her ear. A smile creased Jay's handsome face, and Coal's heart faltered. She knew that sexy grin well. But this time, it wasn't meant for her. *Roommate, yeah, whatever!*

Paralyzed to move, all she could do was stare at Shiloh's hand where it rested on Jay's midriff. When Jay's eyes searched the dance floor, Coal wished she were somewhere else. What struck her as strange was why Jay appeared to be unresponsive to Shiloh's attentions. Jay's gaze was flat, bordering on uninterested. She knew this because only hours before, she'd witnessed Jay's desire. Recalled how Jay's arousal had sparked a need in her so intense that she had nearly succumbed in her arms. Back then, she had been the cause of that need. They'd almost kissed. Had nearly been given the chance to become completely lost in each other. Yet nothing had happened between them because her father once again intruded upon her life. Now Jay was in the arms of another woman. Someone else was touching her. And she refused to sit there any longer and pretend as if it didn't matter.

A k.d. lang song poured from the speakers, and Coal watched helplessly as Jay led Shiloh out onto the dance floor. When k.d. started singing about constant craving and Jay opened her arms to admit

Shiloh, Coal shot to her feet sending her stool crashing to the floor. She swayed and grabbed the table for support, cursing under her breath as the alcohol rendered her lower limbs useless. But dizziness be damned, she needed out of that bar, and the front door was ten feet away.

"Whoa, there," Angel said. She grabbed Coal's arm to steady her. "Where are you going?"

"Home. I'm exhausted."

"Not in your condition, you're not. And what's the rush?" Angel followed Coal's gaze with her own and tightened her grip. "Never mind. Let's dance."

"Let go of me," Coal whispered, but Angel ignored her and yanked her toward the dance floor.

"Shut up and talk with me for a minute. You're in no condition to drive. Besides, I saw who you were looking at, and I'm saving you from yourself."

"You have no idea what you're talking about."

"That tune's about as old as the one that's playing." Angel gripped Coal tighter around the waist. "Now calm down and tell me what the hell is going on between the two of you."

"Nothing...obviously," Coal said through a jaw so tight her teeth ached.

"Do you know who that is with her?"

"Her roommate, supposedly."

God, why couldn't Angel have just let her leave? Seeing Jay in that woman's arms was slowly killing her. She focused on Jay's hands, remembering how they had caressed her back in long strokes. She knew what those hands were capable of. They held the power to create new from old. To thrill and excite. To comfort and protect. Now they were wrapped around someone else and she was seconds from going postal.

She wanted to be held like Jay was holding Shiloh. The last time she'd been held in a similar fashion, she'd been dancing with Taylor. Life with Taylor had been all about lust and sex and the excitement of her first time being with a woman. Taylor had been wild and reckless and passionate. She'd loved making love with Taylor, but this time was so very different. She didn't have this incessant craving that clawed at her to be released like she did when she was anywhere near

Jay. And whereas Taylor's arrogant attitude had been a turn off most times, she loved Jay's shit-eating grin and youthful exuberance when she talked about things she loved. Even though Jay's stubbornness and pride angered her sometimes, she also had to admire those traits. If Coal possessed the ability to be a little more like Jay, maybe then she would be sure of her own actions and decisions and finally have the guts to stand up to her family.

"Roommates, interesting," Angel said. "They look to me to be more than that. And you know, now that I've seen her for the second time, she looks vaguely familiar."

"Funny, your dad said the same thing."

"Like I said, interesting. He never notices anyone. So what's the roommate's story?"

"No idea. I know her name is Shiloh, and supposedly they're not an item. The rest is a mystery."

"So what's the problem then?"

"No problem because it's none of my fucking business," Coal said in frustration, drawing a few curious stares.

"Oh, well, that was convincing. And even if I believed you, which I don't, you might be interested to know that she's spotted you. And by the way she's glaring at me, I think she wants it to be."

Jay had spent most of the evening clinging to Shiloh, afraid that if she'd let go she'd drown in her own pity pool. The evening had started out with the intention of drinking Coal's memory away. She'd hoped to find some companionship, anyone to help take her mind off Coal and her date. But the more time she'd spent staring at the unfamiliar faces of the needy and intoxicated, the more the idea of sex with a stranger didn't appeal to her. All she wanted was for the suffering to end. She hoped that the images of Jefferson touching Coal would vanish. But not even being in the comforting arms of her friend could help her forget.

"You've been awful quiet tonight, darlin'," Shiloh said.

Jay spun them toward the center of the packed floor. "I know. Sorry. I told you I wouldn't be good company tonight."

"I remember. But you're being unusually needy. Want to tell me who you wish you were dancing with?"

Jay pulled away and stared at her. "That's a weird question. And I'm dancing with you."

"Physically, that's true, but I know you. You're holding me, but another woman's troubling that mind of yours. Tell me I'm wrong."

Man, why did Shiloh have to pick this moment to play shrink? Shiloh had always been perceptive, but Jay wasn't there to remember. She wanted to forget. Forget that Coal was somewhere right now with that smug pretty boy probably sitting under a blanket of stars. That he would pull her close. Lean forward in an effort to kiss her...

"Jay?"

"Hmm? I'm sorry, Shi. What did you say?" Jay sighed, laying her head back on Shiloh's shoulder.

"Don't worry, darlin'. You already answered my question."

Thankful that Shiloh had stopped with the inquisition, she closed her eyes and recalled the kiss she had shared with Coal that morning. No one's lips compared to Coal's. They'd been soft, welcoming, hungry. Then there was her scent of hay warming in the sunshine. From the moment they'd met, that scent had the power to ignite all her senses. Today, when they'd almost kissed for the second time, she'd felt a feeling of belonging that she'd never experienced before. Then Jefferson presented a barrier between them, and the tenuous tie that had bound them snapped and she'd felt completely adrift once more.

When the memories became too painful to bear, she opened her eyes and released Shiloh, intent on calling it a night, when she spotted Coal dancing in the arms of a familiar redhead. At first she thought she was hallucinating, that is until Coal's gaze locked on her own. And she looked pissed.

"Shi, I'll catch up with you later."

"You bet."

Forgetting all about how miserable she'd been moments before, she pushed through the crowd until she stood directly in front of Coal and her dance partner. Ignoring the woman who held Coal in a tight embrace, she extended her hand. "May I cut in?"

Coal studied Jay's hand for a long moment, and for a second, Jay thought she might refuse. Eventually, though, Coal released her partner, and without a word, moved into the circle of Jay's arms.

Jay sighed into Coal's hair the instant their bodies became reacquainted. They moved in a tight circle as Jay clung to Coal afraid she'd let go. Coal's cheek brushed against Jay's breast, and Jay's skin tingled where Coal's fingertips glided along the back of her neck. She buried her face into Coal's golden hair and inhaled the scent she'd been remembering for hours, content to stay that way forever. And even when the slow melody faded and the crowd began to scatter, neither one moved as if scared the fragile truce between them would evaporate along with the music.

"I'm sorry if I interrupted your dance," Jay whispered against Coal's temple. *I don't want to let you go.*

"I'm glad you did. But I'm the one who should be sorry. I didn't mean to stare. But I couldn't stop myself," Coal said brokenly and buried her face into Jay's chest.

"Oh, baby, don't…please…It's not what you think."

"Really? Then explain it to me, Jay." Coal stepped out of Jay's arms and wiped a shaky hand across her face. "Because you two looked pretty cozy together."

Jay brushed a shaky hand through her disheveled hair, caught off guard by the turn of events. How could Coal question her relationship with Shiloh after she'd gone out on a date? And then to make matters worse, she'd come here to forget Coal and found her dancing with the same woman Coal had been talking to the first day they'd met.

"Nothing to say?"

"Oh, I have plenty to say, but I think we've made a big enough scene. Let's take this outside." Jay guided Coal by the arm to a quiet spot away from the noisy crowd. In the rear of the poorly lit parking lot, Jay leaned against her truck, facing away from the club, which afforded them the maximum privacy given their location.

"Okay, you dragged me out here. Are you going to answer my question?"

"Sure, but only if you tell me what you and hot pants were doing on the dance floor before I cut in?"

Coal crossed her arms defensively over her chest. "That's none of your business."

"How convenient. You want to grill me about Shiloh but won't answer a simple question about the redhead or why you're here when you were supposed to be on a date with Jefferson." Jay knew she sounded angry, but she was tired and so fucking confused. Besides, the desire to pull Coal back into her arms and kiss her until they both forgot everything was too great. This night was turning out to be a true test of her power of restraint, which when it came to Coal, was always being pushed to its breaking point.

"You made your point. What you do is none of my business. Good night."

"Don't leave." Jay grasped Coal by the shoulders and pinned her against her truck. She pressed along the length of Coal's body as heat raced along her spine. When Coal gasped, something inside Jay twisted pleasurably. Trying to control her body's demand to take the lips that were a breath from her own, she whispered, "Don't you get it? I don't know what's happening between us, but whatever it is, it's twisting me up inside. This morning, I know you were unconscious of that kiss. Not that I'm complaining. But in the barn…while you were in my arms…that was no accident. You wanted to kiss me. I know because I felt it. In here." She placed Coal's hand over her heart.

Coal looked at Jay, her expression full of pain. "You're right. I did. I still do."

Jay cupped Coal's face between her hands and brushed her thumbs over Coal's bottom lip. Without another word, she tilted her head and lowered her lips to Coal's. The kiss was slow. A soft meeting of lips, a touch so feather light it left Jay aching for more.

"So soft," she whispered right before she swept her tongue along Coal's. She moaned and deepened the kiss. Her body screamed for more. More than she even knew what to ask for.

"I could get lost in you," Coal said breathlessly.

Jay pressed her hips further in between Coal's legs. "I feel like a starved tiger being given its first meal. Every time I have a taste of you, I crave more."

Coal ran her tongue along Jay's bottom lip. "You can feed off me anytime."

Jay growled and leaned closer to tug at Coal's ear with her teeth. "Don't tempt me. I've been hungry for you for what seems like forever."

"I don't think I can make that promise." Coal ran her hands along Jay's sides, making her shiver. "You have to know I want you so much it hurts."

"Sometimes I want to cry I want you so badly." Jay placed a kiss on the tip of Coal's nose moving slightly away from her so that their bodies no longer touched. "But I think we need to slow things down."

"Why's that?" Coal lifted her thigh against Jay's crotch and Jay's head shot back.

"Easy."

"Screw easy. I want you."

"Coal, please," Jay said, on the verge of breaking. "Wait."

"I don't understand." Coal laid her forehead against Jay's as they both fought the urge to do what their bodies demanded of them to finish. "I guess I'm a little surprised."

"Uh, newsflash. I think I am too," Jay said. She'd never been the one to put on the brakes before. "But we do have a lot to talk about."

"Yes, we do." Coal threaded her arms around Jay's waist. "Look, I'm sorry about earlier. I was mad at you. Seeing another woman in your arms was killing me. I overreacted…"

"Shh," Jay said and silenced her with a finger over her lips. "Don't think it's any different for me. But I'm still confused about this afternoon. What was with that scene with that clown and your dad?"

Coal's laugh helped lighten the moment. "That clown, as you so eloquently put it, is a friend of my father's. I'm so sorry about that. But you've met my dad. And for reasons I can't explain tonight, I don't want to make waves with him. I agreed to show Jefferson around San Francisco as a favor to my dad. I came home as soon as I could, and I hated it. Every minute."

"I know I have no right to ask." Jay braced for the answer. "But did he touch you?"

"No," Coal said and stroked her jaw. "I would never allow that to happen."

"And the woman you were dancing with?"

"Her name is Angel. We've been best friends since grade school. We're close, but there is zero between us. Promise."

Jay let out a sigh of relief. "Same for me and Shiloh, but I haven't known her as long as you've known Angel. Like I told you before, Shiloh is my roommate. Nothing more."

"She's really beautiful." Coal glanced away as Jay picked up the hint of insecurity in her voice.

"She is beautiful." Jay grasped Coal gently by the chin to look into her eyes. "But you're all I think about."

"I want to believe that."

"Believe it."

Coal placed her hand on Jay's chest and ran her thumb over an erect nipple. "I love how your body responds when I touch you."

"Careful. I'm wired."

"I like that. Knowing I do that to you. What if I want to see that wire snap?"

Jay gritted her teeth and pulled Coal's hand away from her chest. "You will, if you're not careful."

"Then let's get out of here. Go somewhere more private."

Jay struggled with her desire; wanting nothing more than to take Coal back to her place and ravish her until neither one of them could walk the next day. But this thing with Coal was different, special. She wouldn't cave to her urges, not until she voiced the one thing she feared most. "I want that too. Believe me, baby. But I don't think it's a good idea. Not yet."

"You keep saying that. Is it something I'm doing wrong?"

"Hell no!" She pulled Coal back against her body, wanting her to feel the heat that only Coal had the power to create. "Feel me shaking. This need for you that I have is threatening to derail me. I'm hanging on by a thread. But you're special. And I want to treat you that way. Besides, I want to make sure this is what you want. That I'm who you want. Because I don't want you to regret anything that happens between us. I don't think I could survive if you decided this was a mistake."

Jay had spent most of her adult life indulging in one-night stands or quick fucks in any dark corner she could find. She could pick up a woman faster than she could order a beer, but her experiences, even though they fulfilled a basic need, had always left her feeling unsatisfied afterward. She'd never questioned those feelings before because she'd never experienced that all-consuming hunger. But with Coal, she had that insatiable desire to devour, to take. She wanted nothing more than to please her, but she also wanted to prove that Coal was worth so much more even if that meant going against her body's ferocious need to claim Coal right where she stood.

"I could never see anything happening between us as being a mistake. But if it makes you feel better, we could slow down. Take it one step at a time."

"I hear a 'but' coming."

"But I'm going to hate moving out of your arms. Normally, I'm not this aggressive, but I can't seem to keep my hands off of you."

Jay laughed, bringing her lips closer to Coal's. "Well, I trust you."

Coal's eyes darkened dangerously. "Big mistake."

Coal placed her hand between Jay's legs and pressed, causing Jay's vision to dim and moisture to flood between her thighs. Her legs shook. Her core hardened. She was losing her grip fast, and if Coal applied a bit more pressure, she'd release her tenuous hold and fall helplessly, hopelessly.

"Coal, we have to stop. Please, baby." She placed her hand over Coal's. Another few strokes and she'd forget where she was and why she thought they should wait.

"I know…I'm sorry. I can't help myself."

"No apologies." She pulled Coal's hand from between her legs and took a shaky breath. "I'm not complaining. And I'm usually not ready to blast off this easy, but you excite me."

She traced Coal's face with her fingertip, brushing it along one golden brow before running the tip across the lips that were still swollen from their kiss. When Coal caught Jay's finger between her teeth and sucked on the end of it, she reignited the embers that had been smoldering between them into a raging forest fire.

"You're dangerous," Jay said and broke their contact before she went up in flames.

"You have no idea."

"Maybe not, but I want to find out. When can I see you again?"

"How about Friday night?"

With her body under better control, she placed her hands on Coal's hips and tugged her close. She loved the way Coal's body molded to hers, and she didn't think she'd ever get enough. "Eight o'clock sound good? We can do dinner, a movie, whatever. Your choice."

"Wait. You want to go on an actual date, date?"

"Well…yeah. What were you expecting?"

Coal smiled evilly. "Let's say it was more hoping."

"I like the way you think. But I want an old-school date. Does that shock you?"

"A little."

"Want to tell me why?"

"Because, sexy. You don't strike me as the dating type."

"You're right," Jay said, her tone contrite. If Coal only knew. "But I told you, I want to do this right with you. You make everything fresh and exciting. So please say yes."

"And you call me dangerous." Coal pulled Jay's head down for all too brief a kiss. "Friday it is then. You pick the restaurant."

"Any suggestions?"

"Oh, I have a lot of suggestions, but none of them include food."

Speechless, Jay followed Coal back inside, her eyes glued to her firm ass. If everything went as planned Friday, she just might have a few ideas of her own.

Chapter Twelve

Coal sat on top of Dax admiring the scenic view from the eastern ridge high above her hometown. From her vantage point, she could make out her home nestled beneath a canopy of oak trees. Another month or so and the remodel would be complete. She looked forward to the finished product but not the part where seeing Jay every day would come to an end.

For the last few days, her body had been constantly set to simmer. When the memory of Jay's touch burned too hot, she'd had to extinguish the flames under her own touch. But even her skillful hands couldn't banish the memories that touched her deeper than flesh. Jay's musky scent reminded her of wild horses racing through the wind. Jay's strong hands made her feel secure whenever they were wrapped around her. And just remembering how Jay's abdomen tightened when she touched her sent a new course of arousal surging through her body. She adjusted in her saddle. Anything to alleviate the constant building pressure.

She loved seeing Jay working with the sun as a backdrop, the muscles rock-hard beneath her skin flexing with every swing of a hammer. Loved how the sun kissed Jay's bronze body causing the sweat to glisten like diamonds. Then there were Jay's cocky moments when she would flash that quirky grin that she was slowly coming to love. But what turned her insides to jelly was the vulnerable way Jay had shuddered in her arms last night. They hadn't made love, but oh, how she'd enjoyed nearly bringing Jay to her knees with something as simple as a touch. She'd never had that kind of power over a woman before. And most times, she hadn't wanted it. With Taylor, she didn't mind being more passive and had allowed Taylor to take the reins in bed more often than not. But with Jay, she thirsted for that power. Her desire to touch, to draw a moan from Jay had her once again all keyed up. Her skin tingled from the memory of raking her fingers over one of Jay's nipples. She liked the way it had hardened against her palm. She could only imagine touching more of her with her hands. What it would be like to use her lips, her tongue, to feel her heat glide along Jay's thigh....

Dax whined in protest when she pressed her legs together. She'd nearly gone over from the visual. Talk about a first time for everything. "Sorry, boy. I was a bit lost in thought there."

Turning to more serious matters, she thought about the ranch and her responsibilities. Much had changed since the reading of the will. The day she'd returned from New York, she couldn't remember which way was up. She'd been so confused, so lost, that all she could do was what she felt was right at the time. But now, with the possibility of Jay being a part of her life, she was seriously questioning her decisions. Could she say fuck it and give total control to her father? Could she still live with that decision knowing she'd be responsible for destroying so many dreams for kids who had few dreams left? The answer was she still didn't think so. Regardless, time was running out, and she had no idea how she was going to play her cards given the odds of her situation. She wasn't a gambler. Not that it mattered, considering the odds would never be in her favor when the opponent was her family. Her dad was powerful and domineering, and no matter how much he cared about her, her needs would always take a backseat to his political aspirations and what he deemed his moral responsibilities.

The longer she sat there thinking about her destiny, her family, and Jay, the more she understood that somehow she'd overlooked what she'd truly longed for. Sometime in her past she'd all but given up and had resigned herself to the idea that her life was all about sacrificing for her family in some way. She'd buried her wants and desires for so long that it had taken Jay to awaken that passion within her. Now that her all-consuming thirst had been unleashed, she couldn't cage the beast. One taste of happiness was all it took to make her question every other aspect of her life.

The distinct sound of gravel crunching beneath tires made her divert her attention toward the front gate. She grunted in disgust as the recognizable Jaguar headed toward her parents' house. *Jefferson.*

What a perfect pawn her father found to play in one of his chess games. Unfortunately, the naïve Jefferson had no idea how her father operated and wasn't aware that he was just another piece to be moved strategically around the board until her father sacrificed him for a more strategic play. At least she was used to his manipulative behavior, unlike the clueless young Jefferson who seemed to idolize Judge Thomas Davis.

The more she thought about her bullshit night out with him, the angrier she became. Her father had orchestrated the perfect evening with the goal to be seen by every prominent face in his tight knit circle. Every time Jefferson had introduced her as Judge Thomas Davis's daughter, she wanted to run screaming from the room. Not willing to waste any more precious energy on things she couldn't change, she led Dax down the backside of the hill in search of a quiet place to relax. She stretched out under a willow tree, allowing the sounds of a nearby stream to help release the tension from her body and quickly dozed off.

A sturdy prodding to her ribs jarred her from sleep. Rubbing her arms from the chill, she sat up in a daze wondering why the sun had started to fade above the treetops. It couldn't be later than—

"Oh shit!" She looked at her watch and jumped to her feet. "I'm going to be late for my date!" Dax bobbed his head with a whine as she grabbed the reins and mounted him. "You're right. I owe you extra carrots for this one."

They sped through the open meadow and stopped at the top of the hill to make sure the silver Jaguar was nowhere in sight. Once they returned home and she secured the horses for the night, she raced home and rummaged through her bedroom closet in search of something to wear. The knock on her front door brought her up short, and she prayed it wasn't Jay arriving early, or worse, Jefferson making a surprise appearance. She exhaled in relief when she glanced through the peephole to find Angel standing on the porch with her hands perched on her hips.

"You're just in time," Coal said. She grabbed Angel by the arm to pull her into the house.

"Where the hell have you been? I tried calling you all afternoon."

"Sorry. I took Dax for a ride and cell reception sucks up on the hill. Jefferson stopped by to see my dad so I stayed gone for most of the day. Now I'm trying to get ready for my date with Jay and I have nothing to wear!"

"Damn, woman, take a chill pill." Angel dragged Coal toward her bedroom and into the massive walk-in closet. "You call this nothing to wear? You have more clothes than Nordstrom's. Go on. Model something for me."

Fifteen minutes later, Coal had tried on numerous combinations from slacks to skirts. After hearing Angel say "that's cute" for the hundredth time, she was ready to strangle her with the Gucci belt in her hand.

"Why did you stop?" Angel asked.

"Because you're not helping," Coal said. She knew she sounded desperate. Because she was. "Please, Angel. This is important. Help me find something."

"Honey, you'll be beautiful no matter what you decide to wear. If I were you, though, I'd be more worried about that rat's nest you call hair. It's still damp and Jay will be here any minute."

"Oh no!" Coal flew into the bathroom and pulled out her hairdryer. "Angel, please. You have to pick out something for me."

While Coal used a straightener to put the finishing touches on her hair, Angel sifted through a dozen or so items, finally choosing a pair of designer white jeans and a sheer yellow scooped neck shirt with a matching silk shell for underneath.

"You think she'll like that?"

"I think it's perfect. Besides," she pointed to Coal's iPad. "It says right here in *Fashion Weekly*, yellow is in."

Coal grabbed the jeans and had them halfway up her thighs when Angel began to laugh. "What's so funny?" Coal asked around the toothbrush sticking out of her mouth.

"I've never seen you this nervous before. It's kind of cute."

"Glad I can amuse you." Coal threw her hands over her face. "Seriously though, Angel. What am I doing? I'm supposed to be lying low, not going out on a date with her."

"Then why are you doing it?"

She'd been asking herself this question since Jay asked her out. She could lie and say she needed a night out. She could be grateful and say that someone had wanted to date her not because of who her family was but who she was as a person. That it felt good knowing that Jay wanted no one but her. But the truth was, she wanted Jay with everything in her. Being near Jay was more intoxicating than any liquor she'd ever encountered. But most of all, every time Jay looked at her, she could see that unreserved hunger written all over her face. And if given the chance, she planned to unleash that beast and all its fury. "Because I can't control myself around her any longer. And I know she feels the same way. I'm really falling for her, Angel."

"And that's a bad thing?"

"I guess not. Neither is wanting to rip her clothes off."

Angel let out a hardy laugh and stood to place a comforting arm around her shoulders. "Promise me you'll go out and have a lot of fun tonight. And I mean a *lot*."

Coal's spirits lifted as the doorbell rang. "God, Angel, what would I do without you?"

"No use wasting brain power on something you'll never have to worry about. Now go enjoy your night with that stud of yours. I expect a full report, complete with mouth-watering details, in the morning."

Coal laughed. "My mouth is watering just thinking about those details."

Jay stood on Coal's front porch holding a fresh bouquet of purple and yellow wildflowers. She couldn't stop her hands from shaking, considering this whole dating idea was a new experience for her. Maybe the idea was crazy and Coal was right. People like her didn't date. People with her track record screwed and didn't commit because commitment meant responsibility and putting someone else's interests above your own. But here she stood wanting to prove that she could be so much more than someone only good enough to share a bed with for a few hours. With a trembling hand, she raised her fist to knock again when the door swung open, revealing the woman who had been starring in her fantasies for weeks.

"Hi," Coal said shyly.

Angel exited the house and pushed past both of them with a huge, cat got the canary grin.

"You two have fun," Angel said from somewhere behind, but Jay was too focused on the hint of cleavage beneath Coal's sheer scoop-neck blouse to pay any attention to her.

"You look incredible." Jay held out the flowers. "For you."

"Thank you."

"You're welcome," she whispered. She cradled Coal's jaw with her palm and tilted her head for a kiss.

"Mmm," Coal said when she finally opened her eyes. "That was nice."

"Nice, huh? I was going for hot and tempting."

"You are both of those." Coal wrapped her arms around Jay's neck.

Jay leaned forward and kissed her again, this time with a bit more urgency. As Coal broke the kiss, she angled her head back giving Jay better access to her neck.

"I see you're not going to make this easy for me."

"I don't want it to be easy. *Hard* is definitely the plan."

"Then you're on the right track and we need to stop. Because dating rules be damned, if those sensual lips touch my skin one more time, I'm going to drag you inside and finish this."

"Ooh, I think I'm going to like being with someone so forceful." Jay grabbed Coal around the waist and crushed their bodies together. She could think of nothing but assuaging the aching need within her that she knew only Coal's touch could banish. "I think I broke one of your rules. What's the punishment?"

"I can think of several—"

Like a startled cat wary of impending danger, Coal froze and dug her fingers into Jay's shoulders when the sounds of a car could be heard through the thick patch of trees. The stress was so clearly etched in the deep creases between Coal's brows that Jay didn't resist when Coal grabbed her by the hand and swiftly led her to the truck.

"Everything okay?" Jay asked.

Tightly, Coal said, "Of course. Let's go enjoy that meal you promised me."

With every mile travelled, Coal's hands twitched less where they rested on her legs, and she stopped surveying the passing landscape as if she expected someone to materialize out of thin air. This wasn't the first time Jay had witnessed Coal's curious behavior, and whatever was causing this tightly coiled tension was obviously taking its toll on Coal. In an effort to help relax Coal, Jay kept the conversation light as they made their way to a small Italian restaurant located not too far from the Stanford campus. Jay listened intently as Coal told her all about the years she had spent at Stanford and how much she enjoyed the college experience.

"So if you loved it so much, how come you went to New York to get your master's?"

Jay regretted her question when the tension returned to Coal's body and her eyes hardened. "Circumstance. Besides, I needed away from my dad for a while, and New York seemed like the perfect choice. I returned not too long before you and I met."

"What was your major?"

"Business with a minor in economics. After I got my MBA, I planned to own and operate my own horse ranch. I just didn't imagine it would happen so soon."

Jay recalled the conversation they'd shared that day in Half Moon Bay regarding why Coal had been put in charge of the ranch. She reached for her hand. "I'm really sorry about your grandfather. Is your grandmother still alive?"

"No," Coal said. "She died in the accident with my grandfather."

"Oh, baby. I'm so sorry."

"Thanks. But enough about my life. Let's talk about you. I'm sure working with your cousin is great, but you're really talented. Ever aspire to owning your own contracting business someday?"

"Yes," Jay said but wasn't sure how much she should elaborate. When her college dreams ended, she'd given up on the idea of owning anything and settled for a task-oriented job with a steady paycheck. She'd never discussed her dreams with anyone before, partly because she didn't want people, her family especially, to think she was being foolish. What were dreams without money to support them?

Jay pulled into the parking lot of the restaurant and cut the engine. She turned to face Coal. "I'd love to go back to school and get my contractor's license, but I can't find the time."

"Well, if you did, you'd have clients beating down your door. And I have inside information on one client who would like to see much more of your…handiwork."

Even though Coal's words were full of innuendo, Jay couldn't see past her own self-doubt to allow them to affect her. She stared at their joined hands and rubbed Coal's palm with her thumb. She fought with telling Coal about her past family issues, a topic that was never discussed outside of a few close family members.

"Hey." Coal shook her hand lightly. "Something I said?"

"I'm fighting whether to tell you something. I want to, but I'm worried it will make you think less of me."

"Not possible." Coal intertwined her fingers through Jay's. "Look, I know this dating stuff is all new for you. But if this becomes something more, I want you to be able to trust me. To know that I'll be there for you."

Jay took a deep breath wanting to believe everything Coal was saying, but some genies couldn't be put back into the bottle once freed. If she wanted a chance with Coal though, Jay had to make Coal aware of her day-to-day reality. "Because I do want more, I want to share something with you, but we haven't even started our first date and I don't want to scare you off."

"Oh, honey. One thing I do understand is that life is difficult. Whatever you tell me, I promise, I won't judge you."

Jay nodded and squeezed Coal's hand. "A few years ago, my father worked as a handyman for a family in Woodside and stole some items to feed his habit. The day he was arrested, I got a call to come bail him out. I didn't have fifty thousand lying around so I had to put my aunt's house up for collateral. She left it to me when she died, and I promised her on her deathbed that it would always stay in the family."

"That's a lot to take on," Coal said carefully. "Honestly, I think you're amazing for doing it all."

"Thanks, but wait, there's more." She cleared her throat, hating to have to admit what came next. "The bail bondsman was a friend of the family so he felt comfortable putting up the bond so my dad could get out. I gave him the five thousand, which was my entire savings, because I had to put up ten percent, and he covered the rest using the house for collateral. The only way to screw up was if my dad didn't show for the court date. All he had to do was show for the damn date."

Coal gasped. "Oh no!"

"Not quite what I said." Jay smiled ruefully. "They finally caught him in Oregon during a random drug bust and sent him back to California. He was sentenced for three to five, and I became responsible for that debt. I took out another loan on the house to pay off the bond, and now with the bigger mortgage, I can't afford to live there so I rent it out. That's why I live in a small, two-room apartment with Shiloh. So you see, I'm always struggling. Now do you understand why I was scared about whatever this is happening between us? I see people like Jefferson and know they can give you so much more than me. You're so damn beautiful and deserve everything—"

Coal grabbed Jay with both hands by the collar of her jacket and shook her. "Don't you ever say something like that to me again. Do you hear?"

"But, Coal. You need to know what you're getting yourself into."

"God, you're stubborn!" With that, she kissed Jay, hard. "Listen to me. You are more than enough for me. There's not one thing about you that I would change. And honestly, I'm hurt you think so little of me."

"You can't be serious. I think the world of you. Christ, you're all I think about."

"Then why do you think it's any different for me? As for your dad, I know firsthand what it's like for a parent to let us down. I don't blame you for his mistakes, although I could kill him for hurting you and leaving you with his mess."

Feeling lighthearted, Jay walked around to Coal's side of the truck to open her door. She offered Coal her arm, feeling richer than any other time in her life. "You know, I really lucked out when I met you," Jay said with a small smile.

Coal laughed and hugged Jay's side. "I know. And don't you forget it."

CHAPTER THIRTEEN

Coal liked the possessive way Jay threaded her arm around her waist as they walked into the charming bistro. After Jay spoke a few words in Italian to the host, they were seated at a small corner booth next to a beautiful stone fireplace.

"I didn't realize you spoke Italian."

"I know enough to get by," Jay said. "My uncle and aunt tried to teach me when I was a kid. Sometimes I wish I had paid more attention."

Coal's knee brushed against Jay's under the table, and she fought to keep her hands to herself, knowing that if she started touching Jay again, she wouldn't be able to stop. "I can't believe I went to school down the street and never heard of this place."

"Probably because my uncle Mario has only owned it for the last few years. He bought it for my aunt because she loves to cook, and now she cooks for hundreds of people a day. Guido, his son, and of course one of my other cousins, promised to help me out by keeping our special evening just between us."

Jay winked at a young waiter who arrived with a bottle of Merlot and an order of bruschetta. After pouring them both a glass, he quickly disappeared behind the swinging kitchen doors.

"Was that Guido?

"How did you guess?"

"He looks a little bit like Dino, but he's got your shit-eating grin," Coal said around a sip of wine.

"Yep, he's Dino's younger brother. And what shit-eating grin?"

Coal laughed and leaned into Jay to kiss the corner of her mouth. "That one."

"What can I say? It's a famous DiAngelo trait."

"Maybe. But the others don't wear it as well as you. Is this their only restaurant?"

Jay nodded. "This is the only one around here, but some other members of my family have restaurants elsewhere. For instance, my cousin, Dakota, owns Santini's in Seattle."

"Interesting. So, if your family enjoys the restaurant business, how did you and Dino become contractors?"

"Dino hated working in a restaurant so he took the college route. He was the first one in the family to graduate college and soon after got his contractor's license. I washed dishes for my uncle for two years before Dino pulled me out of the kitchen and gave me a job. Uncle Mario actually owns two businesses. One is this restaurant and the other is an auto shop that he owns with his other two sons in the city."

Coal raised her eyebrows in surprise. "A restaurant and an auto shop?"

"I know. Crazy, right?"

Coal intertwined her fingers with Jay's liking the way the strong fingers squeezed back. "No. Not crazy at all."

"I thought you said no touching."

"Did I?" Coal smiled seductively as Jay's eyes ignited. She loved teasing her, but they were in a restaurant and what she wanted to do would surely get her arrested in public. Once she released Jay's hand, she took her time to peruse the menu choices. "It says here, old world Sicilian cuisine. Aren't Sicilian and Italian the same thing?"

"It depends on who you ask," Jay said around a bite of home-made focaccia bread. "It's a sore subject in some circles. Sicily is located south of Italy, and the joke is that it's the island that the boot is kicking. Sicily's population tends to be poorer than Italy's. And centuries ago, it was a major trading port that was invaded frequently by many different cultures. Between the mix of cultures and the Italian prisoners that were sent there, the Italians eventually believed that the Sicilians could never be considered of pure blood."

"Pure blood? Sounds like a bad vampire novel. Who is pure anything anymore?"

"Right?" Jay said lightly, but her look was contemplative.

"So what do you consider yourself then?"

"Well, my dad told me once that I'm half Sicilian, but my mother was from a small town in northern Italy that he conveniently can't remember!" Jay said as Coal laughed.

"That's funny. Couldn't you ask your mom where she's from?"

Jay's laughter died and her expression became pensive once more. "No. She split when I was young."

"I'm sorry. That must have been tough."

"It was, but I survived. Anyway, I got the dark skin and the big nose from my dad's side, which are prominent Sicilian traits."

"Why are you frowning?"

"The nose...why else? It's another famous DiAngelo trait. Unfortunately, it's not very attractive."

Coal reached across the seat, placing her hand on Jay's cheek. "That's where you're wrong. There isn't one part of your body that's not attractive. Trust me on this."

"You're doing that touching thing again," Jay said, her voice husky. "No fair, Ms. Davis."

Coal leaned forward, and with her lips a whisper from Jay's said, "Who said life was fair, Ms. DiAngelo?"

For the next hour, Coal kept her hands preoccupied by either holding a utensil while she ate or by hiding them under the table. She'd made Jay promise not to touch her, but as the evening progressed, the need for Jay to reach for her became almost painful. Over the course of dinner, she had inched closer to Jay and soon became fascinated by the slow circles Jay was unconsciously making with the tip of her finger along the rim of her wineglass. She wondered what it would be like to have those fingers touching her intimately. And when the need to be closer to her became too great, she closed the distance between them in the booth and molded her thigh to Jay's. "So, what do you have in mind for the rest of this evening?"

"Honestly, I couldn't think that far ahead," Jay said. She laced her fingers through Coal's. "Do you know how very beautiful you are?"

"I know how beautiful you make me feel," Coal said. She glanced beyond Jay, avoiding her gaze for the first time that night.

The evening was turning out to be more than she could have ever hoped for. She'd planned on keeping things between them simple. Maybe even partake in some mindless hot sex. But the more she learned about Jay, the more Jay had come to mean to her. If she didn't put the brakes on all these emotions she was warring with, she wouldn't be strong enough to stop what was happening between them.

"Hey, I'm sorry if I embarrassed you." Jay gave Coal's hand a shake.

"You didn't. I guess I'm not used to compliments."

Jay gave her an incredulous look. "You can't be serious. You are the hottest woman I've ever laid eyes on."

"Jay, you've really got to stop."

Jay leaned forward and brushed a kiss across Coal's lips. Coal's heart began to pound loudly in her chest, and she was certain Jay could hear it. "That's not stopping," Coal said breathlessly.

"I know, but I'm not going to apologize."

"Oh, baby," Coal whispered. "I'm so glad because I don't want you to. I guess I'm also a little afraid about what's happening between us. I have a lot going on in my life, and you've come to mean so much to me so fast."

Jay brought Coal's hand to her lips and kissed her knuckles. "Nothing has to happen tonight. In fact, I'm enjoying this dating stuff. Not that I haven't thought about getting naked with you, because that would be a lie. But it's giving me a chance to hone my skills."

"You amaze me. The flowers. Holding the door open for me. This restaurant. That sizzling 'I want you' look in your eyes all night. You hone those skills of yours any more and I'm going to have to beat the women off of you."

"You would do that?"

Jay received a playful punch in the shoulder and a deadly look. "Try me."

Jay stood and extended a hand to Coal. Pulling Coal into her arms, she said, "You have nothing to worry about. I crave only these lips and this beautiful body." When she slanted her head for a kiss, the question hung heavily between them.

"Yes," Coal whispered.

Coal replayed the night's events as they traveled the road that would end at her front door. They made small talk until Jay pulled into the driveway and cut the engine. An eternity seemed to tick by in the silence as they held one another's hand, neither one making the move to break the connection. They had both agreed that slowing things down would be for the best, but the last thing Coal wanted to do was say good night, at least not until she knew when she'd get the chance to see Jay again.

"Jay, do you ride?"

"Excuse me?" Jay choked, coughing into her hand.

"Horses." Coal smirked, shaking her head. "Do you ride horses?"

"I'm no expert, but I can hold my own. Why?"

"Tomorrow's Saturday and I usually take Dax for an early ride on a trail not far from here. Would you like to join me?"

Jay unbuckled her seat belt and swiveled to face Coal. She ran her finger along Coal's jaw. "A *ride* sounds perfect."

Maybe it was the double entendre. Maybe it was because Coal couldn't stand being on the opposite side of that predatory gaze all evening and not do anything about it any longer. Or maybe it was because she simply wanted Jay. Wanted her mind, body, and soul. Whatever the reason, it was cause enough to propel her into Jay's lap and wrap her arms around her neck.

The kiss wasn't gentle nor was it meant to be. Too much passion and need had built up for far too long. As their tongues dueled for dominance, Coal realized she couldn't get close enough. She couldn't touch her enough. Finally remembering that they both agreed to wait, she broke the kiss and leaned her forehead against Jay's.

"Wow," Jay said.

"Wow? I'm straddling your lap ready to rip my clothes off for you, and that's all you can come up with?"

Jay ran her hands up Coal's sides making her shudder. "You're going to rip your clothes off?"

"I planned on doing more than that."

Coal ran her hand down her own body as Jay followed her every move. She hissed when her fingertips brushed over her nipples and slowly worked their way down her abdomen. Coal was nearly gasping by the time she reached her thigh, a combination of her own touch and Jay's feral gaze pushing her so close to an edge she was dangerously close to not being able to step back from. With her hand resting between them, she cupped Jay between her legs and squeezed. Jay's head fell back against the truck window and her ass lifted off the seat. Heat radiated against Coal's palm. She pressed her fingers more firmly against the tight denim, feeling Jay's need swell against her fingertips. Jay's eyes grew hazy. Coal licked her lips, reveling in this new power. When Jay closed her eyes and shuddered, taking things slow was the last thing on Coal's mind.

"Coal, stop," Jay said hoarsely. "Please. I can't fight you. Just a little more and..."

"Seriously?" Coal stilled her hand. "You'd go over that easy?"

"Easy?" Jay looked at Coal as if she'd lost her mind. "Baby, you're in my lap grinding against me. Your hands are on me. You smell and taste amazing. Jesus, I'm only human."

Jay removed Coal's hand and placed it over her heart as Coal leaned forward and nuzzled her neck. "I guess you're right. But I can't keep my hands off you."

"And I'm so glad. But we said slow, remember?"

"I remember. But since you're all fired up, maybe I could watch—"

"No!" Jay said a little stronger. "The first time we make love, I want it to be special. I want you naked in my arms while I watch you succumb to my touch. To show you how you make me feel. I want you to experience what our connection means to me."

Coal trembled and rested her forehead against Jay's. "I'm so hot for you, your voice could bring me over."

"We'll have to try that sometime."

When Jay ran her tongue over the sensitive ridges of Coal's ear, Coal had to push her away. Her restraint was paper thin, especially after the last few hours of teasing. One more brush of Jay's lips over her flesh and that paper would disintegrate. "Okay, enough! It's time to go before I change my mind. See you at nine tomorrow?"

"Perfect."

As Coal kissed Jay and stepped from the truck, she realized that everything between them was perfect. Too perfect. Maybe that's what worried her the most.

CHAPTER FOURTEEN

Jay pulled into a parking stall, and spotted Coal in the process of unloading two horses from a long white trailer that was attached to a green Ford Super Duty truck. Coal had already tied one of the horses to a post and was in the process of adjusting Dax's saddle when Jay wrapped her arms around her waist from behind.

"Good morning," Jay said. She nuzzled Coal's neck as Coal tilted her head back against Jay's shoulder to give her full access.

"Good start. I see you found the park without any problems."

"I could find you in a whiteout in the middle of a snow storm." Jay tickled Coal's ear with her tongue, making her laugh.

"Is that so?" Coal pivoted in Jay's arms and wrapped her arms around Jay's neck. "How about you give me a proper hello?"

After a brief but thorough kiss, Coal pulled out of Jay's arms and moved to the chestnut mare tied next to Dax. She placed one hand right above the animal's nose and handed the reins to Jay. "This is Oak. She's really sweet and will follow your every command."

"That's good to know." Jay scratched underneath Oak's chin. *I wonder if her owner is that compliant.*

Coal must have sensed Jay's thoughts because she knocked the reins out of Jay's hands and slipped back into her waiting arms. "And yes, so will her trainer if the treat is worth it." Coal's eyes sparkled with mischief.

Jay smiled at Coal, taking a moment to study her classic beauty. Coal's thick golden hair sparkled as it hung in a ponytail held in place by her black Stetson. Her high cheekbones became accentuated when she smiled that genuine smile that pulled at Jay's heartstrings. To say she'd missed her since they'd parted last night would have been an understatement. All it took was one brush of Coal's tongue against hers, and every cell in her body reignited. She slipped her hands underneath Coal's T-shirt and placed them on her lower back, feeling the warmth of her skin beneath soft cotton. Coal palmed Jay's ass and squeezed, the pressure sending a quick rush of blood into the second heartbeat thumping wildly between her legs. "You're killing me. You know that, right?"

"Good," Coal said. She shoved her away playfully. "Because I hate suffering alone."

Suffering. What a perfect word to describe how not being able to touch Coal made her feel. When she was with Coal, she constantly had to fight for self-control, and all this teasing was asking for trouble. Teasing was another new experience for her. She'd never taken the time to tease and slowly draw out another woman's desire. Sex had always been about enjoying the moment. At no time did she ever try to engage any of her sexual conquests on a more personal level when that moment was over. And if need be, she could go for hours before detonating from another's touch. But why then did the mere brush of Coal's fingers along her flesh make her restraint slip like sand through her fingers?

Coal unhooked Dax's reins and mounted him effortlessly as Jay climbed into Oak's saddle and spent a moment getting used to the feel of the stocky thoroughbred between her legs. She adjusted uncomfortably in her seat, not appreciating the heavy leather rubbing against her still swollen body parts.

"We're going to take the horse trail up to the right," Coal said and pointed to a narrow dirt path that disappeared around a bend a few hundred yards away. "Follow me until the path widens. If you want to take the lead after that you can."

"I'd rather follow if you don't mind."

"Are you sure?"

"Very," Jay murmured. She tilted her head to admire the way Coal's butt molded to the saddle and didn't care in the least that Coal had caught her.

"You need to stop," Coal said, her tone a warning. "Or we're not going to make it up the trail."

They moved slowly along the rocky path, stopping frequently to enjoy the sights and sounds of nature alive in all its wonder. What remained of the spring rains had created mini waterfalls that trickled down rocks and disappeared into the ravine below. Birds chirped atop trees, squirrels ran about, and once, they were lucky enough to catch a glimpse of a fox chasing some animal off into the distance.

"Don't tell me. You collect twigs as a hobby," Jay said when Coal stopped to admire a large pile of sticks next to a Manzanita bush.

"Funny. I see we can add comedian to your list of charms. But no. That pile of twigs belongs to the home of a very large wood rat."

"What in the world is a wood rat?" *And is it going to come out of there and pay me a visit?*

"Don't worry. It'll stay in there if it is in there."

"I hope so. But just in case, where else *would* it be?" Jay surveyed the ground by her horse's feet, hoping that this giant rat wouldn't appear out of nowhere and scare the crap out of her and her horse. Coal began to laugh hysterically. "What's so funny?"

"You. You're adorable."

"Stop that!"

"And even cuter when you blush. But you can relax. A large wood rat would be about the size of a hamster. They're kind of like pack rats and prefer stuff to collect that shines, like bottle caps. In a lot of ways, they inadvertently help keep the trails clean."

Jay began to feel a little foolish. "So this is you toying with me."

"You started it with your twig comment."

"Truce, then. So is there anything else I should know about this monster?"

"Actually, they're quite interesting. The shelter they build is so durable they say it can last up to forty years. Maybe you construction types could learn something from them."

Jay moved her horse beside Coal's and leaned close. "Glad to see I'm not the only comedian. Any other fascinating traits I should know about you?"

"Too many to count." Coal ran her tongue seductively along her bottom lip. "And I'm looking forward to experiencing all of them with you."

"Any place," Jay whispered, her gaze locked on Coal's lips. "Any time."

They continued their ascent as Coal explained in detail about the many flowers that were local favorites such as the purple Chinese houses and the buttercups that were starting to overtake the surrounding fields. The tall yellow flowers made for nice camouflage as they finally reached the summit. Coal instructed Jay to tie the horses to a nearby tree while she placed a blanket down and unloaded a few goodies from the satchel attached to her saddle.

Jay soon joined Coal underneath a huge eucalyptus tree that provided them with ample shade and even more privacy from hikers and riders alike. Coal was kneeling on the blanket unloading a couple of sandwiches and a bottle of wine when Jay knelt behind her and wrapped her arms around Coal's waist.

"Wow, you thought of everything," Jay said.

Coal groaned as Jay nuzzled her neck. "I love your lips."

Coal smelled of tropical islands and sunshine, so edible and so damn delicious. "What are you wearing today? It smells fruity."

"I hoped you would like it."

"I like it a little too much. It makes me want to eat the rest of you."

"It's a coconut and mango lotion I picked up the last time I was in Hawaii. Guess I'll have to wear it more often."

"Like I need any more reasons to want to jump your bones."

Coal turned and pushed Jay backward onto the blanket to straddle her hips. She pinned Jay's wrists to both sides of her head, locking her thighs against Jay's torso. "Your lips against my skin are driving me out of my mind."

"Says the person grinding their hips into my—" Jay's words were smothered by a kiss, and soon she became lost in all that was Coal. She felt her everywhere. Coal's fingertips gliding down her bare arms. Coal's lips warm and soft against her own. She groaned. "I don't know how much more of this I can take. This slow crap is killing me. I want to get naked with you. So bad."

"I like that."

Coal trailed kisses along Jay's throat, the motion mimicking her hips as she rode up and down on Jay's abs. When Coal's thighs tightened and heat radiated from her core, Jay's control snapped. For the first time since they'd met, she didn't care that they could be making a mistake by moving too fast. She needed Coal—now.

"We need to go," Jay said and sat up with Coal still in her lap. She moved to a standing position, taking Coal with her and began to gather their things.

"Jay, is everything okay?"

"No, it's not. I thought I could do this, but I can't." As soon as she'd said the words, a look of hurt and confusion crossed over Coal's face. Jay moved to her and quickly gathered her back into her arms. "What I'm saying is that I can't wait anymore. It's time to get naked. What do you say?"

Coal's expression turned heated. "Yes. I want that too."

Chapter Fifteen

The apartment door barely had time to shut behind them before Jay had Coal pinned to the back of it. They kissed fiercely, hurriedly. She couldn't touch Coal enough. She couldn't get close enough. And all these damn clothes had to go.

"I want your skin against mine." Jay growled and tugged at Coal's earlobe with her teeth.

"I want that too. Hurry."

The ride over to her apartment had felt like an eternity. After they'd dropped off the horses, Coal relayed that she wanted to see Jay's place so without questioning why, they climbed into Jay's truck and made the short drive in near silence. The sexual tension was in the red zone by the time she pulled into her parking stall and turned to find Coal looking as though she were ready to pounce. By the time they reached her front door, Jay's hands had been shaking so badly she'd had a hard time unlocking the deadbolt. Her intention had been to take things slow. She wanted to experience every inch of Coal's body, first with her hands and then with her mouth. But with every piece of clothing that Coal peeled off her body, the idea of slow was becoming a distant memory.

"I want to get all this dust off of me," Coal said. "Where's the shower?"

Jay slipped her shirt up and over her head and grabbed Coal's hand. "Come with me."

"That's the plan."

Jay impatiently yanked on the faucet and swiveled around. With her hand on her fly, she began to unbutton her pants but froze halfway through the process. She didn't want to miss a second of Coal's seductive striptease as the last remaining articles of clothing slipped to the floor. She guided Coal into the shower, admiring her body as she would a fine work of art. "You're so damn hot."

"Coming from the person who looks as though they've been etched out of granite. I've never seen this much muscle on one person's body in my life." Coal ran her hands up Jay's sides and over her taut abdomen. Jay shivered but was far from cold.

"Turn around," Jay said. She reached for the shampoo and poured a quarter-sized amount into her palm. She massaged the soap into Coal's scalp, enjoying the sounds of pleasure as she worked her hair into a thick lather. She massaged the base of her neck and slowly rubbed her temples in small soft circles. After helping Coal rinse her hair, she picked up the liquid soap and a loofah and began to massage Coal's back in long, languid strokes. She worked her way across Coal's shoulder blades and down her spine, making sure to stop and pay extra attention to Coal's firm, muscled ass. She knelt to work her way down Coal's legs before turning her around, focusing on the golden triangle of hair dripping with moisture. She placed one of her palms a fraction below Coal's breasts and held her firmly against the glass enclosure. She stared up at her, ignoring the beads of water dripping down her face. "I can't wait to taste you."

Coal widened her stance and framed her center. "What's stopping you?"

As if Jay had been offered a priceless gift, she placed her mouth over Coal and took her between her lips. She sucked gently, pulling Coal deeper into her mouth, the warm water mixed with Coal's unique taste was more satisfying than any liquid she'd ever encountered. Coal's fingers tightened in Jay's hair as incoherent sounds broke from her.

"You make me feel so much."

Jay released her before running her tongue a little firmer along her length. "I want you to feel everything."

"Then come up here and I will."

Unsteadily, Jay moved to her feet and pressed her body against Coal's. Leaning forward for a kiss, she reached between them and slid two fingers along each side of Coal's clitoris. Coal's hips pitched forward. The pressure from her own hand against her sex sent a wave of arousal coursing through Jay's body. "You feel incredible."

"I've dreamt of your hands on me."

Coal covered Jay's hand with her own, urging her deeper. Coal felt so damn good. Jay widened her stance, placing one leg between Coal's while using the other to brace against the wall. As Coal's thrusts became more urgent, the motion was causing her solid thigh to rub along Jay's clit. Jay gritted her teeth. She was seconds from exploding.

"I can feel how close you are," Coal said.

"Funny, I can feel the same thing." Jay squeezed Coal's clit a bit harder and her eyes fluttered closed. "I want to see you come."

"Then take me to bed and cover my body with yours. And I will."

Jay shut off the hot spray, wasting no time drying their bodies off with a towel before they moved into the bedroom. She laid Coal beneath her on the cool sheets, covering half of Coal's body with her own. She traced one of Coal's breasts with her fingertip, marveling at the way the nipple pebbled against her skin. Too impatient to wait to experience the sensation against her tongue, she leaned forward and took the firm tip between her teeth.

"I'd wanted you to take your time," Coal said. She moaned as Jay pulled her nipple firmly between her lips. "But you got me so pumped I don't know how much longer I can last."

"That sounds like a challenge I can rise to. Let's find out."

Jay lowered her lips to Coal's and taunted her with a kiss, slowly darting her tongue in and out from between her lips, daring Coal to chase it. She dipped one finger into the heat between Coal's legs, matching the rhythm she'd set with her tongue. Coal growled in frustration.

"Enough teasing. I want to come."

"Soon, baby. I want to explore more of you first."

"Fine, but just so you know, payback's a bitch."

Jay smiled against Coal's lips and trailed kisses down her neck. When she reached her breasts, she stopped to take a velvety tip between her teeth.

"More," Coal said. She placed her hand over Jay's urging her deeper. "See what you do to me."

Jay pushed up onto her free hand and hovered above Coal. "I've wanted to touch you for so long."

"Same here." Coal rubbed her hands down Jay's chest and across her abdomen. The muscles in Jay's stomach flexed and her clit twitched with warning shocks.

"Careful."

"You're so sensitive there. I love watching your abs twitch when I touch you. And you feel amazing. Do you like it when I touch you there?"

"Yes." She shivered as Coal ran her hands down her spine and stopped to palm her ass. "Makes me want to come."

"If I have to wait, lover, so do you."

Coal raked her nails along Jay's sides and stopped to toy with one of her nipples. She rolled it between her fingertips, receiving grunts of encouragement from Jay. Jay's mind and body were at war. Too many sensations were assaulting her all at once. Her hips pumped in time with each thrust between Coal's legs. The more her desire flared, the more difficult it became to hold back. Not helping were Coal's quiet moans. Urging her on. Urging her deeper.

"Look at me, baby," Coal said. She pushed a few sweat-soaked strands of hair out of Jay's eyes.

Jay gazed down the lengths of their bodies, reveling in the slickness of her skin gliding along Coal's. She'd had sex with a lot of women, but no one had ever stoked the fire within her until she was so hot she'd thought the core of her would melt. She'd also never wanted to please a woman so much. And with every graze of Coal's fingertips over her heated flesh, her restraint was vanishing like smoke in the wind. "I need to taste you."

"Then put your mouth on me, baby."

Jay pushed up with both arms and slid between Coal's legs. She parted Coal with her hands, and pulled back the hood, running her tongue along the length of her.

"Enough. I can't take it. Make me come, lover."

Closing her eyes, Jay felt Coal's words deep in her own belly. Her clit twitched with warning spasms, and she crossed her legs, trying to combat the building pressure. She sucked Coal's clitoris between her lips and entered her with her fingers. Coal anchored her hands to the sheets as she lifted her hips, engulfing Jay's fingers in a tight, warm embrace.

"Almost...there."

Jay positioned her hands underneath Coal's hips and pulled her more firmly to her. Alternating between quick flicks and long strokes of her tongue, she felt Coal swell against her tongue and grow incredibly hard.

Coal's thighs tensed. Jay's tongue moved faster. Firm, long strokes against her vibrating slick skin. As Coal cried out, and ripples coursed deep within her body, Jay entered her again, sensing a more powerful storm brewing.

Pumping harder, faster, deeper, she climbed up Coal's body. The sight of her fingers disappearing between Coal's legs sent tendrils of electricity racing along her spine and caused the blood to race rapidly beneath her skin. She wanted to give Coal every part of her. Wanted Coal to experience how the sight of Jay claiming her fueled her own desire.

"Straddle my thigh, baby," Coal said. "And come with me."

Jay let out a part moan, part sob as she placed one of her legs over Coal's. Coal reached between them, grasping Jay's sex between her fingers. Her hips bucked frantically. Her blood turned to liquid fire. Her body rose until it crested on the brink of shattering. And then with one final stroke, she tumbled.

❖

Coal held Jay while she slept, reveling in the sensation of their naked bodies pressed together. Jay's lovemaking was as she had expected, passionate and fierce. Jay was a skilled lover. Something she'd never considered of herself. The longer she stared at Jay the more some of her old insecurities crept in until she'd immersed herself in a tidal wave of self-doubt.

Could she be enough for Jay? She'd never been enough for anyone before, not Taylor, her family, or anyone who hadn't agreed with her more liberal ideals. Not being able to measure up in her world had forced her to be cautious. Made her wary of other's motives. Jay had never done anything to garner skepticism, but after seeing Jay with someone like Shiloh, she still wasn't sure she'd ever be able to measure up. Sure, Jay had said they were nothing more than friends. But the Shilohs of the world were the ones she'd have to compete with. She glanced down at their intertwined limbs and compared her body to Jay's. Her legs weren't as long. Her pink-tipped nipples, so very different from Jay's chocolate ones, weren't as firm as when she'd been in her early twenties. Jay was strong and lean, where she was stocky and short. The differences were endless. But Jay had said she was special, beautiful. Why couldn't she see that herself?

When she'd been with Taylor, it had always been about Taylor's needs. Nothing much had changed with some of her one-night stands. The sex was hot and she could usually reach orgasm but at no time had she ever been tempted to forge an emotional connection with anyone since Taylor. But with Jay, she was already bound to her in more than body. She'd had a shattering, bone-melting orgasm, but still she hungered for more. More of Jay's body cresting. More of Jay's skin gliding across her own. When Jay stirred beneath her, she straddled Jay's stomach again, painting Jay's abs with her wetness.

"Christ!" Jay groaned. "You're so wet. Let me touch you."

"Not so fast, lover." She ran her tongue along Jay's bottom lip. "I want to taste you."

"If that's what you want."

"Of course it's what I want, sweetheart." Coal stared deeply into Jay's eyes knowing that as long as they had that connection, neither one of them would be able to hide from the other. Jay's evident withdrawal brought her up short. Had she been right? Had she not been enough to satisfy her?

"Hey, look, I'm sorry," Jay said. She held Coal in place as she tried to move away. "Guess I'm feeling a little insecure."

Coal moved to recline along Jay's length and rested her head on her shoulder. A moment ago, she'd been the one feeling insecure and wondered what could have possibly happened in Jay's past to cause the worry lines forming between her brows. "Want to talk about it?"

"It's nothing. Probably all in my head."

"Honey, you're being vague, and I'm still a little fuzzy ever since you nearly sexed me into a coma. Now spit out what's going on in that crazy brain of yours." Coal massaged Jay's abdomen in tight, small circles, causing the already rigid abdomen to stiffen even further.

"I want to tell you, but....I can't...think when you do that."

"Do what, baby, this?" Coal raked her nails down Jay's side.

"Yes," Jay hissed.

"How about this?" Coal cupped Jay's sex and squeezed.

"Even better."

"Tell me what you want."

"Your mouth on me. I want to look into those gorgeous eyes when I come."

Forgetting all about both their uncertainties, she slid between Jay's legs and took her into her mouth. She pressed her palm against Jay's abdomen feeling her belly vibrate under her touch.

"That makes me want to come."

"You're so hard." She ran her tongue along the length of her. "Is this what you need?"

"I need you." Jay propped her body up onto one elbow and placed her hand on the back of Coal's head. "Suck me. And I'll come."

With a groan, Coal took Jay into her mouth. She rolled her clitoris between her lips. Alternated between sucking and tugging until Jay grew incredibly hard. When Jay begged, Coal could feel her own body begin to stir. As she coated her lips with Jay's essence, she could feel the moisture pool between her own thighs. When Jay's orgasm consumed her, drove through her, and ultimately undid her, Coal gave in to her own body's demands until they both collapsed haphazardly onto the bed.

"You're incredible," Jay said breathlessly.

Coal slowly crawled up Jay's body leaving a trail of kisses along the way. "I could say the same thing about you. It's a good thing I train horses. I don't think I know of any bucking broncos that are as strong as you are when you come."

Jay tried to hide her humiliation by grabbing a pillow and placing it over her face. "So much for my sexiness card."

Coal yanked the pillow away from Jay's face and kissed her hard. "After that performance, you just earned the lifetime membership card. But as long as you understand, I'm the only one who can redeem it for you."

"I like you jealous."

"You're in luck then. Now, are you going to tell me what was bothering you earlier, or do I make you suffer?" Coal ran her hand down Jay's abdomen once more and dipped one finger between the damp curls at the base of her belly. Jay gasped and her eyes fluttered closed.

"If this is suffering, I'll gladly take whatever punishment you want to dish out."

Coal rolled her thumb over Jay's still sensitive clit, and Jay trembled once more. "Okay, okay. I surrender!" Jay's head thrashed from side to side and her thighs shook. She placed her hand over Coal's pleading for her to stop.

"Tell me."

"Damn, you're persistent!"

"Duh! I've worked with horses my whole life. Now stop dodging my question."

"But I want to touch you."

Coal moved to her knees and ran a hand over her own breasts, stopping when she reached the apex of her thighs. Jay's eyes glittered madly as Coal dipped her fingers between her legs and slowly stroked in and out. "Talk. To. Me."

"I want to do that," Jay said. She licked her lips.

"I want you to do it." Coal dipped deeper. "But not until you tell me what's going on with you."

"You're evil."

"You love it." Coal groaned as her body responded to her own touch and Jay's scorching expression. "Now talk before I make myself come."

"After we made love, I felt you pull away from me when I was lying in your arms. I already explained, I'm scared you're going to regret this. Now that I've touched you, tasted you, have parts of you embedded under my skin, I don't know what I'd do if I lost you."

"Oh, sweetheart." Coal removed her hand and reached for one of Jay's. Guiding Jay's fingers between her legs, she wanted to convey with her body and soul that every touch was real. "Truthfully, while you were asleep, I was starting to feel a little self-conscious too. My fear is that I won't be enough for you."

"You are more than I can ever imagine." Jay curved her fingers upward and circled her thumb over Coal's clit. "I want you and only you. Please believe me."

"And you're dangerous when you talk like that." Coal rotated her hips, feeling something twist pleasurably inside. "I want you too, and I promise I won't regret this. Ever."

After recovering from another earth-shattering orgasm, Coal felt content to let Jay hold her until Coal's rumbling stomach had other ideas.

"You got a tiger in there," Jay said. She bent to kiss Coal's belly.

"No, I have a tiger right here." Coal pulled Jay on top of her and Jay settled between her parted legs. "But she's going to have to wait to get fed again. I, on the other hand, need food immediately. If you forgot, we skipped lunch earlier because someone was in a hurry to get me into bed."

"You complaining?"

"Never! But you need to get dressed, sexy, and feed me before I become evil."

"Oh no! Not again. I almost didn't survive the last time."

"And it only gets worse. So get moving, lover."

Jay leaned over the side of the bed and picked her pants up off the floor. She stood to pull them on, stopping with them halfway zipped to gawk at Coal's nude body. Seeing the look of pure lust on Jay's face forced Coal to her knees. She wrapped her arms around Jay's middle, pulling her close.

"Food first," Coal said then sucked one of Jay's nipples into her mouth, releasing it with a pop. "Then you can have me for dessert later."

"And you called me dangerous." Jay broke their contact and moved out of Coal's reach. "If you want me to cook for you, I think I'm going to need to invoke your no touching rule."

"You cook?" Coal asked, pleasantly surprised.

Jay grinned and leaned forward just enough to steal a kiss. "Baby, I'm Italian. Of course I cook."

"My, my, Miss DiAngelo. You are full of surprises."

"Ms. Davis, you haven't seen anything yet."

CHAPTER SIXTEEN

The morning was bright and cheery, matching Coal's mood. After leaving Jay's yesterday, she'd thought of not much else except for the next time she could see her again. Getting out of Jay's bed and returning home had been a true test of her mental strength. What she wouldn't give for the opportunity to lie in Jay's arms forever and forget the rest of her responsibilities. But as she stood outside her father's office door, she was reminded that life would never be that simple.

The door was slightly ajar, and she raised her fist to knock but stopped short when she heard another voice inside. She peeked through the small crack and noticed Judge Parker sitting in the chair across from her father's desk. From the sounds of their raised voices and her father's no-nonsense tone, whatever they were discussing was serious.

"Justin, how the hell can you say that?" her father asked. "You know if this law is deemed constitutional, this state will be made a mockery for the rest of the country. God didn't intend for two men or two women to wed. It's our duty as judges to protect the law and vote that the gay marriage ban stands. If we don't, the term *marriage* will lose its true meaning.

"That's a bunch of *shit,* and you know it." Judge Parker reached into his briefcase and threw a sheet of paper onto her father's desk. "Look at these stats. The state of Massachusetts already allows gay people to wed, and there's no proof that they're struggling with problems of morality. Honestly, I never understood what everyone's problem is with this issue. It's not like gay people are manning booths looking for enrollment. Think about that, Tom... Massafuckinchusetttts! This is California, for Christ's sakes. If any state should allow gay marriage to pave the way for other states, it should be ours."

Coal remained stone still, afraid to exhale as her father stood and began to pace in front of the large office window. Her dad placed a cigar in his mouth, chewing on the end of it as he appeared to be contemplating what to say to his liberal friend. "Justin, the people of this state want to set forth an amendment to our constitution that marriage is between one man and one woman. Not two women—not two men—not two *Goddamn* animals! How can we vote on something that the people of this state clearly do not want?"

"You know as well as I do any law that discriminates on the basis of sexual orientation, race, or gender is ethically wrong. It is our duty to uphold the law in this state, Tom, not make this a personal battle between you and your daughter."

Coal gasped as she watched her father's eyes narrow and his nostrils flare. The last time she'd seen a similar look, another rider had brought their stallion too close to Dax. Thankfully she hadn't been on the back of him when both horses reared onto their back legs in preparation to fight to the death.

"How *dare* you bring my daughter into this," her father said, his jaw so tight every tiny wrinkle around his mouth became nonexistent. "Coal is not gay and has nothing to do with this issue. Don't ever bring her name up to me again when discussing this topic. Do you understand?"

Judge Parker bowed his head and nodded solemnly. "My apologies. I didn't mean—"

"I'm going to pass on lunch," her father said gruffly. "I have work to do, and I'm assuming so do you."

"You're right." Judge Parker stood and grabbed his briefcase. "I'll go. Again, I apologize for stepping out of line."

"Justin?"

Justin stopped with his hand on the doorknob as Coal scrambled to the end of the hallway, straining to hear her father's next words.

"I'm sure you're aware that it really doesn't matter how you vote. There are six conservative judges on this court. When it's all said and done, I'm pretty confident that the correct decision will be made fairly and lawfully."

The sound of her father's door closing echoed loudly in the empty hallway. She'd always appreciated Angel's father for accepting her choices and her lifestyle, and after today, Coal respected him even more. It took guts for anyone to stand up to her dad. Unfortunately, in this instance it wouldn't get Judge Parker anywhere. He was outnumbered in the court system, and from the sounds of their conversation, would be outvoted. As her mood soured, she decided it wasn't the time to discuss more of the details regarding the ranch today. Sagging against the wall in defeat, she realized that whatever hope she'd had for her father's acceptance had diminished along with the rights for gay couples in California to wed.

Jay spent most of Monday morning finishing up the trim work in the downstairs living room, trying to keep her mind from wandering back to Coal and their one night of passion. She hadn't seen her all morning, which was probably a good thing since she was a bit behind schedule, but nevertheless, she was disappointed. She was positive that if she ran into Coal, there would be no way she would be able to keep her hands off her. With Dino in the next room and Jane Davis constantly popping in unexpectedly, it probably wasn't a good idea to focus on anything but the job at hand.

She ran her hand along the smooth, unpainted surface, remembering the sensation of touching Coal's naked body. Her skin prickled at the memory of the way Coal's eyes had darkened when she had wrapped her lips around her intimately. How Coal's entire body tensed right before she soared toward orgasm. Those images had kept her awake all night. When the memories became overwhelming, she'd even taken the edge off under her own touch.

Masturbation wasn't a new concept for her, but one she didn't entertain often. Being a solo flyer was something she engaged in more when she was in high school. Christ, back then, just seeing a pinup of a woman had her going off like a missile at blastoff. Even then, she couldn't remember being this keyed up over anyone. Before

Coal, relying on her own hand had never been necessary since she could always count on the touch from another. But this situation was different. She didn't want anyone else to touch her. Coal had somehow changed the rules, and she didn't know when that had happened exactly. All she knew was that Coal consumed her every thought and she wanted more.

Being with Coal helped her forget. Forget that she was twenty-seven and was still struggling to reach her dreams. Helped her forget her mother walked out on them when she was an infant and was never heard from again. That her father never thought she'd amount to anything. But maybe she should consider the source. Because of his actions, she had to work long hours with little to show for it. Those actions had almost cost her a promise, and a promise to her meant everything. When she said something she meant it or she wouldn't say it at all. She may not have much, but what no one could take away from her was her pride.

She checked her watch and wondered where the morning had gone. She sat on the floor with her back against the wall and her feet stretched out in front of her intent on eating her sandwich when Dino appeared with a broken hammer dangling from one of his hands. She raised her eyebrow at him in question, wondering how the sturdy Craftsman had met its demise. "Hit yourself in the head again?"

"Very funny, smartass! And getting hit by tools is more of your problem than mine. I can't believe this. This is the second one in a month. They definitely don't make them like they used to."

"No, they don't. I have a screwdriver in the toolbox that met the same fate. Haven't had time to return it though."

"There's a hardware store down the road next to that sandwich shop. Think you can handle all of this while I return them both?"

"Piece of cake. Not to worry. If I can't, you'll be the first one I call."

"Ha, ha." He tossed a crumpled up piece of paper at her that he pulled off her tool chest. "Let's see how funny you think you are when I forget to write out your paycheck."

Jay laughed at Dino and polished off her sandwich in three quick bites. She jumped to her feet and jogged up the staircase with the intention of installing the new cabinet in the master bathroom when she noticed Coal's mattress sitting on the floor next to the still disassembled bed frame.

A short time later, she tightened the last screw that connected the headboard to the frame. She shook the heavy wood a few times, making sure it was secure, and couldn't control a grin when a particular fantasy of making love to Coal in that very bed surfaced. As the familiar tingling in her belly returned with a vengeance, she dropped the screwdriver at her feet and went in search of the only woman who could fulfill that fantasy.

❖

After the disappointing morning events, Coal decided to ditch going to Half Moon Bay and decided to stay with Dax. She needed his company and his solid strength to help put all thoughts of her father aside for a while. After feeding and washing him, she cleaned out his stall, figuring she'd put her frustrations to good use. Besides, she was avoiding Jay while she worked, worried that she couldn't be around her without wanting to rip Jay's clothes off. She'd already made an appointment for next week to have a lawyer look at all the legal documents concerning the transfer of her grandfather's ranch and took Dax for a short ride. With energy still to burn, she decided to brush her trustworthy companion and tell him a little secret.

"I don't know what to do, boy. She's so hot and so damn sexy. I can't stop thinking about her."

Dax nudged her with his nose, making her drop the brush.

"Rude! And okay, you're right. I don't *want* to stop thinking about her. Happy?"

Dax bobbed his head, obviously enjoying the extra attention she had been giving him lately. When she needed to talk, Dax was always there to lend an ear. He listened, didn't give advice, and wouldn't scold her even if he thought she was making a mistake. He was her psychologist, her rock.

"Well, what do you think, Mr. Stallion? Still think I'm ready for the loony bin?"

Dax snorted, making her laugh.

"Whatever. Guess you don't want to hear what she did to me yesterday. But let me tell you, I'm surprised I can still walk. God, this is killing me." She groaned and leaned against him. "I want to go up there and see her, but I know I won't be able to control myself. Did you see her earlier? All tanned and hot in those blue jeans and that sleeveless white T-shirt. I just wanted to reach out and touch her skin."

"Then touch it."

Coal spun around so quickly that Jay didn't have time to react. She gripped Jay roughly by her shirt and pressed her mouth heavily, possessively to hers. Jay backed them up so that Coal's back rested against a pile of hay bales and pressed her long form against Coal's body.

"What are you doing here?" Coal popped the button open on Jay's Levi's.

"I had to see you. I've been going crazy all day."

"Good. That makes two of us." She slipped her hand past every one of Jay's barriers, already finding her slick and hard.

"Ah...Coal...baby, we can't here."

"Yes, we can."

Coal grasped Jay between her thumb and index finger, pinching lightly on her swollen clitoris. Jay widened her stance to give Coal more access and rested her forehead against Coal's. "Baby, you got to slow down. I've been primed all morning. You're going to make me come."

"Good."

Jay grabbed Coal's face with both hands as her orgasm turned her legs to jelly. Jay sagged against Coal as Coal kissed her firmly, muffling the cries that threatened to tear from Jay's throat. As Jay's body continued to convulse, Coal could feel another powerful surge deep within. Eventually, Jay succumbed in Coal's arms and sank to her knees.

"Jesus!" Jay wrapped her arms around Coal's waist and rested her head against her stomach.

"Funny thing how the whole religion thing plays such a big part in sex." Coal stroked Jay's hair. "Especially since God supposedly doesn't approve of this." *Or my dad wants to think that's the truth anyway, to make him feel justified.*

"Cute." Jay moved onto unsteady legs. "I'll show you how true that is."

Jay covered a pile of hay with a clean horse blanket and lifted Coal up so that she was sitting on them. She moved between Coal's legs as Coal wrapped her arms around her neck.

"And just what do you think you're doing?"

"What I've wanted to do since the last time I saw you."

Jay knelt in front of Coal and removed both of her boots. "Lift up," she said after unhooking Coal's belt buckle. She quickly removed Coal's pants and underwear with a single tug and placed Coal's feet on her shoulders.

"Oh!"

Coal threw her head back and closed her eyes as Jay's lips enclosed around her. She didn't hurry, taking her time to kiss every sweet slick inch. Coal tasted sweet and reminded her of fresh honey glistening in the midday sun. As Coal's thighs tightened, Jay pulled her more firmly into her mouth and sucked, knowing right then she would never get enough of her. The hard nub between her lips was a pulsing ball of fire ready to ignite and all Coal needed was a few more well-placed strokes.

"Make me come," Coal pleaded. "Yes…right there…yes!"

Coal's eyes flew open, and Jay saw the flash of light in them right before Coal's orgasm rippled through her. The pulse between her legs fluttered wildly against Jay's tongue. Jay held on, taking more, taking everything. When the pulsing slowed to a calmer beat, Jay stood and entered her with one swift motion. Coal groaned and wrapped her legs around Jay's waist, their gazes locked and held. In that one moment, where they were connected by more than flesh, Jay knew without a doubt she found the one woman who completed her.

"Take me deep, baby. I want to come again," Coal said and pumped her hips into Jay's hand. "And I want you to come with me."

"Fuck! Anything you want."

Jay took Coal's lips in a ferocious kiss as she pumped her hips in between Coal's legs, the motion sending her hand deeper with each thrust. She was so close already, and when Coal whispered she was ready to come again, Jay slid into her one final time and brought them both over.

They fell limply into each other's arms, but it was Jay who guided them onto the dusty floor and pulled Coal into her lap. She placed a kiss on Coal's temple, content just to hold her.

"God, that was amazing," Coal said around a shaky breath.

"Told you I'd make you find religion," Jay said with a huge grin.

"Very funny. At this rate, I'm going to have to believe in some kind of afterlife because you're going to kill me."

"Well, you destroy me so how about we call it even?"

"You telling me you want more of this?" Coal licked the thin sheen of sweat that had accumulated on Jay's neck.

"I do want more. A whole lot more," Jay said seriously. She rested her chin on Coal's head with a contented sigh. "I will never get enough of you and those talented hands."

"Good to know. But my hands are nowhere as talented as yours. In fact, they play me like a fiddle."

"Go on. I'm liking where this is headed."

"Since you asked, this fiddle constantly needs fine tuning. Do you know where I can find a talented musician to help me keep it in top shape? It seems to need tuning often lately, especially since someone has been tugging magically on its strings," Coal said and lifted her head to stare at Jay's lips.

"Did I ever tell you I was a fiddle master?" Jay reached between Coal's legs, and Coal's body responded again instantly.

"No," Coal said and covered Jay's hand with her own, urging her inside. "But I hoped."

CHAPTER SEVENTEEN

J ay drove the last nail into the custom tigerwood deck before taking a sip of her soda to admire her handiwork. The orange tinted wood with random black stripes nicely complimented the sand and chocolate accent color choices of the recently painted exterior. She'd been working hard all morning trying to play catch up. She should have been exhausted after spending a sleepless night of thinking about Coal. But not only was she not tired, she had energy to burn, sexual energy that hadn't subsided even after two orgasms by her own hand.

They hadn't seen one another since they parted yesterday, but the countless replays from their tryst in the barn left a smile on her face and her libido jammed in high gear. Earlier that morning, she'd caught a glimpse of Coal outside talking with her mother and had wanted to say hello but couldn't find any reason to interrupt their conversation. From the few times she'd witnessed Coal's behavior around her parents, she'd always wondered about the cause of Coal's underlying anxiety. She'd never considered it before, but could it be that Coal was uncomfortable with her own sexuality?

Maybe her parents had no clue she was gay. But even if that were true and they found out, Coal was an adult and didn't have to answer to anyone. Personally, she didn't care if Coal's mom knew about their relationship. She'd been comfortable with her sexuality ever since she and Danielle Whitmore had sex in the back of her father's '65 T-Bird. She'd been fifteen then and never questioned why she preferred women over men; it was just the way her door swung.

But Coal's father was a different story. From what she could tell from the few times they'd met, Thomas Davis struck her as demanding and calculating, not that she wasn't familiar with the do-it-my-way or else attitude. She'd grown up with a father who also demanded respect, but in his case, didn't show it in return and was quick to use his hand if he felt he was being insulted. The difference now though was she was older and could choose whether she wanted to have a relationship with her dad. The night she and Coal had kissed outside in the bar parking lot, Coal did explain that she didn't want to cause problems with her father for reasons she hadn't wanted to discuss. Even if that conversation hadn't taken place, Jay would have to be blind not to notice Coal's stiff posture and cautious nature around her father. Their relationship was strained, but the question was why, and would Coal ever tell her?

She thought about broaching the subject last night on the phone with Coal, but when the conversation had turned heated, she'd had other ideas. Phone sex was something she'd never done with a lover before and was amazed by how rapidly her body responded to something as simple as Coal's whispered words.

"Hey," Coal said when Jay answered the phone. "Did I wake you?"

"No, actually. I've just been sitting here thinking."

"Want to share?"

Jay chuckled softly. "Only if you want the x-rated version."

"Hmmm...sounds interesting."

"Oh, it is." She'd spent the last hour staring at the ceiling, thinking about the last time she'd touched Coal. Her body had been primed ever since she thought about her lips wrapping around Coal intimately. That visual combined with the familiar rumble of excitement in Coal's voice was only adding fuel to the flames of desire. "We could make it more interesting."

"I'm listening."

"Well, for starters, you can tell me how much you want me."

"I wish I could show you instead. Show you how wet I am for you." A soft moan escaped Coal's lips. "I love your hands on me."

"Explain to me how you want to be touched." Jay dipped her hand into her boxers, her fingers drenched from imagining she was touching Coal. Imagining it was Coal's hands stroking her.

"Rub my clit, baby. Feel how hard I'm getting for you."

"God, you feel so good."

"Tell me what it feels like to touch me."

Jay dipped her hand deeper, the muscles tensing and relaxing under her fingertips. "You feel like warm satin. So soft. I wish I could put my mouth there."

"Next time, baby. Stroke me harder. Feel how full I am for you."

Jay's hand pumped faster, harder. She couldn't stop even if she wanted to. She could almost feel Coal's whispered words, floating over her skin. She could almost feel Coal's hands dipping deeper. She pictured Coal's desire dripping onto her hand and could almost feel Coal's lips enclosing around her. "I feel you. Everywhere."

"Good," Coal said breathlessly. "Imagine my lips around your clit. Me sucking—"

"Yes!"

Jay's eyes flew open as a stiff wind blew through the French doors, forcing her out of her daydream. She latched on to her toolbox right before the impending orgasm brought her to her knees.

"Jesus."

Glancing around the empty room, she was thankful no one was close by to see her sexually weakened state. As the heavy beat between her legs dulled to a distant throbbing, she moved on shaky legs into the bathroom and filled the sink with cold water. She closed her eyes and splashed her face, needing to clear the haze of arousal. She braced both hands against the sink. Talk about no control.

"Hey," Coal said from the doorway forcing Jay to open her eyes. "Are you all right?"

"No." Jay stared at Coal in the mirror before spinning around and advancing on her. She pulled Coal into her arms and walked her backward into the bedroom where they toppled onto the bed. "I told you this mattress would come in handy."

Coal lifted her leg so that her thigh rested between both of Jay's. "Ooh, is that for me?"

"Careful," Jay said tightly. "I'm already so close."

"I know. I can see it in your eyes. Hear it in your voice. Feel it in your touch."

"We shouldn't do this here. What if someone walks in…" Jay hissed as Coal ran her hand along her tightening abdomen.

"You were saying?"

"Too many clothes. Need them off."

"Then you know what to do, lover."

Jay sat up and removed her T-shirt before helping Coal to remove her shirt and bra. They quickly kicked out of their jeans and shoes, returning to each other's arms with Jay pulling Coal on top of her.

"I can't get enough of you." Jay ran her hands up Coal's sides, stopping just under her breasts.

"The same goes for me. I love how your muscles tense under my fingertips. I'm so keyed up and so need for you to make love to me."

"God, you make me crazy." She pinched Coal's nipples as Coal shuddered. "I don't want to hurt you, but I want to take you hard. Take you deep. I have this aching need…"

"Baby, you're not hurting me. I came to find you because all I can think about is being naked in your arms. I know this seems crazy, but I crave you in the farthest reaches of my soul." Coal reached for one of Jay's hands and thrust it between her legs. "Feel this? Feel me?"

"Christ, yes." Jay's head was reeling. The reins that bound her were about to snap, and she was losing control and fast.

"Jay," Coal said. She held Jay's face between her hands. "Look at me, baby."

Fighting through the thick fog clouding her judgment, she did as Coal asked. "I need…"

"You need to fuck me, Jay. To take me with everything you have."

Jay groaned and threw her head back, the roaring in her ears matching the one that ripped from her throat. She flipped Coal onto her back and knelt between her legs. She entered her with long strokes watching in awe as Coal's body responded to her touch.

"More," Coal groaned. "I want it all. Everything. Harder."

Jay straddled one of Coal's legs and braced her body above Coal's. She drove Coal hard and fast, feeling as her sex hummed and tightened. Coal's excitement coated her palm as she wet Coal's thigh with her own pleasure. She bit back a moan as waves of electricity shot down her spine. Jay's thighs tightened. She was seconds from shattering.

Coal's entire body went rigid just as her climax consumed her forcing a strangled cry from her throat. Jay held tight to Coal as she battled through the storm never remembering seeing anything more beautiful than Coal succumbing in her arms. Coal's body expertly rode each rise and fall until the waves of passion receded leaving her lying exhausted in Jay's arms.

"Please don't go," Coal whimpered when Jay tried to pull her hand from between Coal's legs.

"Oh, baby, I never want to let go." Jay buried her face in Coal's neck and shivered uncontrollably as her own orgasm threatened to undo her.

"Jay," Coal said breathlessly, apparently aware of Jay's plight. "Let me touch you."

"I'm okay."

"No, you're not." Coal pushed Jay off her and instructed her to move to the edge of the bed while she knelt on the floor between her legs. Coal used her shoulders to force Jay's legs further apart and framed her sex with her hands. She brushed a soft kiss along Jay's clitoris, her eyes never leaving Jay's.

"Not this time." Jay said. She tightened her hand in Coal's hair and guided Coal's mouth to her. "I can't take any more teasing."

Coal smiled then flattened her tongue and slowly but firmly ran it along the tense shaft. Jay's eyes closed involuntarily, the coolness a welcome balm over her heated flesh. "You're so ready for me."

"You're all I need. Make me come."

Tears formed on Coal's lashes, but Jay didn't have time to ask about them as Coal leaned forward and enfolded her lips around her clitoris. Jay's hands tightened in Coal's hair as the momentum that began in her toes sent tingles of excitement coursing through her veins. The pressure built. Her body braced. And with a hoarse shout, Coal unleashed all Jay's fury.

"What's so amusing?" Jay asked moments later when awareness returned and she opened her eyes to find Coal cuddled up next to her with a silly grin on her face.

"Simple. I'm happy."

"Me too."

But maybe that's what frightened her the most. Simple was a term she didn't recognize. For the last few years, she'd come to count on no one but herself. Lately though, she was starting to wonder how she ever lived before Coal. Loneliness was not an emotion she'd entertained in the past. She had a large family, a network of friends. And if she wanted company, more often than not, she could find it. But the more time she spent with Coal the more she realized she'd been missing out on the best part of life, the part that included a partner, a life with the one person she'd always put above her own needs. All those women in the past had made her feel good in the moment, but with Coal it went beyond company or sex. Coal challenged her mind and body, but also made her feel as though she mattered.

As she toyed with a lock of Coal's hair, she thought about telling Coal about the Parkers. She'd struggled with telling her since she saw Judge Parker at the Fourth of July party. But since their connection had become stronger, maybe Coal would understand why she'd kept the information from her until now. Or so she hoped.

"Something's bothering you," Coal said.

Jay was once again left amazed with her intuitiveness. "I was thinking you're an incredible lover."

"You're pretty okay yourself."

"Just okay?" Jay tickled Coal.

"Stop!" Coal tried to squirm away from Jay but was unsuccessful. "All right. Better than okay. A-plus material."

"Better," Jay said and hugged her tighter. "But you know, I was always into extra credit. Know of anyone I could fit into my schedule that can help me out?"

Jay had been around her long enough to know what it meant when Coal's blue eyes darkened. It meant she was either turned on or incredibly pissed. In this instance, both responses pleased her.

"There better not be anyone else on *your* schedule."

"Ow, Jesus!" Jay hissed when Coal bit down hard on one of her nipples to drive home her point.

"Now tell me what's really on your mind."

"I want to. I just don't want to mess this up."

"Sweetie, I told you before. You can tell me anything."

"You say that now." Jay closed her eyes and inhaled deeply in an effort to center her mind and body.

"And I meant it. Go on."

"Remember the Fourth of July party when your dad's friend Judge Parker said he thought he knew me?"

"Yeah. Angel said the same thing."

"That's weird. I wonder why?"

"Well, she is his daughter."

What? Jay's pulse skyrocketed and she sat up with Coal still in her arms. "Angel is his kid?"

"Yeah, so?"

Jay pulled her knees to her chest and placed her chin on top of them. "Because, Coal. The Parkers are who my father stole from."

"I see," Coal said calmly.

Jay heard the distance in Coal's voice and turned to look at her. "Are you mad?"

"Kind of. But not for the reason you're probably thinking. I'm upset because you didn't tell me sooner. But more importantly because you thought it was something you had to hide from me."

"I know. And I'm sorry. But I was scared. I didn't want to screw this up. Ever since the moment I touched you, I knew you were it for me. You touch me and I explode into a thousand pieces, shattered, spent. You're all I need."

You're all I need. Coal remembered the last time she'd heard those words. Taylor had said them to her right before her world came tumbling down around her.

"Coal?"

"When I was twenty." Coal continued as if Jay hadn't spoken, "I met this girl. Up until then, I had dated a few guys, but when it came to the sexual part, I wasn't interested, you know? Then one day in college, Taylor walks into one of my classes and into my life. She had this magnetic personality that made people gravitate toward her, me being one of them. So one night, she asks me to join her and a bunch of her friends to go to some party. Turns out, the friends didn't show so it was just her and me. It also turns out we never made it to the party."

Jay grinned. "I bet. Can I assume this was your first time?"

"Yes. And it changed my life forever. For two years after that, we were inseparable. I loved her and I thought she loved me. But then…"

Jay gave her a gentle squeeze. "It's okay."

"No, it's not okay. We fought a lot. Especially when I caught her keeping things from me. She said it was for my own protection, but it made it hard for me to trust her. And then my parents caught us—"

The sound of the downstairs door opening and closing caused a swell of fear to rise inside of Coal. She shot to her feet. "Oh shit," she said under her breath.

They tumbled out of bed and scrambled to put on their clothes that had been hastily discarded all over the room. Heavy footsteps echoed up the winding staircase as Jay made a hasty retreat onto the deck and Coal disappeared into the bathroom.

"Coal," her father said. His deep voice sent a new wave of fear coursing through her.

Her father hadn't stepped foot in her home since she'd moved back. His presence was more than unusual. And with the timing, it was downright unsettling.

"Hold on. In the bathroom. One sec," Coal said over the running faucet as she tried to wash the scent of Jay from her hands and body. When she was satisfied that she didn't look like a hungry lion had mauled her, she opened the bathroom door to find her father staring pensively at Jay's silhouette behind the sheers covering the French doors. "Dad, what are you doing here?"

"We need to speak," he said very clearly, using his authoritative voice.

"Now's really not a good time." She hoped to keep the tremor from her voice but wasn't sure if she'd been successful.

"I think you may want to hear what I have to say." He closed the balcony doors to offer them privacy.

"What's going on?" She hated when he played these games, looking at her as if he had some big secret that only he was privy to.

He used to do the same thing to her when she was a kid. Sometimes when she got into trouble, he'd summon her to his office and make her wait an hour in that damn red chair before deciding to make an appearance. Making her squirm was all part of the power trip.

"What this is, is you breaking your word to this family."

"I have no idea what you're talking about."

"I'm talking about you promising this family that you would never engage in inappropriate activities with a woman again." He glanced in the direction of the balcony again. "I'm talking about Jay DiAngelo."

Coal desperately hoped her face hadn't turned whiter than the newly painted baseboard. She wanted to deny his accusations. Hell, she had to deny it, because she needed to protect Jay, but she didn't think she'd be able to hide her fear brewing directly below the surface. Her father knew how to read her. She opened her mouth to plead her case, but her father held up a hand to silence her.

"Don't try to deny it. I researched the DiAngelo name, and it turns out, they're well known here in Woodside, but not in a good way. You see, Justin couldn't place Jay because he'd only seen her once in court after her father stole some very expensive items from him. Jay is paying for his mistakes by paying the bills to cover his debt."

Coal knew all this, but hearing it again from her father only made her heart bleed more for Jay. But she couldn't allow her father to see just how much this conversation was affecting her. She crossed her arms defiantly over her chest in an effort to hide their shaking. "So? What Jay's father has done has nothing to do with the two people working on my home."

Her father shrugged. "True. But I would hate it if something unexpectedly should happen where her dad had to spend more time in jail. Besides, if news like that got out, I can see how a small company that shares the DiAngelo name could find themselves out of business. Couldn't you?"

Her eyes narrowed. "Are you saying what I think you're saying?"

"I'm stating fact. You know how people talk in this town. No work means she could lose everything. I think that would be a shame."

So you know about us and you'd destroy her because of me. Coal had seen her father in many lights throughout the years, and even though she didn't agree with him most of the time, she'd always respected the powerful individual that others feared. But this man before her made her sick to her stomach. She had no doubt that he would follow through with his threats. He could hurt Jay, Dino's business, and Jay's father, all with something as simple as a phone call. "Are you finished, *Dad?*"

His smirk was answer enough. "Oh, and by the way." He tilted his chin toward the patio doors. "This conversation stays between us or I will dismantle the ranch and sell the pieces to the highest bidder. Do I make myself clear?"

"Crystal."

The moment she heard the front door slam behind him, she collapsed onto her bed and allowed the tears to fall. Eventually, Jay's knocking made her get to her feet. But the moment she unlocked the patio doors and Jay stepped through, she stepped out of Jay's reach when Jay attempted to grasp her hand.

"Hey, what's wrong? I know we almost got caught with our hands in the cookie jar, but tears aren't necessary."

"You need to go, Jay."

"What?"

Coal closed her eyes, dreading her next words. Another minute longer and her father would have caught her in bed with a woman again. But even beyond being humiliated for the second time in her life, her father would destroy Jay and her grandfather's dream and not lose a minute of sleep over it. It went without saying that she loved Jay with everything in her, which made what she was about to say a million times harder. "What's wrong is this. This shouldn't have happened. *We* shouldn't have happened."

Jay paled and her step faltered. "You don't mean that."

"Yes, I do."

Jay advanced on Coal and grabbed her by her shoulders, forcing her to look at her. "Talk to me. Please don't shut me out. Whatever it is, we'll work it out. Damn it, Coal, I love you."

Oh, Jay, no! Please don't say that. Don't you know what those words will do to me? Coal took a deep breath and dug deep, summoning the Davis iron resolve. She knew of only one way to get Jay to leave because what she was about to say would hurt more than anything. "No, Jay, you don't. This was all a mistake, a big mistake."

"Coal," Jay said roughly, turning her head as though absorbing a slap to the face. "Please…"

"Just go."

Without looking back, Jay turned and bounded down the stairs, slamming the door on the way out. Coal collapsed against the bedroom wall, her heart pounding as though it would tear from her chest. When her legs would no longer support her weight, she slumped to the floor and buried her face into her hands.

"Whatever it is, we'll work it out. I love you."

A torrent of tears rained down her cheeks as Jay's words echoed in the empty room. She knew the only way to get Jay to leave was to tell her their being together was a mistake. She remembered it was the one thing Jay feared since the moment they'd begun seeing one another. Coal had been afraid of anyone finding out about their relationship, afraid to stand up for what she wanted instead of what her family wanted for her. But the longer she sat there, the more her fear turned to anger. How could she have let the most precious thing in her life slip away without so much as an explanation? How could she give up Jay to do what she thought was right or what her family thought was right for her? She'd finally found the one person in life that made her feel complete. The one person who loved her wholeheartedly without restrictions. She'd hurt the one person she loved more than life itself, allowing her fear to outweigh her better judgment.

Their earlier conversation came back to haunt her, and she realized she had just done to Jay what Taylor used to do to her. She was the one now keeping secrets. She was the one trying to protect Jay, not giving Jay the opportunity to stand up for herself.

As her strength returned, she realized she needed time to fight for what she wanted. Jay was worth that fight. The ranch was too. And damn it, she would fight this time instead of giving in to her family's demands. She just hoped Jay could wait until she figured this mess out. Because no matter what she did from here on out, a piece of her soul would always be lost. Without Jay, she'd never be whole.

Too emotionally drained to think beyond her own pain, she picked up the phone and called the one person in the world who could give her some perspective. "Angel," she sobbed.

"Coal…honey…what's wrong?"

"Oh, Angel, I blew it. My father…Jay…I made…"

"Calm down. Where are you?"

"I'm home, but you can't come here."

"Why not?" Angel asked in obvious confusion.

"You just can't…okay. But can I come there?"

"Of course. Get your ass over here and tell me what the hell is going on."

❖

Coal barged through Angel's front door and launched her body into her arms. The crying had become uncontrollable, and she feared the tears would never stop.

"Honey," Angel said. She pulled Coal into her arms, gripping her like a mother bear would a cub. "You've got to tell me what's going on." She guided Coal over to the couch so they could both sit down and handed her a tissue. Once Coal got control of her emotions and told Angel the entire story, mother bear looked as though she was ready to tear someone apart. "Fuck this! You can't go along with him. He's a maniac!"

"Yeah, he is, but he's a maniac with power," she said and wiped at her eyes again. "I don't know what to do, Angel."

"You tell Jay, that's what you do. She's in love with you, and she needs to know what's going on."

Coal laughed through her tears. Angel was never one to hold back.

"So are you going to tell her?"

"Not yet. Not until I figure all this crap out. Besides, I don't know if she'll even take me back after what I said. You had to see the look on her face. She hates me, and she has every right to. I love her, I know I do, but we can't be together. My father threatened—"

"Shh…I know," Angel said gently and put a comforting arm around her shoulders. "So what are you going to do?"

She'd been thinking about that same question ever since the conversation with her father. She couldn't let everything Jay had worked so hard for disappear, and she knew that even if she promised Jay she'd help her financially, Jay would never accept her help out of stubborn pride. Besides, what would Jay think of her now if she knew what her father was really like? She could tell her, but would Jay believe her after everything she'd said to her? Then there were her parents to consider. Would their marriage suffer if she told her mom the truth? And would the ranch be destroyed if her father found out about Jay before she had a chance to figure out another alternative? No, she couldn't take any chances, not until she had every detail sorted out.

"What I need to do is get away from here for a little while. I can't be around her. I just can't. The remodel is almost done, and by the time I get back, I'll either have everything worked out or I'll never see her again."

"You want to leave in the middle of the remodel? What will your mother think?"

"She won't think anything. She's been in charge for most of it, and she's been telling me I need a break all summer. I can't think of a better time."

"But where will you go?"

"To the only place that will help me find some answers."

CHAPTER EIGHTEEN

Jay awoke the next morning with cottonmouth and a splitting headache. Hangovers were far from being a new experience for her, but she couldn't ever remember drinking as much as she had last night. As she looked down at her open jeans and bare feet, she wondered how in the hell she got home. And why was her shirt on the floor hanging from one of her wrists?

"Shit," she muttered. She looked around her bedroom, hoping she wouldn't find anyone there with her. She remembered Paula the bartender buying her the first round of tequila, she bought the second, and somewhere between the third and forth, a beautiful redhead appeared in the picture.

She dragged her slack body out of bed and into the bathroom where she took a cold shower and brushed the sour taste of agave out of her mouth. As she stepped through the bedroom threshold, she stopped short when the beautiful redhead from the bar was waiting at the kitchen counter with coffee in hand.

"I thought you might need this," the woman said with a wink as she handed the fresh smelling brew to Jay.

"Thanks," was all she could manage as she grabbed her head and sat on the stool next to her. Normally, waking up with a woman whose name she couldn't remember wouldn't have fazed her, but today not only was she embarrassed, she hoped she hadn't made too much of an ass out of herself. From the looks of things, she guessed it was too late to worry about that now. "What's your name?"

"I'm DC and you're, Jay, correct?"

"Yeah." Jay smiled weakly. *Oh God! What have I done?*

"Can I make you something to eat?" DC asked around a bite of toast. She placed her bare foot on Jay's stool, and Jay scanned the long, pale leg that disappeared beneath a pair of dark blue boxers. Her blue boxers. DC was also wearing one of Jay's button-down white shirts with nothing underneath it. Her curly red hair hung loosely past her shoulders, and her emerald green eyes were the most beautiful shade of jade that she'd ever seen.

"DC, can I ask you a question?" She rubbed her forehead trying to figure out what she wanted to say without further embarrassing DC or herself.

"I know what you're going to ask me, and the answer is no. Not that I didn't want to, but I can't take advantage of a sexy grieving woman. Not my style."

Jay let out a small laugh and placed her forehead on the cool Formica countertop. "Well, I guess I must have made quite the impression last night then."

DC rubbed Jay's back in soothing circles. "On the contrary, you were very sweet. That is until you passed out. Paula happened to know where you lived so I volunteered to take you home."

"Who uh…"

"Undressed you?"

"Yeah."

"I did, and as you can probably tell, you weren't very cooperative." DC laughed.

"I can see that. Look, DC, I—"

DC put her hand up as if to say stop and bent toward Jay, placing a soft kiss on her lips. "You don't have to say anything. I heard you last night. And she's a fool for leaving you."

DC pushed away from the bar, gathering her clothes on the way to the bathroom. "I'm going to get dressed then get out of here. And for what it's worth, I'm sorry she hurt you."

When the bathroom door shut behind DC, Jay groaned and grabbed her head again as if to keep it from falling off her shoulders. "Oh fuck!" *Who else knows?*

She tried to remember anything about last night, but the truth was if she could scrap the whole day she would, except for the part where she and Coal had made love. This couldn't be happening. She lost Coal, ended up with a strange woman in her apartment, and Dino—

Oh fuck, Dino! He's going to kill me! She picked up her cell and pressed one for speed dial. "Hey, Cuz, it's Jay," she said to his voicemail. "I'm going to be late. Be there soon."

She waited for DC to finish up in the bathroom, downing the rest of her coffee and a piece of toast, hoping to settle her queasy stomach. She walked DC to the door and held it open for her. If this was any other time in her life, she didn't think she'd be able to allow DC to leave so soon. "DC...uh...what can I say? Thanks for all of it."

"You really are cute." DC chuckled and placed a kiss on Jay's cheek. "And you're very welcome."

DC disappeared down the hallway as Jay let out a heavy sigh and shut the door. Laying her forehead against the cool wood, she prayed to whatever deity who would listen that today would be better than yesterday.

An hour later, Jay showed up to work and received the cold shoulder from Dino. Italians were never silent unless they were pissed, and by the way he was glaring at her, pissed would be a mild word for how he was probably feeling. He motioned for her to go inside the house, no doubt for privacy. Whatever he had to say to her wasn't for the world to hear.

"Do we need to talk?" Dino asked. He crossed his arms in front of his chest and leaned against the doorjamb, apparently not ready to leave her alone until he got a response.

"What do you want me to say? I fucked up. I'm sorry."

"No you didn't just *fuck up,* Cuz. I listened to your shit story right before you decided to get laid by that redheaded Amazon. This is so past fucked up. I know you love this girl, but you can't. Do you understand you *can't,* because you're not one of them. She comes from money and is educated. What do you have? I'll tell you what you have, nothing! Nothing to offer her except a lot of heartache and a week-to-week paycheck. How could you think that someone like Coal Davis could possibly want someone like you?"

Jay placed her hands against the wall and bowed her head. He wasn't telling her anything she didn't already know, but it still hurt to hear the words. "Well, you have nothing to worry about because she wants nothing more to do with me. I'll keep a low profile until the job is done and make sure we don't run into each other."

"If that's the case, it looks like you're in luck. I spoke to Coal's mother this morning and she's decided to go on an extended vacation."

Jay's head shot up and she pushed forcefully away from the wall. "What do you mean she's going on a vacation? And what the *fuck* did you say to Jane Davis?"

Dino looked at Jay in surprise. "Say? Do I look stupid to you? I didn't say anything to her. All I know is that Coal's gone for a while and she doesn't know when she'll be back. She does, however, have the punch list of everything Coal wants completed before she returns. If we finish by the scheduled completion date, which to remind you, is this Friday, we'll even get a bonus."

Jay paced like a caged animal. *We get a bonus! In other words, she wants us out of here before she returns so she doesn't have to face me!*

"Cuz," Dino said. "Let it go."

He cautiously placed a hand on her shoulder but she shrugged it off. "I'm going back to work."

Jay stormed down the stairs finding a task to help take her mind off the fact that she was hung over and angry. She needed to find a way to overcome the toughest obstacle though, finding a way to put Coal Davis behind her forever.

Coal was jarred awake by the sounds of dozens of horses calling out to one another in the nearby pastures. She glanced around in a daze at the small room her grandfather had furnished for her when she'd been a child and had helped him on the ranch. She pulled the blanket up to her shoulders in an attempt to fight off the early morning chill, but nothing she could do could fill the emptiness of her heart.

It had been two days since she'd seen Jay, two days of crying and bouts of self-pity. She'd escaped to the familiarity of the ranch, needing a safe place to think. Except for a few meals, she hadn't left the safety of her room. She even refused to answer her cell and had missed a few dozen calls from her mom and twice that many from Angel.

As she stared out the bedroom window at a palomino chasing a chestnut colt, she thought about Dax and missed his company. She could use her trusted companion now more than ever, but she couldn't have stayed at home. There were too many opportunities to run into Jay. And Jay was her ultimate temptation, that decadent dessert that she could never say no to and always needed to have one more bite.

She hated the way she had to treat Jay and cried for hours over what they'd shared and what they would miss out on in the future. She missed Jay's smile. She missed watching Jay work. But most of all, she missed being wrapped up in Jay's arms. There had only been one other time where she'd felt that accepted. It had been years ago, but the memories were as fresh as the dew that had accumulated outside her window.

"Coal, do you like it here?" her grandfather asked.

"Yes, Grandpa. Even more than home sometimes," she said. She patted one of the older horses right above the nose.

"Why is that, honey?"

"Because I can be who I want to be here."

"What do you mean?"

She kissed the thoroughbred who placed his large head under her arm. "Daddy wants me to wear dresses and do girl stuff, but I'd rather wear jeans and ride horses."

"And why does your daddy think that girls shouldn't wear jeans and ride horses, honey?"

"I don't know, Grandpa. But I like it here. And if I could stay here forever with you I would."

After that day with her grandfather, she'd thought he, out of everyone in her family, had understood her. When the thought that she'd disappointed him too became too much to bear, she threw on some jeans and a sweatshirt and walked out onto the wooden porch that overlooked the pasture. The low-lying fog, which was typical throughout most of the year in the small seaside town, settled over the ranch like a heavy blanket. A man she'd known for most of her life greeted her with a wave and a toothy smile as he stepped from his Chevy truck. Before she could get down the front steps, two strong hands lifted her up and pulled her into a hug.

"Little Coal Davis," Doug Bransten said. "Well I'll be."

She laughed as he twirled her around in a circle just like when she was a child. "Put me down."

He had greeted her every summer in that exact same manner, and even though he had to be somewhere in his mid sixties, he still reminded her of the young, energetic handsome ranch hand that she'd always known.

Doug had been her grandpa's best friend. The ranch always ran smoothly under his control, not a small task considering he was responsible for over a hundred and fifty horses. He was six-foot-five of all-American cowboy. His leathery skin spoke of years of hard work in the sun, and his Stetson hung low on his forehead as his steely gray eyes appraised her.

"You haven't changed at all," Coal said.

"You have, little lady, but you're as beautiful as always."

"Still a charmer I see. How have you been?"

"I'm good." He looked out over the pasture his eyes losing some of their spark. "Miss your granddaddy though. He was a good man."

Coal grabbed his hand and held it in hers. "I'm sure wherever he is now he would say the same thing about you." *I just wonder what he'd say about me?*

Doug cleared his throat. "Enough of that there nonsense. What brings you out here, girlie? I haven't seen you since you were three hay bales high."

She laughed then her tone turned serious. "I've been here but I heard you took a few months vacation to see your grandkids. How are they?"

"Growing like weeds. Now stop dodging the subject, why you really here?"

"I guess you heard that Grandpa left the ranch to me?"

He nodded. "Yes, ma'am, I did. And I could think of no one better to leave its care too. How does your daddy feel about that?"

Coal swiped at a stubborn tear, cursing its timing. "We'll get to that later. How about I go ditch these slippers for some boots and we take a ride along those acres of beautiful beachfront property? I could use the fresh air. What do you say?"

A smile touched his unshaven face. "I'd say you got yourself a deal there, little lady."

❖

Jay sat on Coal's bed, staring at a picture of Coal riding her horse. Coal had given it to her after their first date and she'd kept it in her wallet ever since. Every time Jay felt a pang of loneliness settle over her, she pulled out the photo, remembering that she'd once had everything she'd ever wanted and more.

She still couldn't figure out how it had all gone so wrong. Nothing in her life had ever been easy, so why did she think that a relationship would be any different? Her mother had walked out on them when she was young, and then her father slowly deteriorated with every drink he took. His drug habit followed soon after, and when he ended up in jail for stealing, she'd spent every earned dollar trying to keep a roof over her head and her pride intact. She'd promised her dying aunt she would always keep the family home in the family, and thankfully, the rent she received paid most of the mortgage, otherwise she'd never be able to keep afloat. As she sat staring at Coal's picture, she knew that she'd give it all up just to have Coal in her arms one more time.

She'd thought about her mom the last few days, wishing she had her to talk to. She'd needed motherly advice many times during her life, but more than anything, she needed someone who would hold her and tell her everything was going to be all right. She sure as hell couldn't get that from her dad even if he wasn't in jail, and since she never looked to family for anything, she wasn't about to go crying to them now.

With one of Coal's sweatshirts in her hand, she brought the cotton to her face and inhaled the familiar scent of warm hay and sunshine. She held the sweatshirt tightly, imagining Coal in her arms. She allowed the burning lump in her throat to turn into hot, flowing tears. She was so consumed by her own grief that she didn't hear the footsteps until someone stopped directly behind her.

"Jay, is everything all right?" Jane Davis asked.

Jay rose, dropped the sweatshirt onto the bed, and stepped back, clearly shocked that Coal's mom had caught her crying on the job, hell, crying at all. She was officially a basket case. How was she going to explain her behavior? "I'm sorry."

"No, I'm sorry if I spooked you. I couldn't help but notice you're upset. Anything I can do?"

"No, ma'am. I'm fine. Hard day is all." Jesus! Could this day get any more fucking embarrassing for her? First DC and now breaking down in front of Coal's mother. If she were a horse, she'd be taken out to pasture and put out of her misery.

"I know I'm a stranger to you, but I'm a good listener. And sometimes it helps to talk out your problems with someone who can be objective."

Objective, not! You're Coal's mother! "I'm okay, ma'am, really. I've just had a few bad days. Thanks for asking though."

"Can I give you some advice?"

"Sure," Jay said warily. Funny how minutes before she'd wished for some motherly advice.

"I don't know who is causing you pain, but whoever that person is, I'm sure they'll be willing to listen if you give them the chance."

"How do you know it's a person?" Jay felt like she was walking on thin ice beginning to crack below her feet. She had to tread cautiously.

"Lucky guess. And if I'm right." Jane's gaze dropped to the sweatshirt on Coal's bed. "I'm sure things can be worked out."

"I wish I was as optimistic as you, but sometimes I don't think everything can be worked out."

Jane shrugged. "You never know. Time heals all they say."

The entire conversation was beginning to feel surreal. Was Jane saying she knew about her past with Coal and was okay with it? She wouldn't take the bait, but she did feel a bit better. "Thank you, ma'am. I see your point."

"Good," Jane said. "So, is the house still on schedule to be completed tomorrow?"

"Yes, ma'am. Everything except for the roof. The roofers said they can't make it until Monday. Scheduling issues."

"Sounds like you have everything under control just like I knew you and Dino would." She placed her hand on Jay's forearm and gave it a gentle squeeze. "Take care of yourself and…if you need to talk… I'll be around."

As soon as Jane Davis disappeared down the winding staircase, Jay took her first full breath. She thought about what Jane had said, but there was no sense in having a conversation with Coal, especially after being told their relationship was a mistake. She was tired of not being enough for someone again. Her mother had abandoned her all those years ago, her father emotionally abandoned her not long after, and when she finally felt like she'd mattered enough to someone else, they walked out on her too. Physically and emotionally drained, she grabbed her hammer and set back to work. One more day and she could put Coal Davis's memory behind her.

CHAPTER NINETEEN

Jay spent her lunch hour alone since her mood hadn't improved. She'd ignored Dino for most of the day, only speaking to him if he had something important to say that pertained to the job. She was edgy and tired and couldn't wait for the day to end.

"Hey, Cuz," Dino said. He moved closer and offered her a can of her favorite soda like some sort of peace offering and his notepad. "I have one more small thing to add to your list."

"Thanks," she said and glanced at his incoherent scribble. Lucky for her she grew up with him and could decipher its meaning. "I'll get to this once I finish the tile work."

"Okay. And don't forget about my dad's party this weekend. You're coming, right?"

Jay glanced over at Dino like he was a foreigner speaking a different language. "Uh…no."

Jay's uncle Mario was Dino's father. Uncle Mario loved to throw parties, and they were usually large family productions. Her father was Uncle Mario's brother, and since Jay had heard they had released him from jail only yesterday, she didn't want to chance running into him.

"Why are you always doggin' us? The family wants to get together for the weekend, and Pop wants all of us to be there. Why don't you want to go? It's not like you have anything better to do."

They'd spent the previous morning discussing this same topic. How many more times could she say no to him? She couldn't think about anything else, not with Coal occupying her every thought.

With the remodel nearly complete, she'd been on a mission to finish the work by tomorrow's deadline. She would have liked to get more done quicker, but fatigue and depression had prevented her usual speed on the job. She wished he'd stop badgering her about a family get-together that she had no desire to partake in. She needed sleep, not socializing, and the sooner he understood that and left her alone the quicker she could finish her work.

"Why can't you get I'm not in the mood for a family thing? Especially since Pop—" Jay stopped mid sentence, shaking her head dismissively. Damn it! She tried so hard not to talk about him.

"Damn, you're still living in the past. Why can't you give your old man a break? So what he made a mistake? Happens to everyone except for you, right?"

"You have no idea what you're talking about. Let it go, Dino," she growled in warning.

"Fuck that! You've been dragging your ass around here like a wounded animal for the past few days. Coal's gone. She doesn't love you. It's time to get over it before—"

Dino didn't have time to finish his sentence before Jay grabbed him and shoved his back hard into the kitchen wall causing a few of the newly inlaid tiles to go crashing to the floor. "Leave her out of this, Dino. Don't mention her name to me again. Do you understand?"

"Let go," he rasped before she came to her senses and released the hold she'd had on his throat.

She stumbled backward, staring at her hands as if they belonged to someone else. "Fuck! What the hell am I doing? Dino, I'm sorry—"

"No," he rasped, massaging his throat. "I'm sorry. I was out of line, Cuz."

"That's no excuse. You're family and the only person I could ever count on. You've given me a job, helped me find a place to live after Dad's trial. I owe you everything." *Jesus, you've sunk to a new low.*

"You don't owe me anything. We're family." He placed a hand on her shoulder. "That's what family does, Cuz."

"Maybe your family, but not mine. If it wasn't for your side… Uncle Mario…you…I'd have nothing." Jay leaned against the wall and slid to the floor. She laid her head in her hands feeling the weight of the world on her shoulders.

Dino sat next to her and placed a hand on her knee to get her to look at him. "Your old man said he was sorry. What more does he have to do to make you forgive him?"

"You don't understand, Dino. He stole from those people and we lost our *home*! They trusted him, and he sold their stuff for drugs." She still hated thinking about the money and the trial, but its lingering effects still ruled her life.

"He had a habit. Things happen that we can't explain."

"I understand, but his habit cost us not just our home, but my college fund, and I'm still paying off the lawyers. He got off easy. He went to jail for three years, and now he's out doing God knows what while I'm stuck with thirty-five thousand in debt. I put up Tia's house as collateral after I swore on her grave that I would keep that house in the family. If I lose it, my word is shit!"

Dino looked shocked. "Cuz, I didn't know. Why didn't you say something?"

"Because it's *my* business, Dino. Not yours—not Uncle Mario's—no one's! Besides, what could you have done?"

"Done? I could have helped you. I have the money. Why didn't you ask?"

"Because I knew you would give it to me."

"And I still will."

"No, you won't. I appreciate it, but I can't let you do that. It's my responsibility and mine alone."

He studied her pensively, and Jay wondered what he was thinking. Instead she moved to her feet and offered him a hand up.

"You sure you don't want help?" he asked one more time.

"I know you mean well, but my pride won't let me allow you or anyone to bail me out. Let's get this job done, and hopefully the bonus will help. In a few years, I plan on having everything paid off and then I'm going back to school. Maybe one of these days, I'll be a successful contractor like you." She bumped his shoulder playfully with her own.

"You're so stubborn." He shook his head but shot her the DiAngelo trademark grin.

"Damn right I am. Now, come on, boss, we have work to do."

❖

Dusk was settling over the ranch as Coal curled up with a blanket on the porch and stared out over the wide open space. She'd spent the afternoon riding one of the horses around the ranch with Doug and found the property to be in perfect condition, not like she expected anything less. As the crickets confirmed night was upon them, she inhaled the rich smell of soil and manure, a scent that would be considered foul to most people but had always helped center her. The familiar aroma fueled some of the memories of the times she'd spent here with her grandfather. She'd thought about him a lot the last few days, especially after spending time with Doug. He seemed to have everything under control, just like she knew he would. She'd even had the opportunity again to work with a few of the children and still loved their unique responses to the large animals. Giddy wasn't a term she would use often to describe how she was feeling, especially after the last few days. But seeing those kids laugh and forget about their illnesses, even for a short time, reminded her of why the ranch was important to so many people.

Doug took the rocker next to her and placed his familiar pipe in his mouth. They were quiet for a moment, as if neither one of them wanted to upset the silence. When he turned to her, Coal broke out in a smile.

"You still have that old thing?" she asked, as he tapped the white and black pipe against his sturdy thigh.

"Yes, ma'am. Your granddaddy gave this to me thirty years ago. Best pipe I ever owned."

"Have you owned a lot of them?"

"Nope. Never had a reason to."

"Does there have to be a reason?"

Doug pulled the pipe out from between his lips, letting the smoke out slowly. "Coal, I knew your granddaddy for a long time. That man meant a lot to me, kinda like this pipe. But he and I had our differences and didn't always share the same views. I think that's what made us such good friends. But to answer your question, I believe a person usually doesn't need to change a thing until they have a damn good reason to."

Why do I think that somehow we are no longer talking about pipes? She had no idea if Doug and her grandfather had ever discussed the details of her life, but she was also aware that he had to know she had a reason for being there, and something was telling her he knew exactly what that reason was. "But that's just it. What if we don't know what's right? What if doing the right thing costs you everything?"

Doug rocked back and forth in his chair, appearing deep in thought. "Did I ever tell you how I met my Rita?"

"Not really." She knew Doug worshipped the ground Rita walked on, but she also knew his wife had died at the very young age of fifty. "I remember you telling me she was beautiful."

"She wasn't just beautiful. My Rita was picture-perfect. Every boy in this town wanted to marry that woman. God only knows why she chose me," he said with a twinkle in his eye. "Anyway, her father owned one of the largest nurseries not too far from here, and I went to work for him one summer and fell head over heels for Rita. One day, her father cornered me and told me he'd shoot me full of holes if I ever came near his daughter again."

"And then what happened?"

"What do you think? We ran away and got married." He laughed then his face turned serious. "When we got back, her daddy was furious. You see, not only did I work for him but so did my daddy and my two brothers."

"Wow, that must have been rough." Coal knew from her conversations with her grandfather that forty years ago, Half Moon Bay was nothing more than farmland. If you didn't work for one of the farms, there wouldn't be much in the way to earn income. And if you pissed off one owner, you might as well have pissed them all off.

"It was for a while, but that's when I met your granddaddy. He had just bought the land and didn't know shit about horses, pardon my French. Anyway, I was drinking at the local pub, feeling a little down on my luck, when he sat next to me and we began talking. He asked me if I knew anything about horses, and whatever I said must have impressed the hell out of him."

"You don't remember?"

"Hell no, girl! I was four shots of Cuervo in by that point." They both laughed. "When he told me his plan about horses working with children, I told him I'd work for next to nothing if he gave me a chance. He gave me a job that day. Within a year, my whole family ended up working for your granddaddy. I've been working here ever since."

"And what happened with Rita's father?"

Doug's grin grew wider. "That ole coot wouldn't have anything to do with either of us for five years until we gave him a grandson."

"I remember Eric." She and Eric used to clean out the horse stalls at night for extra spending money, but she'd have done it for free. "How's he doing?"

"He's running a nursery that he inherited from his granddaddy."

"You're kidding?"

"Nope. Swear on Rita's grave."

She looked into his kind eyes. "Was it worth it, Doug? I mean, you didn't really know how things were going to turn out."

The smile that touched his face could have lit up the night's sky. "A woman makes you do crazy things, Coal. It was worth it, and it was because I took that chance on love that my life ended up the way it did. Things happen for a reason. Don't let people dictate your life or you'll be running away from your problems for the rest of your life."

Coal closed her eyes and pictured Jay. She had to ask the next question, even though she feared the answer. "If you had to do it all over again, would you?"

Doug stood, placing a hand on her shoulder. "Girlie, I'd give my life just to have Rita in my arms one more time. I may be an old fool, but the look you have in your eyes right now, I had all those years ago when Rita's father forbid me to see her. So yes, I'd give up everything to have another chance with her. Remember, real love comes around for most people only once. *If* you're lucky."

Coal waited as the silence once again settled all around her so that she could have a moment to think. She thought about her future, her dreams, and Jay. As a plan began to form, she finally understood what she needed to do. The time had come to face her fears. Hopefully, it wasn't too late.

CHAPTER TWENTY

F riday morning couldn't have come fast enough for Jay. Every hour working on Coal's home had been emotionally painful and physically draining. She'd finally completed the job that she had come to do, but this time she found no pleasure in her finished work.

"Well, ma'am, that's it," Jay said. She shook Jane Davis's outstretched hand. "My cousin said to tell you that he'll be over on Monday to do the walk-through. He also said he will be able to complete the few odd jobs that you have at your home and check on the roofers for you." *God, you remind me of your daughter. I miss her so much.*

"Thank you, Jay, for everything. I'm sure Coal will love it when she returns." Jane glanced up at the completed house, her smile one of pleasure and admiration.

"I hope she does."

"She will. But maybe…"

"Ma'am, is there something else?"

"Well, I was hoping maybe, *you* could do the walk-through with her on Monday instead of Dino. I'm sure she'd love to see you."

There hadn't been a minute that had ticked by that Jay hadn't thought about Coal. When the memories of how it had felt to hold Coal came roaring back, she trembled and buried her hands in her pockets so Jane couldn't see how much her words had affected her. "I don't think that will be possible, but please tell her I hope everything turned out as she expected."

"Somehow, Jay." Jane Davis gave her a regretful smile. "I don't think that's possible either."

Jay sat by the corral gate, taking one final glance at the perfectly manicured grounds and Dax running inside his pasture. She pulled her truck over to the side of the road, spying on the large animal as he ran back and forth in the warm summer heat. She figured he missed Coal, but also knew he had only a few more days before she would return to him. *Lucky horse.*

Since Coal's departure, Jay had made it a ritual to visit him daily to bring Dax carrots. Somehow it made her feel closer to Coal knowing that he was a large part of her life. She'd often observed Coal feeding him the treat when she knew no one was watching. She'd been worried that in Coal's absence, no one would know to keep up with the ritual. After the first two days, Dax started waiting for her by the fence when she arrived in the morning, and Jay understood how this brilliant, beautiful animal had touched Coal so deeply. He represented the final link to Coal and she would miss his company.

"Is everything done?" Dino asked.

Jay had driven to Dino's to deliver the check. She looked around for a safe place to sit, but from the looks of Dino's condo, she was afraid she'd end up with last week's spaghetti dinner on her butt. "Yep, and Jane Davis said we will get our bonus on Monday. But Jesus, Cuz. Don't you ever clean this place?"

"Why? I got no one to share it with."

"Well, if you ever have any aspirations to change that, maybe you should hire a maid so that the poor woman won't run when she gets a load of this hellhole."

"Look who's talking." He picked up a half-eaten bowl of Cheerios that sat on his counter and threw it onto a pile of dirty dishes overflowing in the sink. "It's not like you're Suzy Homemaker. I've seen your pad, and if it weren't for Shiloh cleaning the place when she was home, I bet the items in your refrigerator could be donated to science."

She couldn't argue with him there. In fact, she had a loaf of bread currently sitting on her kitchen counter that fit that description perfectly. "I've got to get out of here, but before I do, Jane Davis wanted me to remind you about a little work that needs to be done on her home."

"I didn't forget. Sure you don't want the work? You can have all the cash if you take it?"

She'd already had this conversation with him after he'd offered the first time. She rightly refused because she couldn't take the risk of running into Coal. "No, but thanks. Do we have anything else lined up?"

"Not until after Labor Day weekend," Dino said apologetically.

"Okay then. Catch you later."

"Jay, wait! If you need some money just ask, okay?"

She nodded her thanks, thinking for the first time that she could survive without money. What was killing her was living without Coal.

After finding out from Angel that Coal's parents were meeting her parents for dinner, Coal made the short trip home but decided if she wanted to fix things with Jay, now was as good a time as any before she lost her nerve. She called Angel to come get her because she needed her words of wisdom and moral support. Besides, she wasn't sure that Jay wouldn't turn her away and she didn't want to take the chance of becoming stranded.

"Hey, sweetie. You sure about this?" Angel asked as Coal climbed into her white BMW.

"Yeah. I need to make things right. Or try anyway."

Angel pinned Coal with a hard stare. "You going to fill me in on this plan of yours?"

"You want to keep your eye on the road before you kill us?"

"Oh crap!" Angel swerved out of the way of an oncoming car, the passing driver's blaring horn signaling they were as unhappy as Coal.

"I guess that answers that question." Coal placed her hand over her pounding heart.

"Sorry, sweetie."

"It's cool. I've been doing a lot of thinking, and—"

"Hold that thought." Angel pressed the answer button on her steering wheel to accept the incoming call. "Yeah."

"Angel," the caller shouted into the phone. "It's Paula from Spice."

"Hey, woman. Why you calling me so early on a Friday night?"

"I'm working tonight," Paula yelled over the loud background noise. "Your cousin Jenn's here. She's drunk and she's making a scene. I don't need any slack, if you know what I mean."

"Shit," Angel muttered. "I'm going to kill her."

"My thought exactly," Paula said. "Can you come get her?"

"I'll be right there. Thanks, babe. I owe you."

Coal listened to the cryptic conversation but sat patiently until Angel disconnected the call. "What the hell was that all about?"

"Oh, sorry." Angel merged onto the freeway, which was in the opposite direction of Jay's. "That was Paula, the bartender from Spice. My underage cousin is drunk, and you heard the rest. She can't go back to her house after she's been drinking, and Paula can get in a shit-load of trouble if the manager finds out she let her in. I hope you don't mind, but we have to take a detour before we visit Jay's?"

"Of course," Coal said. "I would have suggested it even if you didn't ask."

"Thanks. So are you going to tell me about what you're going to say to her?"

"You have enough on your mind. How about we take care of Jenn then I'll tell you everything. Deal?"

Angel nodded as Coal laid her head back against the headrest and closed her eyes. She would help Angel with her problems before the time would come to face her own.

Chapter Twenty-one

The first thing Coal noticed when entering the crowded club was a tall, slender bartender with short dark hair and two gold nose piercings holding a woman Coal didn't recognize from slumping to the floor. The skinny jeans, cropped tank, and baby smooth skin of the young woman screamed this had to be Angel's cousin.

"Thanks for coming. I don't know what I would have done if you didn't answer your phone," the bartender said to Angel as Angel hooked her arm around the young woman's inert form.

"Paula, this is Coal," Angel said. "Thanks for looking out for Jenn. We got it from here."

Coal moved to Jenn's other side and threw one of her limp arms around her shoulders.

"Fuck, Jenn, what the hell have you done to yourself?" Angel held Jenn's head up, but Jenn's body protested the movement. Jenn groaned. "Oh no you don't, chica. Not on *Manolo Blahnik* pumps."

"Does she do this often?" Coal asked. She was having a difficult time maneuvering under the dead weight.

"No. And if my aunt finds out, she and I are both going to get an ass chewing!"

"Do you have this?" Coal asked Angel, but her attention was focused on the dance floor.

"Yeah. We'll meet you outside."

Coal absently waved her off as she tried to get a better view of the jam-packed room. When the dark hair came into view once more, she didn't need to see the woman's face that held the tall redhead in her arms to know that it was Jay. She'd recognize that lean, dangerous body anywhere.

Her eyes remained glued to the two women wrapped in each other's arms as her world once again crumbled all around her. She gasped as her heart hammered violently in her chest. The tears threatened. She was seconds from losing it.

Jay had her arms wrapped loosely around the woman's waist as the redhead's arms were clasped behind Jay's neck. The woman whispered something into Jay's ear, provoking that grin that Coal had come to love. A smile that was no longer for her.

Something snapped inside her, and she felt as though she were falling endlessly. She stood paralyzed with fear—dying inside. Jay couldn't see her among the mass of people, but she was sure that Jay wouldn't notice anything while in the arms of that beautiful woman.

She found her way to the bar, ordered two shots of whiskey, and downed them before motioning the bartender for two more. This wasn't how she'd planned her evening, but she knew of only one way to banish the memory of Jay in the arms of another woman. As the haze of alcohol overtook her, she welcomed the loss of her grief, if only temporarily.

"Honey, what are you doing?" Angel asked

"Drinking. Just go and take Jenn home. Don't worry about me."

"Fuck that! I can't leave you here. I don't know what's going on with you, but we need to go. Now." Angel tried to wrap an arm around Coal's waist to guide her off of the stool, but Coal pushed her hand away.

"Angel, don't—"

When Coal tried to stand on her own, her legs gave out beneath her. Lucky for her, someone else was there to catch her.

"Jay?" Coal said.

Jay tightened her grip around Coal's waist to steady her. "Yeah. What are you doing here?"

"Having a drink. Bartender, one more," Coal said.

"Baby, I think you've had enough."

Coal stiffened. "You know God damned well I'm not your baby!"

Jay ran a shaky hand through her hair. The last few hours had been equivalent to riding an emotional rollercoaster. One minute, she was in DC's arms, trying to banish Coal's memory and the last words she'd spoken to her. The next, she spotted an inebriated Coal arguing with Angel, and she could think of nothing but making sure she was okay. Now that she had, no matter the pain that seeing her was causing, she knew deep in her heart there was no place else she'd rather be.

"You got this?" Angel asked. She threw Jay a sympathetic smile and handed her a piece of paper with an address on it. "In case you need it."

"Thanks." She watched Angel leave and pulled Coal tighter against her. "Come on. Let's get you out of here."

"Why do you care?" Coal pulled away from Jay and, in the process, knocked over her shot glass, shattering it on top of the bar.

Instinctively, Jay shielded Coal from the shattering glass. When Coal pulled away from her, she could overlook the stinging sensation against her forehead, but she couldn't ignore the trickle of blood that seeped its way into her right eye.

"Oh no!" Coal cried. She cupped Jay's chin and brushed the stream of blood away with her thumb. "I've hurt you! Sweetie, I'm so sorry."

Jay closed her eyes, welcoming the heat of Coal's skin brushing against hers. She'd missed the feel of her. The taste of her. And forgetting all about the night's events, she placed her hand over Coal's and kissed her palm.

"I need you," Coal whispered. "Jay, please."

Jay tilted her head and brushed a kiss over her lips. When Coal swayed toward her, Jay parted Coal's lips with her own, searching, needing, wanting something that Coal could no longer give her. She'd spent the last few nights wanting to touch Coal like this again. There'd been a time when Coal's desire for her would have made her blood boil. But this was different. Coal was drunk. And the only words she kept hearing were the ones that forced her to accept that she couldn't allow anything to happen between them. *This is a mistake, Jay.*

"Hey," Jay said breathlessly, breaking the kiss. "It's time to go home."

"But I don't want to go home…" The slurred words died on her lips as she slumped against her.

Jay easily lifted Coal into her arms and carried her without further incident to the truck. As Coal slept off the effects of the alcohol, Jay secured her in the cab with a seat belt and followed the directions that Angel had given her to her house. She kept one hand on Coal's thigh for the entire ride, the simple connection all that remained of their last few moments together.

Angel was waiting for them on the front porch when Jay pulled up to the house. She carried a passed out Coal up two flights of stairs to a spare bedroom where she placed her onto a king-sized bed. She pulled the blankets up to cover Coal's body and placed a tender kiss on her lips. *I love you.*

Jay was headed back to her truck when Angel stopped her on the porch. She'd been so wrapped up with Coal it took her a second to realize she was at the house that her father had once violated.

"Thank you," Angel said.

"Anytime," Jay said, the pain of leaving Coal tearing at her heart. "I'm just glad she's okay."

"You know, for what it's worth, I trust you with my friend. And I'm sure when she wakes up, she'll appreciate all you've done for her."

Jay smiled wanly. *She knows it was my dad and she's okay with it.* "Please take good care of her, Angel."

"I will, honey." Angel hugged her. "Promise."

Chapter Twenty-two

I'm sorry about last night," Coal said. She took the wet rag from Angel and placed it over her forehead. She'd been sitting on the bathroom floor for hours, the light beige tile rendering her butt numb from the cold. She'd forgotten how many times she'd emptied the contents of her stomach, not that there was much left.

"You owe me." Angel wore a light pink bathrobe and matching fuzzy slippers and looked about as exhausted as Coal felt. She handed Coal a glass. "Drink."

"What is it?"

"Ginger ale. It will help with the queasiness. Between you and my cousin, you'd think I was running a drunk tank."

"How's Jenn feeling?" Coal sipped the gold liquid, grateful when it appeared it would stay down.

"She looks worse than you, if that's what you're asking."

Coal grabbed her head, feeling a sharp pain begin to coalesce behind her eyeballs. "I should call a cab. I need to get home and into my own bed. It's going to take a week to sleep this off."

"No need. I have time to take you home before my cousin wakes up. Better you're gone before I have to give her a lecture."

"Hey," Coal said to stop Angel from leaving the room. "I am really sorry about the way I acted yesterday. It was immature and you didn't deserve it."

"Honey, you don't need to apologize to me. I'm your friend, and if that brain of yours is still muddled, you forget that I've seen you so much worse."

"I hear a 'but' coming."

"But." Angel's expression turned serious. "You need to speak with Jay. She's the one who took care of you. She loves you, Coal. It's written all over that sexy face of hers."

Coal shook her head, the motion making her want to vomit again. She desperately wanted to believe what Angel was saying, but she saw Jay last night. Saw her in the arms of that drop-dead gorgeous redhead. She'd been right about being easily replaced. She wasn't surprised, but it hurt so damn much. "I don't doubt she cares for me, but she's made it clear she's moved on. It's my fault. That's clear. But because she has, I have to too."

Angel nodded as if she understood and left Coal alone to gather her things. On the way home, every bump and turn on the short drive made Coal feel as though she were seated on one of those amusement park teacup rides. She spent most of the journey with her hand over her mouth, afraid she'd lose it again but more concerned of the tongue-lashing she'd receive if she puked all over Angel's immaculate white interior. By the time Angel turned into her driveway, Coal was ready to sell her soul to anyone who could get the earth to stop moving.

"I do owe you." Coal gave Angel a quick hug.

"Damn straight. And I plan to cash in."

Angel drove away, leaving Coal to appreciate her newly renovated home for the first time in the daylight. Once she'd returned yesterday, the sun had already set, not allowing her the opportunity to admire the finishing touches such as the new stain or the bay windows that would allow more sunlight into her kitchen. Jay had done everything she'd asked for and more. She should have been more excited that a part of her life had come together, but without Jay in her life, she was more incomplete than ever.

"Coal!"

"Hey, Mom," Coal said. She forced a smile, as her mom stepped from the golf cart. She hoped the shower she'd taken at Angel's had removed the stench of stale alcohol and vomit from her breath, otherwise she'd have a lot of explaining to do. Last night had been unusual for her. She didn't often drink to get drunk. A few beers here and there or a glass of wine among friends was more her speed. The hard stuff had always been reserved for when she felt trapped.

Last night had been the second time in her life where she felt the walls closing in around her. The first time had been when Taylor had disappeared from her life without so much as a fuck you. Her mother had been the only one to see her like that. If her mother witnessed that behavior again, she'd know something was up, and Coal didn't have the energy to explain herself today. Not today.

"Darling, you don't look rested." Her mother leaned forward to kiss Coal on the cheek, staring at her inquisitively. "I thought you were going away to relax."

"I rested, Mom."

"Where? In the barn? Because I can tell you're still not sleeping. And you're so pale. Are you ill?"

"I see the contractors are done," Coal said. She didn't want to be interrogated anymore. "Did you pay them?"

"Yes, but Dino is coming back tomorrow morning to do the walk-through and a few small jobs at my house. He said to tell you he'd be here at eight a.m. The roofers will be here too."

Just Dino? She really is gone for good. "Fine. I guess I'll get settled in and go check on Dax. How is he?"

"He missed you. But why don't you take a nap first? You have the whole day to go see him."

"You're right. Is there anything else?"

Her mother pursed her lips as if she had more to say but instead glanced up at Coal's house one more time and shrugged noncommittally. "Nothing I can think of."

At any other time, Coal would have questioned her mom's odd behavior, but she didn't have the energy. After saying their good-byes, she wearily climbed the stairs and fell into bed, not bothering to take the time to remove her clothes. The sheets beneath her body were soft, and when she rolled over onto her side and her head sank into the pillow, she caught the familiar scent of wood and smoke. Inhaling deeply, she recalled the last time she lay in that bed, Jay had made love to her. She'd felt so carefree then. Similar to the way she felt when she rode her horse in the wind. Effortless motion without thought. The give and take between two individuals who connected in mind, body, and soul. Jay had possessed a way of making her feel whole. A way of making her feel accepted. Now, not only did she no longer feel complete, she felt numb. Somewhere between now and when she'd been a child she'd lost her identity, her true sense of self. As she cried herself to sleep, she wondered if she ever really knew who she was at all.

❖

"Jay, you gotta go," Dino said.

"No, I don't. And you know damn well why."

Jay had been having this same argument with Dino for the last five minutes. She ditched the family party on Saturday and was glad she had after hearing that her father had attended and was drunk for most of the day. She couldn't handle any more heartache, especially after leaving Coal at Angel's the previous night. She was tired, weary in body and soul. And Dino was crazy if he thought she'd cover for him because he had a two-day hangover. Wild horses couldn't drag her over to the Davis house today.

"Damn it, Jay. I can't tell Jane Davis I'm hung over and can't do the work. Besides, don't you want the bonus check? I know you need it."

Dino was right. She did need the money, but it wasn't worth the price her heart would have to pay if she had to see Coal. She'd spent all day Sunday barely able to find the energy to get out of bed. She'd wanted to go check on Coal. Make sure she was all right. But Coal had made it clear that wasn't her job. "I could wait a few days until you feel better."

"Oh, bullshit!" Dino said. "Get your ass over there right now and do what needs to be done or you can find yourself a new job!"

Jay stared at her phone, listening to the dial tone. "Shit."

She slammed the receiver into its cradle and grabbed her keys. She took a pit stop at a local grocery store before heading over to the Davis home. She pulled over next to the wooden fence and climbed out of the cab. She called over to Dax then waited for him to approach while she pulled a carrot out of a brown paper bag. She took her time removing it and laughed when he snorted at her, his obvious way of telling her to hurry up.

"Hey, big guy." She tickled underneath his chin and offered him the first carrot.

The large stallion nodded as his nostrils flared then kicked the ground hard with his front foot.

"Yeah, I know. It's been a few days. I'm sorry, big man."

Dax pushed open Jay's bomber jacket and found the second carrot hidden in her pocket.

"Man, you're smart. I can see why Coal loves you so much." Jay tangled her fingers through Dax's mane, tugging him closer to tell him a secret. "I miss her so much, boy. I wish she could love me like I love her, but she doesn't. Don't worry though. I know she loves you and that you mean more to her than anything."

Dax laid his large head on top of her shoulder, as if offering the only comfort he was capable of to her.

"Thanks for the hug, boy," she said and placed a kiss on his nose. "See you around."

❖

Coal was leaning against the barn door, waiting until Jay's truck headed down the road. She had not been expecting Jay to be there that morning, and her thumping heart told her that her body wasn't expecting it either. After hearing Jay's voice and watching discreetly through the window as Jay hugged Dax and fed him carrots, she had no idea how she was going to handle the rest of her day knowing that Jay was almost close enough to touch.

It went without saying that Jay had taken the time to check on Dax while she'd been gone and that the two of them had formed their own special bond. She couldn't hear what Jay was saying to him, but she'd never known anyone to get Dax to stand so still while they spoke to him, besides her. Dax had always been there to listen to her and she wanted to believe he understood her pain. Could Jay possibly be in pain? Miss her as much as she did Jay?

"Coal? Honey?" Her mother yelled out to her from the other side of the door. "Jay's here for the walk-through."

"Coming, Mom." Coal ran a hand through her hair in an effort to pull herself together. As she emerged from the barn she spotted Jay wearing her trademark jeans and work boots, her muscles rippling against the soft white of her T-shirt. Jay's tousled short hair was as wild as ever but her eyes lacked their usual glow. She hated not seeing that spark of recognition that she'd come to crave. Instead, the indifference in them angered her. *So that's how it's going to be?* "Let's get this done."

Jay remained silent as Coal climbed into the front of the golf cart as Jay slid in behind her mother. They rode in silence, Coal keeping her gaze forward, trying not to squirm even though she could sense Jay's eyes on her. As they reached the house, a tall, burly man approached from one of three roofing trucks parked next to the garage.

"Hey, Jay. Ladies," the man said in greeting. "Man, am I glad to see you."

"Everything okay?" Jay asked.

"Not really. I got to show you something. Ladies, would you please excuse us?"

"I'll be right back," Jay said.

"Jay, wait!" Coal jogged a few feet to catch up with her. She hated this distance between them. Distance that she caused. With her nerve returning, she wanted to tell Jay everything. To explain her behavior. But with all these people around, now was not the time.

"Everything okay?" Jay asked.

"No. It's not." God she wanted to touch her. "When you're done, can we talk? Alone."

When Jay's smile returned, Coal's heart felt a hundred pounds lighter. "Absolutely. Wait here and I'll be right back."

Coal watched as Jay followed the man up the ladder to the top of the roof. The glare of the morning sun made it difficult to see what the man was pointing to but her eyes were glued to Jay's ass anyway.

"What's going on, Jer?" Jay asked.

"Termites, that's what's going on." He pointed to a rotting section of roof. "When we ripped off the old paper, we found large sections of rotted plywood."

"So it's going to be more than just tile."

"Afraid so. There's a larger section over there if you want to go see, but be careful of those stray branches. The tree guys still haven't cut them back, and we told them we're not going to touch this roof until they do."

"Let me check it out then I'll give them another call. They're supposed to be here today too."

Coal watched Jay move around on the roof, remembering the hours she'd spent doing the exact same thing when Jay hadn't noticed. Today was different though. Back then, there wasn't this wall separating them. The silence between them had hurt more than any harsh words that had ever been thrown in her direction. She couldn't wait to get her alone. To tell her she was sorry for the way she'd acted last night. She didn't know if she could repair the damage she'd caused between them, but if that meant building back her trust with Jay one brick at a time, she'd spend the rest of her life doing so.

She turned to answer one of her mother's questions when a loud crash caused her to jump. Men began shouting. A large cloud of dust mushroomed into the air. The cloud was as thick as smoke, billowing higher and higher as men began to scramble from all directions. Fear clutched at Coal, a feeling of dread so strong she gasped sharply as if someone had a hold over her throat. Chaos reigned. And Jay was nowhere to be seen.

"Jesus fucking Christ!" the man yelled who had been standing with Jay moments ago. He scurried down the ladder, jumping from the last few rungs to the ground.

Coal raced toward him and grabbed him by the arm. "Where's Jay?"

He coughed into his arm, expelling some of the dust from his legs. He rasped. "She was inspecting the roof where we discovered some termite damage. She tripped over one of the tree branches that was impeding the roof and it gave way under her weight. She fell through—"

"Jay!"

Coal ran into the house, finding a group of men huddled in her living room. She pushed her way through the solemn crowd, finding Jay sprawled out onto the hardwood floor with her arm bent in an unnatural fashion. Her T-shirt was ripped, and blood trickled from a small cut above her right eye. She wasn't conscious, and the sight of her motionless body sent ripples of despair through Coal, sending her to her knees. "No! Baby, please. Talk to me."

"Honey, we called an ambulance," her mom whispered softly into Coal's ear. "They'll be here any moment."

Coal placed her palm on Jay's cheek feeling as though she were dying inside. Jay was hurt, could possibly die. Forgetting there were people gathered around her and her mother kneeling beside her, she did the only thing she could think of, which was to lean forward to kiss Jay softly on the lips. "Baby, I'm here. Please don't leave me."

Slowly, the men started to file out, their hats held firmly in their hands. The sounds of an ambulance pierced the silence and her mother stood over her, squeezing Coal's shoulder.

"How could I have let her go?"

"Just keep hold of her hand, honey. She needs you now."

"No, Mom, that's where you're wrong," Coal said bitterly. "*I* need her. I have since the day she walked into my life." *I just wished I had told you instead of pushing you away.* "Oh, Jay, what have I done? I love you. I will always love you. I'm so sorry I didn't tell you sooner. Please stay with me."

Just then, two very capable looking paramedics pushed their way through the door and made their way to Jay. A hefty blonde motioned for Coal and her mom to move out of the way as she reached into her kit to start an IV.

"Ma'am," the older paramedic said. He fastened a collar around Jay's neck to stabilize her. "Do you know what hospital she'd prefer?"

The question was simple enough, but Coal was so emotionally distraught she had a hard time organizing her thoughts. After the incident with Jay's hand, she wasn't sure about the current insurance situation, and there was no way in hell she'd ever send her to County. Without giving it another thought, she turned to the paramedic and said, "Stanford Medical Center."

CHAPTER TWENTY-THREE

Coal looked up from her plastic hospital chair just in time to see Dino storm through the waiting room doors looking frazzled and distraught. Her mother had never left her side, gripping her hand for added support when, a little more than two hours before, Jay had been wheeled into surgery. Coal was thankful that Dino had finally arrived because the hospital wouldn't allow non-family members to make medical decisions.

"Have you heard anything yet?" Dino asked.

Her mother stood, and placed her hand on his shoulders. "No. We haven't, but the doctors assured us that they would come and find us as soon as they know something. Are *you* okay? Jay told me earlier you weren't feeling well."

Dino colored. "I'm fine, ma'am. Just a little headache."

"Sit." Her mother's tone left no room for argument.

"Do you know what happened?"

"She fell," Coal finally said around the lump in her throat. "She was on my roof and fell through it. It's all my fault."

"Ms. Davis," he said, his voice a lot calmer than when he'd first entered the waiting room. "It was an accident. Please don't blame yourself."

Not blame myself? She could die and will never know how much I love her. What if I don't get the chance to tell her? Coal gripped her thighs, her hands shaking.

"Hey, she'll be okay." He took one of her hands in his. "My cousin's tough."

"That's what I told her," her mother said gently. "I'm going to get us all some coffee. Would you mind waiting with Coal until I return?"

"Sure." Her mom disappeared into the elevators as Dino sagged in the chair. "Sorry it took me so long to get here. I thought they took her to Sequoia. Does anyone know why they brought her here instead?"

"I told them to come here," Coal said. "After she injured her hand, she confided in me that she didn't want to use your insurance if she got hurt. She was worried your premiums would go up. This is where I go, so I made the choice."

Dino bowed his head and shook it in anger. "Damn her. I told her never to worry about that stuff. She's always so concerned about being a burden to someone. When it comes to her, she knows I don't care about the damn money! If she..." Dino's entire body shook, and Coal wrapped an arm around his shoulders.

"It's okay. She'll be okay. I know because you told me she's tough, remember?"

He used his shirtsleeve to wipe his eyes and smiled through his tears. "That's right."

"She's a lot like you, you know?"

"How so?"

"When she's nervous, she has to do something with her hands." She pointed to the ball cap he was torturing between his fingers. "She usually shoves them into her pockets or picks something up to work with."

"It's a DiAngelo trait." He stared at the crushed hat. "One of many."

"I'm familiar with a few." She thought about Jay's grin. How the quirking of those lips could make her forget everything except wanting to kiss Jay senseless. Then she remembered a trickle of blood that fell across them. Jay lying so still. Her face pale... "God, Dino! I can't take this waiting. There's so much I need to say to her."

"Then promise me one thing?"

Coal glanced at him quizzically. "Anything."

"Promise me, when she wakes, you tell her that. My cousin will probably kick my ass for saying this, but she wants others to think that she doesn't need anyone. Her parents have never been there for her, so she's always tried to prove to everyone, including herself, that she can do everything on her own. Until she met you. Now that's changed, even though she's too damn stubborn to admit it."

Coal gasped, burying her face in Dino's broad shoulders. She needed Jay too, with everything in her, and she would tell her that and more if she got the chance. "I'm so sorry. The things I said to her."

"Excuse me."

Coal looked up at the person in scrubs who stood in the doorway. "Yes?"

"Are you Jay DiAngelo's family?"

"I'm her cousin," Dino said. He and Coal both stood as he extended his hand to the doctor with the confident demeanor that reminded Coal a lot of Jay. "And this is Coal Davis, her—"

"Lover," Coal interjected quickly. If Dino was surprised by the admission, he didn't show it. She also shook the doctor's hand, the warmth in the woman's skin matching the gentleness and understanding in her appraising eyes.

"Nice to meet you both. I'm Dr. Ammini. Jay's surgeon."

"Could you tell us how she is, doctor?" Coal asked.

"She fractured her arm and broke her collarbone. The collarbone will heal with time but we had to use a metal plate and a few screws to help keep the bones in place in her forearm. She also had a nasty gash above her right eye that has been sutured."

"Is that all?" Coal asked. When the doctor's expression turned serious, a sense of dread fell over Coal, and she wrapped her arms around herself bracing for the news.

"When she fell, she hit her head pretty hard. We'll be monitoring her for the next few days but I'm sorry to tell you she's in a coma."

The room spun, and Coal reached blindly for the chair behind her. Coma? Was this how it was going to end between them? Her legs gave way as strong hands wrapped around her waist.

"Whoa, there," the doctor said. "Easy now. Into the chair."

"Should I get her some water?" Dino asked quickly.

"That would be great," the doctor said, her eyes glued to Coal.

"I'm sorry." Coal's voice sounded distant even to her own ears. "Will she come out of it?"

"Head injuries are unpredictable. We're going to keep a close eye on her. The first twenty-four hours are the most critical. Then we'll see."

"When can I see her?" Coal asked.

"We're getting her situated now. I'll have a nurse come and get you in a few minutes."

"Thank you, doctor." The surgeon nodded and walked away as Dino appeared with a bottle of spring water and sat next to her. He looked as lost as she felt. She reached for his hand, needing the feel of another to steady her. "What am I going to do, Dino? Coma. She's in a coma."

"I told you she's tough," he said. "My cousin will fight. She's fought her whole life, and this won't stop her."

"How could you say that?"

"Because this time, she has you to fight for."

She wanted to say, "You don't know what I've said to her. How I pushed her away." But she couldn't. Tears gathered once more. He handed her a few tissues. "How did you know?" she finally asked.

Dino chuckled softly. "Believe me, Coal, *everyone* knows. Neither one of you are good at hiding it."

Just then, a nurse in pink scrubs entered the waiting room. "If you'd like to go see Ms. DiAngelo now, you can go on back."

Coal halted in the doorway at the sight of Jay hooked up to different machines, beeping and buzzing above her bed. Her right arm was casted, and she had a six-inch piece of gauze taped above her left eye. Jay was breathing steadily without any type of breathing apparatus, and except for an IV tube sticking out of her left arm, Coal would have guessed she was sleeping.

Her mom had returned shortly after and sat quietly by Coal's side while Coal held on to Jay's hand. They had not spoken in hours, yet her mother's presence comforted Coal and made her feel accepted in a way that she hadn't felt by any of her family members in a long time.

When visiting hours ended, her mom tried to persuade Coal to go home, shower, and take a nap, but Coal refused. If Jay woke up, she didn't want her to be alone. She'd been away from Jay for far too long, and she wasn't going to let another precious moment slip by, especially since she didn't know how many precious moments they had left.

She rubbed the back of Jay's hand against her cheek. She thought of all the moments they shared—all the moments they could have shared—and she was angry for allowing her duty to her family to push Jay away. If she were given another chance, there would be no more wasted moments. Only special ones.

"Hey, girlie," Angel said softly from the doorway.

"What are you doing here? It's after hours."

"Your mother called me. Thought I could talk some sense into you. The question is why didn't you?"

"I'm sorry," Coal said, her voice thick with worry and exhaustion. "I didn't think. I haven't been able to think since she...since she..."

"Oh, honey." Angel rushed to Coal's side, sliding her arms around her neck from behind. "How is she doing?"

"They don't know. All they can say is that head injuries are unpredictable."

"Jay, what have you done to yourself?" Angel ran her fingers down Jay's arm.

"I don't know if I'm strong enough for this," Coal whispered.

"Sure you are. Have you eaten anything today?"

"No, but I'm not hungry." She brushed a strand of hair out of Jay's face. "It seems I'm always doing that, isn't that right, baby?"

"Sweetie, you need to eat something. You're shaking."

"I'm not leaving her, Angel. Not again."

"You're not leaving her. You're gaining your strength and taking care of yourself. Jay would want you to."

"I can't."

"And you think Jay's stubborn. Fine. I'll get you something and be right back."

Coal rested her head on Jay's chest, feeling the stress of the day wash over her. Fatigue had set in, the type of fatigue that paralyzed the body and mind. She needed sleep. She needed food. But most of all she needed to see Jay sit up in that bed and flash that electric grin that only Jay knew how to do. When she couldn't hear anything except both their heartbeats, she leaned over her and whispered a story into her ear.

"Do you remember that day up on the ridge? We were on that hillside overlooking the valley. You came up behind me, wrapping your arms around my waist below that tree. Jay, do you remember?" She stretched out on the bed next to Jay, placing her head in between the crevice where Jay's neck and shoulder met. "Do you remember me straddling you? My body so hot for you I wanted to scream because I felt like I was going to melt. I knew for sure I was in love with you that day. You know why? Because that day, I saw beyond that ridge. I saw us together. Building a life. I saw…forever in your eyes. I need you to open those eyes for me. Please, baby, I need you so much."

Coal ran her fingers gently up and down Jay's midriff, secretly hoping that Jay could sense her lying there beside her. She closed her eyes, eventually falling asleep with the cadence of Jay's breathing as her only music.

CHAPTER TWENTY-FOUR

C oal," her mom whispered in her ear.

Coal stirred and lifted her head. She paused and glanced around the room, forgetting where she was. She turned to find Jay still asleep, still unresponsive.

"Hi, Mom."

"Did she wake at all last night?"

"No," Coal said tiredly and leaned forward to kiss Jay on the lips. "Good morning, baby."

She climbed out of the hospital bed built for one, surprised that her mother's first question hadn't been how she managed to remain in the room long after visiting hours had ended. At one point, one of the nurses had insisted that she leave until the morning, but Coal reminded the woman who she was and how much her family had donated to the hospital. For once, the perks of being a Davis had paid off.

After splashing some water on her face and finger-combing her hair, she plopped down into the same avocado-colored chair as the day before and reached up to brush a stray lock of hair as it fell into Jay's eyes. Jay hadn't moved in two days, and Coal was starting to wonder if she ever would again.

"Honey, you have to go home and get some rest."

"I'm not having this conversation again, Mom." *Especially after Dino telling me she's gone it alone for most of her life. This is not going to be one of those times. Not now, not ever, if I have a say.*

"How about if I stay with her until you at least grab a shower and a change of clothes?"

"Mom, I appreciate the offer, but the answer is still no."

Coal glanced up when Dino appeared, thankful that his presence would save her from a mom lecture. "How is she?" he asked.

"There's been no change since last night."

"Well, you heard the doctor," he said, his tone optimistic. "It could be days before she wakes up."

"Yeah, and the longer we wait the more hope we give up!"

Coal pushed away from the bed and strode to the window. All the waiting, the not sleeping, and the little bit of food she'd consumed since yesterday was finally getting the better of her. Dino paled as sadness plagued his dark features but she didn't have the energy to comfort him.

"Coal Davis, that is not helping the situation," her mom scolded her.

"Why? Because I'm telling the truth—"

"Could you all go and fight somewhere else? I have the worst headache, and my arm is killing me," Jay said but it came out more as a groan. Her eyes fluttered open then closed just as quickly.

"Jay." Coal grabbed Jay's hand. "Hey, open your eyes. Stay with me, baby."

"Coal? What...ow..." Jay used one hand to shield her eyes in an attempt to block out the overhead lights. "What's with the stadium lighting?"

Coal leaned forward and kissed her on the forehead. "Shh, it's okay. I'll turn it down."

"Hey, Cuz," Dino said, his eyes misty as he placed a hand on her uninjured shoulder. "How you feeling?"

"Like crap." She weakly lifted her arm and inspected the IV tube before dropping it back on the bed. "What the hell happened?"

Coal wasn't surprised that Jay didn't remember anything regarding the accident, especially after sustaining a head trauma. "What do you remember?"

"I remember being on your roof. There was termite damage. I looked down and then tripped..." Jay gripped Coal's hand hard. "Did anyone else get hurt?"

"No, baby," Coal said. "Only you."

"Good. That's good." Jay closed her eyes.

"Dino," Coal's mom said. "How about we go and notify the nurses that she's awake?"

Nodding, Dino followed Coal's mother as Coal twisted in her chair to find Jay staring inquisitively at her.

"Now that everyone's gone, how are you really feeling? And no macho tough guy routine with me, got it?" She knew Jay would try to hold it together in front of Dino. Now that they were alone, she wasn't going to allow her to hold back until every ache in her sexy body was discussed in vivid detail.

"I'm groggy, my head hurts, and my arm is killing me. Otherwise, I think I'll survive."

"Are you sure?" Coal said. "You had me so worried."

"I'm sure. You didn't get hurt, did you?"

"Me? I was nowhere near the roof when it collapsed." Coal stared at Jay, confused by the question. *Probably the concussion. I couldn't have gotten hurt. I remember her looking in my direction right before...*

Forgetting that Jay was lying in the hospital injured or that she'd just spent the last twenty-four hours worried to death that she'd never wake up—or worse, die—she leaned forward, fury sweeping through every pore. "God damn it, Jay! You weren't looking where you were going. You were focused on me instead of keeping yourself safe up on that damn roof! You could have gotten killed—"

Jay slipped her hand behind Coal's neck and pulled her close, silencing her with a kiss. The kiss was one of passion and relief, and though it was all too brief, it had its desired effect. As if being doused with cold water, Coal's ire subsided, and she stretched out on the bed next to Jay with Jay resting her chin on the top of Coal's head.

"Baby, you could have killed yourself. What were you thinking?"

"I *wasn't* thinking. I couldn't take my eyes off of you, and then all I remember is falling."

Coal remembered the scene all too well. The smoke and dust. Men screaming. And Jay gone. "I was so scared."

Jay didn't have time to answer because a couple of nurses appeared and took stock of Jay's condition. A swirl of activity filled the room as they checked Jay's heart rate and blood pressure. They were nearly finished with their quick examination when Jay's doctor appeared with clipboard in hand.

"Good to see you awake. I'm Dr. Ammini. How are you feeling?"

"Like I've been hit by a sledgehammer."

The doctor chuckled. "I'm sure your body agrees with that assessment. I'm going to do a routine exam. First, though, do you have a headache...blurry vision...nausea?"

"A headache."

"On a scale from one to ten?" She shone a light in Jay's eyes, making her wince.

"I'll say seven, and now I change my mind about the nausea thing."

"You sustained a head injury," the doctor said calmly, but her eyes maintained a certain level of intensity that Coal had seen on people like her father when they were assessing a serious situation. "It's going to take a few days before the side effects diminish."

"How about my arm?"

"That, I'm afraid, will take a lot longer to heal. You broke both bones in your forearm and your collarbone. You'll be in a cast for about six weeks. After that, you may have to do a little physical therapy and some light work until you're fully recovered."

Jay studied her arm. Not only was she right-handed, she needed both hands for work. Six weeks or more without a paycheck was bat crazy. She needed out of that hospital and would sign out against medical advice if that's what it took. "Doc, I appreciate everything you've done for me, but I have to speed this recovery thing up. I got to get back to work." Jay threw the covers off her body and tried sitting up when a wave of dizziness hit. She wavered and sank back into the pillows with a groan.

"Unbelievable," Coal said angrily. She placed her face within inches of Jay. "You try that stunt again, and I will have them handcuff you to this bed if necessary. This is not the time to be pig-headed. You will not give the doctors trouble. And you will *not* go back to work until Dr. Ammini tells you it's okay. Got it?"

"Coal, you know my situation. I have to—"

"What you have to do is get better. Don't worry about work. We'll figure something out."

"Easy for you to say," Jay shot back. She was tired, and this entire day was surreal. Having a head injury. Coal by her side acting as if nothing had happened between them. Maybe it was a dream and she hadn't awakened yet. When Coal linked their fingers, Jay relented with a sigh. "And you call me pig-headed."

"I can see you're in good hands," the doctor said with a wink. "I'll be by to check on you later."

Coal adjusted Jay's pillow and pulled the sheet up to cover her chest. She sat back down in the chair, placing her hand in Jay's once more.

"Are you always this bossy?"

"You haven't seen anything yet." She leaned forward and kissed Jay softly on the lips. "Now sleep. You need your rest."

"I don't...want to...sleep."

"I know. But close your eyes anyway. I promise, I'll be here when you wake up."

As Jay began to drift off, the last thing she thought she heard was something about wild horses and Coal not being dragged away.

Chapter Twenty-five

I s she asleep?" Dino asked.
    "Yeah, for the last few hours."
Since Jay had slept off and on since that morning, Dino had decided to go get lunch while Coal sat by her bedside. Every time Jay woke, she appeared stronger than the time before. They had argued with one another about Coal not going home and getting rest. But Jay had lost every argument and Coal decided she'd take the arguing over the silence any day.

"Does she remember anything?"

"She remembers everything," Coal said in relief, kissing her hand.

"Great. When she wakes up she's going to kill me."

"I'm not going to kill you, Cuz," Jay said with a grin, never opening her eyes. "But I think I deserve hazard pay."

"Ha! You're lucky I don't garnish your wages for the hole you made in Ms. Davis's roof." In what appeared to be an unusual gesture between the cousins, Dino leaned forward and kissed Jay on the forehead. "How you feeling, Cuz?"

Coal smiled, enjoying their childish bantering. They needed each other even if neither one of them knew it.

"I keep telling everyone I'm fine." Jay scowled. "But the doctor said six fucking weeks before I can work."

"That's not exactly what the doctor said, sweetie. She said six weeks in a cast. After that you *might* be ready for light work. And you will *not* work before then." Coal threw Dino an "agree with me or else" look.

"If that's what Doc says then that's how it has to be."

Jay spoke softly, calmly. "Coal, I need to talk with Dino alone. Can you give us a minute?"

"Of course. I'll grab a cup of coffee and be right back."

Jay waited until she could no longer hear Coal's footsteps before she unloaded on Dino. "Cuz, I can't be laid up for almost two months. I can't afford it and you know it. Coal doesn't understand. She forgets that I'm different from her. You know my situation. I'll lose everything."

When Jay hadn't been able to sleep, she thought of nothing but how she was going to get back to work and what she would say to Coal about whatever it was that was going on between them. She was still confused as to why Coal was there with her after basically telling her to get lost less than a week ago. But the truth remained, she wanted Coal there, even though she knew she was being selfish.

"Calm down. I've got everything covered. Including Tia's house."

"I don't need charity. I need to get out of here!" Jay tried to push out of bed, but she was still weak and her collarbone protested the movement. A stabbing pain shot down her arm, and she grunted, biting back a string of curses.

"Jesus, Jay! You need to stay put until the doc releases you."

Jay tried a second time to get out of bed when Coal appeared and threw her an incredulous look. "What do you think you're doing?"

"Why doesn't anyone understand I can't stay here any longer?" Jay slammed her head back into the pillows, ignoring the pain the motion had caused.

"Look. You just came out of a coma, your arm is useless, and now you're being combative. If you don't knock this shit off right now, you're going to piss me off!"

Jay studied Coal in shock. No one had ever talked to her that way before. She hoped Dino would offer his support, but the chicken shit was already halfway out the door.

"I have errands to run," he said. But Jay caught him suppressing a smirk. "I'll drop by tomorrow. Feel better, Cuz."

"Great." She let out a weary sigh and closed her eyes. "Think you're pretty tough, don't you?"

"Only when I have to be," Coal said, but the anger was gone.

Left wounded in body and soul, Jay hung her head. She was bleeding from some deep place inside that she'd never allowed anyone access to except for Coal, and now she couldn't stop the tears even if she tried.

"Oh, God, Jay. What's wrong?"

Coal moved onto the bed and leaned Jay into her arms. Jay shook uncontrollably. She allowed the tears to come, letting the only woman she'd ever loved ease her suffering. But Coal didn't love her in return. And the longer Coal held her, the more Coal's parting words slammed into her like heavy surf after a storm.

This was a mistake, Jay. A big mistake.

That's what Coal had said to her. That's what left the cloud of doubt hanging over her until she was bogged down with so much uncertainty, she crumbled. "I don't know what to think, Coal. You tell me I'm a mistake. That what we had was a mistake. Then you show up here after disappearing for a week and act as if the past didn't exist."

"Look, I know you don't trust me. And I don't blame you. And for all I know, after seeing you with that woman at the club, you may have even moved on. I don't know what to say except that I'm sorry I hurt you. These last few months, my life has been more complicated than usual, and I wasn't sure how to explain my situation to you before, but now I want to try."

"But that's just it. You shouldn't have to try. You said you loved me. So telling me things should come natural. I gave you my heart and you cast me aside without so much as an explanation." The pain in Jay's heart matched the pounding behind her eyeballs. She couldn't do this again. Not without losing some vital part of herself.

"Jay," Coal said desperately. "I know you don't understand, but I had to say those things. I had to protect you from my father. He's a powerful man. And you don't know what he's capable of."

"Your father?" What could Coal's dad possibly have said or done that could force Coal to break things off with her? "Now I'm really confused."

"I know you are. And I promise, after today, I will tell you everything. Even if you choose not to be with me, I at least owe you the truth."

"Damn it, Coal!" Jay's frustration with the entire situation finally getting the best of her. "Just tell me."

"Not yet." Coal leaned down and kissed Jay quickly. "There's something I need to do first. Something I should have done a long time ago. I just hope when it's all over, you'll forgive me."

"Hold on—" Jay called out to her. But Coal was already out the door.

CHAPTER TWENTY-SIX

Jay tried to down a few bites of pudding, but she'd lost her appetite. She'd snapped at the nurses, refused any more pain medication, and had hung up on Dino when he called to check on her after a lengthy chastising from him. After he had used the terms dumbass and moron in the same sentence, she hadn't wanted to listen to him anymore and slammed the phone in his ear. The more she stared into the empty room, the more Dino's words rang true.

All she'd been thinking about for the last few hours was what Coal had said to her. What did Coal's father have to do with their breakup and was Coal planning to face him and do something she was going to regret? More importantly though, what exactly would that be?

The longer she lay there, the more she understood that it was time to stop feeling sorry for herself. Maybe she hadn't amounted to much at this point in her life, but damn it, she wasn't a slacker. She was worth something in this world. When she'd been younger, she'd spent years blaming herself for her mother leaving. She hated the fact that her mom left her with her dad and wished she had taken her with her. But then she'd never have grown up with Dino. Would have never spent summers hanging out in a tree house that she'd built with him and laid around lazily with her cousin Dakota. Wouldn't have worked in her uncle and aunt's restaurant only to be given the chance to work as a contractor with Dino. That job had led to her meeting Coal. She'd finally fallen in love. Thought about building a life with someone for the first time. Then Coal took a hammer to the idea and shattered her dreams along with the foundation they had tried to build.

She'd spent so many years trying to build things that in the process she'd forgotten to forge a foundation for her future. What she wanted now, she never would have considered a few months ago. A family, a loving partner. These were the foundations that shaped her future, but none of that would be possible without the stability Coal offered her. Coal's strength, her conviction, her iron will. Jay had come to love all those traits. She knew in the deepest reaches of her soul that Coal was everything to her, and this time, she wouldn't allow someone to walk out of her life. No, this time, she had the power to make things right.

She knew with every beat of her heart that Coal was the one person who made her feel as though her life had purpose. Coal's optimistic attitude and why she didn't just embrace life but commanded it like she would a horse made Jay want to be a stronger person. Whatever Coal's deal was with her father, it had to be major for Coal to push her away. In the past, she'd seen the fear in Coal's eyes when her father had been near. If he did have something to do with separating them, no way could she allow Coal to face him alone. Besides, she refused to sit there any longer and pretend that being with Coal was a bigger mistake than being without her. The time had come to swallow her pride and fight for the one thing she shouldn't have allowed to slip through her fingers in the first place. As she picked up the phone, the only thing she could do was pray it wasn't too late.

Coal called her dad and asked him to meet her at her house. With papers in hand, she sat nervously and waited for the knock at the door. She inhaled deeply, trying to settle her queasy stomach. *Just relax. In less than an hour, it will all be over.*

Even though she'd been expecting him, the knock at the door startled her and she jumped. "Here we go."

"You wanted to see me," her father said. He stood stiffly on the porch.

"Yes, I did. It's about the ranch." She handed him the manila folder.

"Well," he said. "I'm glad to see you've come to your senses."

"Actually, Dad, I've decided I don't want it. Any of it. I told you before I'm not going to hide who I am because you have a different agenda. I'm a lesbian, Dad, whether you accept it or not, and I'm tired of fighting you. You can keep the inheritance, destroy Grandpa's dream, and shove the Davis name right up your conservative ass! All I want is to be free from the shackles that this family has kept me bound by for all these years."

Her father's face turned crimson. His neck bulged over his collar, and his blue eyes blazed. "You dare talk like this to me? For what? That loser contractor?"

"She is not a loser! You say that because she doesn't fit your mold. Doesn't bathe in money. Doesn't dress like your uptight friends. I don't understand what could be so wrong about two people loving each other."

"I will not discuss this topic with you. If it's your decision to give up your inheritance then that's your choice. But I'm warning you, Coal. Stay away from Jay DiAngelo, or she will regret coming anywhere near you."

Coal narrowed her eyes as she refused to release his cold, challenging stare. "She is *not* a part of this conversation! And you can't destroy someone's life or their family's simply because I refuse to live my life the way you want."

"I have said my piece. Let's see if you truly are a Davis and make the right decision."

"Sounds like she's already made up her mind," Jay said, surprising them both. She was standing at the bottom of Coal's porch looking exhausted, in pain, and like the best thing Coal had ever seen.

"Jay?" Coal stepped past her father and placed an arm around her waist.

Jay's Metallica T-shirt was soaked with sweat, and she was finding it hard to catch her breath. "What are you doing here?"

"Had to see you."

"I can't believe they released you," Coal said.

"They didn't." Jay smiled weakly. "I signed out against doctor's orders."

"So stubborn." Coal wiped a strand of hair out of Jay's eyes as Jay swayed toward her.

"Ms. DiAngelo," Coal's father said coolly. "What business do you have with my daughter?"

"I needed to be here for her, sir."

"Jay, dear," Jane said. She climbed out of her golf cart and approached them all. "Shouldn't you be in the hospital?"

"Not now, Jane. Why don't you go back home and let me deal with this."

"Thomas, what is this all about?" Jane asked.

"It's nothing, dear. I said please stay out of it. Ms. DiAngelo," he said, turning his attention back to Jay. "If you'd like to speak with Coal, I suggest the telephone. Otherwise, I think it's time you leave our daughter's property."

"Sir, I'm not leaving her. I love her."

"You do?" Coal wanted to cry. She tightened her grip on Jay's waist noting that every second Jay remained standing was zapping what was left of her energy.

"Yes. I'm so sorry that I let my pride get in the way, and it almost cost me the most important thing in my life."

"And what's that?"

"You."

"Oh, sweetheart." Coal placed a hand on her face. "I love you too."

"Coal Davis," her father said angrily. He grabbed her by the arm and pulled her out of Jay's embrace. With his face inches from hers he growled, "This deviant behavior stops now!"

"You know what, Dad?" She yanked out of his iron grip. "You're right. This does stop now. All of it."

"Everyone stop!" Her mother stood with her hand stretched out between Coal and her father, her expression one of caution and concern. "Someone tell me what the hell is going on."

"Mom, I'm sorry. But this is Dad trying to run my life and destroy someone else's because they love me."

"Thomas, what is she saying?"

"Beats me. I don't think she knows what she's saying. Do you, Coal?" Her father's tone was lethal.

"Actually, Dad, I know exactly what I'm saying."

She started at the beginning, explaining to Jay and her mother about the ranch and her father's threats. When she was done, the sound of shocked silence hung over them like a heavy cloud.

"Thomas, please tell me these allegations aren't true," her mother finally said.

"And this is why you pushed me away?" Jay pulled Coal close and buried her face in her hair.

"Yes. I couldn't have him ruin everything you've worked so hard for. You've already sacrificed so much. No way could I be the cause of any more pain for you."

"Jesus, don't you get it? All that other stuff is meaningless without you in my life. The only pain I've ever suffered is when I thought I lost you. I love you."

"And I love you."

Jay dipped her head to kiss Coal and pulled her close to the uninjured side of her body. Feeling stronger and more confident than she'd ever been in her life, she faced Coal's father once more. "Sir, you can take everything I own if you think that matters to me. I thought I knew what I valued before, that is until I met your daughter. Turns out, she makes my life richer just being in it."

"You're making a mistake, Ms. DiAngelo," he said.

Jay laughed, thinking how ironic that statement was. "I have made enough of those in my life—some of them forgivable—some of them not. But what I know with all my heart is that no part of my love for Coal is a mistake."

"Thomas," Jane seethed. "I can't believe this. You threatened Jay, her family, and tried to blackmail our daughter?"

"We will discuss this later." Thomas didn't look in Jane's direction dismissing her as if she were an insignificant underling. "As for you, Coal, I will file those papers that you've signed regarding the transfer of the ranch immediately. I'm also requesting you leave the area as soon as possible. I can't have your objectionable behavior affect my election chances."

"That's enough!" The hardness in Jane's voice caused Thomas to turn back in her direction. He took one step back. "If you think I'm going to stand by while you throw our daughter out of our lives, you're sadly mistaken. If anyone will be leaving, Thomas, it will be you."

"Since when do you speak to me—"

Jane held up her hand to silence him. "We will discuss this in private. Coal." Jane turned toward her daughter, her facial features softening. "I know you really wanted to try to follow the rules that had been set for you by this family."

"Mom, I'm sorry. I can't—"

"That's just it, honey. You shouldn't have any rules. What kind of family sets guidelines for their children's happiness?" The comment was directed at Thomas who was no longer looking at any of them.

"Mom, I love Jay. You know that, don't you?"

Jane smiled, placing a hand on her cheek. "It's not what I know that's important. Only that she understands how much you love her."

"You do know that, don't you?" Coal looked up uncertainly at Jay.

"I think I know. But how about you tell me again?"

Coal pulled Jay's head down to whisper into her ear. "How about I show you instead? In private."

"What a great idea."

Coal called out to her dad who still wouldn't look at any of them. "I wanted you to know that I'd already made up my mind to leave before you asked me to go. I can't be partners with you, especially not after all this. So, after you read over the paperwork, you'll notice that I've found a way to keep the ranch operational. But that means selling my house and moving the ranch to a smaller plot of land. At least that way, I can continue with the program that has meant so much to so many people."

"Over my dead body," Jane said. "You are not selling this house. And the ranch details can wait."

"But, Mom—"

"No buts." She took the envelope from her husband without an argument from him. "Jay needs to lie down, and your father and I have a lot to discuss. Oh and, Jay, I expect you to join us for breakfast tomorrow morning."

"Yes, ma'am. I wouldn't miss it."

As Coal's parents drove off, Jay waved to Dino who had watched the entire conversation from the safety of his pickup. Finally alone, Jay sagged against Coal, wondering how the hell she'd remained standing for this long.

"Honey, we need to get you to bed," Coal said.

"I like the way that sounds. I'm worried about your mom though. Will she be okay?"

"I think so. I've never seen her that mad before. She's a lot tougher than I thought. But I guess I shouldn't be surprised. My grandfather told me long ago, anyone who marries a Davis needs to have balls of steel."

Jay bent forward and kissed her. "I'll have to remember that."

CHAPTER TWENTY-SEVEN

One Year Later

"Angel, are you sure you have the ring?"

"Jesus, Coal." Angel walked out of one of the adjoining rooms. "How many times are you going to ask me that question?"

"Sorry. I'm nervous." She ironed out an imaginary wrinkle in her Vera Wang wedding dress, the tapered neckline showing a hint of cleavage underneath an elegant pattern of lace. "How do I look?"

"Do you even need to ask?" Angel placed her arm around Coal's shoulders. "I would be surprised if Jay can remain standing after seeing you in this."

"Well, if I get my way, she won't have to wait very long to take it off of me."

"That's the Coal I know. Now enough with the bullshit. Tell me what else is bothering you?"

"My dad. What else? I really thought after last week he'd make an appearance."

Since the day Jay had shown up declaring her love, Coal had spent the last few months trying to salvage some relationship with her father. It hadn't taken them long to settle the affairs of the ranch, her father coming to the decision that it was best for Coal to take over complete control. Coal wasn't shocked. She knew it was her mother's influence that had most likely swayed his decision. Coal also kept the house and finally persuaded Jay to move in a few months later. They visited Coal's mother often, but except for a few perfunctory hellos and good-byes, her father seemed to try his best to avoid them. Coal had had one glimmer of hope at a dinner not too long ago. Her father was not only present with both of them there, he'd started a conversation with Jay about the advantages and disadvantages of granite versus marble countertops. Talk about awkward, but at least it was a start.

"Shh," Angel said. "Not today. This is not about him. It's about you and Jay."

"You're right." Coal closed her eyes, taking a deep breath.

"Of course I am." Angel hugged her. "It's time."

Coal couldn't have asked for a more perfect day to celebrate her love with Jay. As they stood surrounded by their family and friends, they recited their vows like thousands of gay couples had since the Supreme Court of California legalized gay marriage. It was a four to three decision in a predominately conservative court. As she stood there in front of Judge Parker, who had agreed to marry them, she knew without a doubt that his influence had been a large factor in the ruling.

Jay was stunning in a black Versace tux and white silk dress shirt. Her eyes were as vibrant and sparkling as the black pearl studs she wore encased with diamonds, and as Coal slipped the gold band onto Jay's ring finger, she could never remember being happier.

When the ceremony ended at dusk, Coal's mother enveloped Coal and Jay into a hug. Her mom had spent the last few weeks transforming her backyard into what some would consider the outdoor wedding of the year. No details were spared, from the backlit silk canopies crisscrossing overhead to the floating candle blocks moving around in the pool.

"You both look beautiful."

"Thanks, Mom."

"Jay, I need to speak to my daughter for a second. If you don't mind me pulling her away?"

"No, ma'am."

Her mother threw her a stern look. "Cut the ma'am stuff. If you're going to use any words around me from now on that start with the letter M, it's going to be Mom, understood?"

Jay blushed. She couldn't remember the last time she used that word, but she accepted the endearment and all that it implied. "Yes, ma...Mom."

Jane winked as Coal laughed. "Much better."

Jay watched them disappear and was overcome with so many different emotions she spoke without thinking. "Christ, I hope I can make her happy."

"Are you kidding me?" Dino asked. "Look at that beautiful woman. She's crazy for you."

"I know," Jay said. "And I'm crazy for her. I just hope it's enough."

"I'm no expert. But I would think that's everything."

"It is."

"Look, Cuz. I know you're still worried about a few things. Why don't you let her help you? You're married now, and that's what couples do. They help each other."

Jay's eyes narrowed. "We are not having this discussion today," she said through clenched teeth as she tried to keep a smile pasted on her face.

"That's what we all figured." He handed her a card. "Congratulations, Cuz."

"Dino what the—"

"Just open it."

"What did you do?"

Dino put up his hand. "It wasn't just me. This is a gift from your family. Me, Uncle Mario, and the rest of your family. We want you to accept it because we love you and you deserve it."

Jay stared in disbelief as the implications regarding the details inside the card hit her hard. "Dino, I can't. You don't understand..."

"No, *you* don't understand. You've always been there when any of us needed you. Now, we wanted to be there for you. Tia's house is yours. Free and clear."

Jay reached for him, pulling him into a bear hug. "Thanks, Dino. I guess this means I'm going to owe you a few Saturdays."

"Uh, not exactly."

She placed him at arm's length. "What's with the tone?"

"No tone. Hell, I guess now is as good a time as any to tell you I've got to let you go."

Jay couldn't have possibly heard him correctly. She'd just married the woman of her dreams and Dino was firing her? The next words died on her lips when he handed her another envelope. She opened the flaps, blinking a few times to make sure she was reading the words correctly. She held the paper tightly that confirmed she'd passed her state test to become a licensed contractor. She'd been waiting in anticipation for this letter to arrive for weeks. "How did you get this?"

"Coal has been scoping out the mailbox. When it arrived, we took it upon ourselves to open it, knowing that you passed. She thought you'd like to open it on your wedding day."

"But how did you know I'd pass? Nobody knows those results until these letters arrive."

Dino rolled his eyes. "Whatever! Anyone that knows you could see that you could have passed that test with your eyes closed. You did nothing but work or study for six straight months!"

Jay let out a shaky breath. This day was turning out to be more than her heart could handle. "I can't believe this."

"Believe it, lover." Coal wrapped her arms around Jay's waist from behind.

Dino mumbled something about Angel and a dance, but Jay was already too lost in Coal to hear the rest of it. She swiveled in Coal's arms and pulled her along her body. "You put too much faith in me, baby."

"Yes, I do. I believe in you and I love you. So get used to it."

Jay slanted her head and kissed her finally believing she could build that promising future one step at a time.

About the Author

L.T. Marie is a career martial artist who writes during her free time. She believes strongly in the philosophy of yin and yang and sees her writing as a necessary form of relaxation to combat the intensity of her training. Her writing career started in high school where she met her English teacher, Mr. C., who pressed her to reach her potential or, as she would say, "pushed her to her limits." During this time, she won back-to-back English awards and went on to minor in English in college.

L.T. was born and raised in the great state of California where she still resides with her loving partner and two children. Her hobbies are reading every lesbian romance she can get her hands on and working out religiously.

Books Available from Bold Strokes Books

One Last Thing by Kim Baldwin & Xenia Alexiou. Blood is thicker than pride. The final book in the Elite Operative Series brings together foes, family, and friends to start a new order. (978-1-62639-230-4)

Songs Unfinished by Holly Stratimore. Two aspiring rock stars learn that falling in love while pursuing their dreams can be harmonious—if they can only keep their pasts from throwing them out of tune. (978-1-62639-231-1)

Beyond the Ridge by L.T. Marie. Will a contractor and a horse rancher overcome their family differences and find common ground to build a life together? (978-1-62639-232-8)

Swordfish by Andrea Bramhall. Four women battle the demons from their pasts. Will they learn to let go, or will happiness be forever beyond their grasp? (978-1-62639-233-5)

The Fiend Queen by Barbara Ann Wright. Princess Katya and her consort Starbride must turn evil against evil in order to banish Fiendish power from their kingdom, and only love will pull them back from the brink. (978-1-62639-234-2)

Up the Ante by PJ Trebelhorn. When Jordan Stryker and Ashley Noble meet again fifteen years after a short-lived affair, are either of them prepared to gamble on a chance at love? (978-1-62639-237-3)

Speakeasy by MJ Williamz. When mob leader Helen Byrne sets her sights on the girlfriend of Al Capone's right-hand man, passion and tempers flare on the streets of Chicago. (978-1-62639-238-0)

Venus in Love by Tina Michele. Morgan Blake can't afford any distractions and Ainsley Dencourt can't afford to lose control—but the beauty of life and art usually lies in the unpredictable strokes of the artist's brush. (978-1-62639-220-5)

Rules of Revenge by AJ Quinn. When a lethal operative on a collision course with her past agrees to help a CIA analyst on a critical assignment, the encounter proves explosive in ways neither woman anticipated. (978-1-62639-221-2)

The Romance Vote by Ali Vali. Chili Alexander is a sought-after campaign consultant who isn't prepared when her boss's daughter, Samantha Pellegrin, comes to work at the firm and shakes up Chili's life from the first day. (978-1-62639-222-9)

Advance: Exodus Book One by Gun Brooke. Admiral Dael Caydoc's mission to find a new homeworld for the Oconodian people is hazardous, but working with the infuriating Commander Aniwyn "Spinner" Seclan endangers her heart and soul. (978-1-62639-224-3)

UnCatholic Conduct by Stevie Mikayne. Jil Kidd goes undercover to investigate fraud at St. Marguerite's Catholic School, but life gets complicated when her student is killed—and she begins to fall for her prime target. (978-1-62639-304-2)

Season's Meetings by Amy Dunne. Catherine Birch reluctantly ventures on the festive road trip from hell with beautiful stranger Holly Daniels only to discover the road to true love has its own obstacles to maneuver. (978-1-62639-227-4)

Myth and Magic: Queer Fairy Tales edited by Radclyffe and Stacia Seaman. Myth, magic, and monsters—the stuff of childhood dreams (or nightmares) and adult fantasies. (978-1-62639-225-0)

Nine Nights on the Windy Tree by Martha Miller. Recovering drug addict, Bertha Brannon, is an attorney who is trying to stay clean when a murder sends her back to the bad end of town. (978-1-62639-179-6)

Driving Lessons by Annameekee Hesik. Dive into Abbey Brooks's sophomore year as she attempts to figure out the amazing, but sometimes complicated, life of a you-know-who girl at Gila High School. (978-1-62639-228-1)

Asher's Shot by Elizabeth Wheeler. Asher Price's candid photographs capture the truth, but when his success requires exposing an enemy, Asher discovers his only shot at happiness involves revealing secrets of his own. (978-1-62639-229-8)

Courtship by Carsen Taite. Love and justice—a lethal mix or a perfect match? (978-1-62639-210-6)

Against Doctor's Orders by Radclyffe. Corporate financier Presley Worth wants to shut down Argyle Community Hospital, but Dr. Harper Rivers will fight her every step of the way, if she can also fight their growing attraction. (978-1-62639-211-3)

A Spark of Heavenly Fire by Kathleen Knowles. Kerry and Beth are building their life together, but unexpected circumstances could destroy their happiness. (978-1-62639-212-0)

Never Too Late by Julie Blair. When Dr. Jamie Hammond is forced to hire a new office manager, she's shocked to come face to face with Carla Grant and memories from her past. (978-1-62639-213-7)

Widow by Martha Miller. Judge Bertha Brannon must solve the murder of her lover, a policewoman she thought she'd grow old with. As more bodies pile up, the murderer starts coming for her. (978-1-62639-214-4)

Twisted Echoes by Sheri Lewis Wohl. What's a woman to do when she realizes the voices in her head are real? (978-1-62639-215-1)

Criminal Gold by Ann Aptaker. Through a dangerous night in New York in 1949, Cantor Gold, dapper dyke-about-town, smuggler of fine art, is forced by a crime lord to be his instrument of vengeance. (978-1-62639-216-8)

The Melody of Light by M.L. Rice. After surviving abuse and loss, will Riley Gordon be able to navigate her first year of college and accept true love and family? (978-1-62639-219-9)

Because of You by Julie Cannon. What would you do for the woman you were forced to leave behind? (978-1-62639-199-4)

The Job by Jove Belle. Sera always dreamed that she would one day reunite with Tor. She just didn't think it would involve terrorists, firearms, and hostages. (978-1-62639-200-7)

Making Time by C.J. Harte. Two women going in different directions meet after fifteen years and struggle to reconnect in spite of the past that separated them. (978-1-62639-201-4)

Once The Clouds Have Gone by KE Payne. Overwhelmed by the dark clouds of her past, Tag Grainger is lost until the intriguing and spirited Freddie Metcalfe unexpectedly forces her to reevaluate her life. (978-1-62639-202-1)

The Acquittal by Anne Laughlin. Chicago private investigator Josie Harper searches for the real killer of a woman whose lover has been acquitted of the crime. (978-1-62639-203-8)

An American Queer: The Amazon Trail by Lee Lynch. Lee Lynch's heartening and heart-rending history of gay life from the turbulence of the late 1900s to the triumphs of the early 2000s are recorded in this selection of her columns. (978-1-62639-204-5)

Stick McLaughlin: The Prohibition Years by CF Frizzell. Corruption in 1918 cost Stick her lover, her freedom, and her identity, but a very special flapper and the family bond of her own gang could help win them back—even if it means outwitting the Boston Mob. (978-1-62639-205-2)

Edge of Awareness by C.A. Popovich. When Maria, a woman in the middle of her third divorce, meets Dana, an out lesbian, awareness of her feelings brings up reservations about the teachings of her church. (978-1-62639-188-8)

Taken by Storm by Kim Baldwin. Lives depend on two women when a train derails high in the remote Alps, but an unforgiving mountain, avalanches, crevasses, and other perils stand between them and safety. (978-1-62639-189-5)

The Common Thread by Jaime Maddox. Dr. Nicole Coussart's life is falling apart, but fortunately, DEA Attorney Rae Rhodes is there to pick up the pieces and help Nic put them back together. (978-1-62639-190-1)

Jolt by Kris Bryant. Mystery writer Bethany Lange wasn't prepared for the twisting emotions that left her breathless the moment she laid eyes on folk singer sensation Ali Hart. (978-1-62639-191-8)

Searching For Forever by Emily Smith. Dr. Natalie Jenner's life has always been about saving others, until young paramedic Charlie Thompson comes along and shows her maybe she's the one who needs saving. (978-1-62639-186-4)

A Queer Sort of Justice: Prison Tales Across Time by Rebecca S. Buck. When liberty is only a memory, and all seems lost, what freedoms and hopes can be found within us? (978-1-62639-195-6E)

Blue Water Dreams by Dena Hankins. Lania Marchiol keeps her wary sailor's gaze trained on the horizon until Oly Rassmussen, a wickedly handsome trans man, sends her trusty compass spinning off course. (978-1-62639-192-5)

Rest Home Runaways by Clifford Henderson. Baby boomer Morgan Ronzio's troubled marriage is the least of her worries when she gets the call that her addled, eighty-six-year-old, half-blind dad has escaped the rest home. (978-1-62639-169-7)

Charm City by Mason Dixon. Raq Overstreet's loyalty to her drug kingpin boss is put to the test when she begins to fall for Bathsheba Morris, the undercover cop assigned to bring him down. (978-1-62639-198-7)

Let the Lover Be by Sheree Greer. Kiana Lewis, a functional alcoholic on the verge of destruction, finally faces the demons of her past while finding love and earning redemption in New Orleans. (978-1-62639-077-5)

Blindsided by Karis Walsh. Blindsided by love, guide dog trainer Lenae McIntyre and media personality Cara Bradley learn to trust what they see with their hearts. (978-1-62639-078-2)

About Face by VK Powell. Forensic artist Macy Sheridan and Detective Leigh Monroe work on a case that has troubled them both for years, but they're hampered by the past and their unlikely yet undeniable attraction. (978-1-62639-079-9)

Blackstone by Shea Godfrey. For Darry and Jessa, their chance at a life of freedom is stolen by the arrival of war and an ancient prophecy that just might destroy their love. (978-1-62639-080-5)

Out of This World by Maggie Morton. Iris decided to cross an ocean to get over her ex. But instead, she ends up traveling much farther, all the way to another world. Once there, only a mysterious, sexy, and magical woman can help her return home. (978-1-62639-083-6)